BARLEN
WOU

. . . when the Earthman casually reached down, scooped him up and placed him on top of the strange crawling machine. To a Mesklinite, a fall of inches would be fatal . . . and now he was six feet off the ground.

In a few moments, he had calmed down and was fascinated, almost giddy, at the new experience.

But to the crew of the <u>Bree</u>, seeing their captain brought toward them atop the crawler was pure horror. They could have been no more dismayed if the alien had displayed Barlennan's severed head on a pole.

Flexing their pincers—powerful enough to snip through steel—the sailors flowed in a red and black tide from their ship toward the unsuspecting Earthman . . .

Mission
of
Gravity

Hal Clement

A Del Rey Book

BALLANTINE BOOKS • NEW YORK

All of the characters in this book are fictitious, and any resemblance to actual persons, living or dead, is purely coincidental.

A Del Rey Book
Published by Ballantine Books

ISBN 0-345-27092-4

This edition published by arrangement with
Doubleday and Company, Inc.

Manufactured in the United States of America

First Ballantine Books Edition: January 1978

Cover art by H. R. Van Dongen

CONTENTS

I: WINTER STORM

The wind came across the bay like something living. It tore the surface so thoroughly to shreds that it was hard to tell where liquid ended and atmosphere began; it tried to raise waves that would have swamped the *Bree* like a chip, and blew them into impalpable spray before they had risen a foot.

The spray alone reached Barlennan, crouched high on the *Bree*'s poop raft. His ship had long since been hauled safely ashore. That had been done the moment he had been sure that he would stay here for the winter; but he could not help feeling a little uneasy even so. Those waves were many times as high as any he had faced at sea, and somehow it was not completely reassuring to reflect that the lack of weight which permitted them to rise so high would also prevent their doing real damage if they did roll this far up the beach.

Barlennan was not particularly superstitious, but this close to the Rim of the World there was really no telling what could happen. Even his crew, an unimaginative lot by any reckoning, showed occasional signs of uneasiness. There was bad luck here, they muttered —whatever dwelt beyond the Rim and sent the fearful winter gales blasting thousands of miles into the world might resent being disturbed. At every accident the muttering broke out anew, and accidents were frequent. The fact that anyone is apt to make a misstep when he weighs about two and a quarter pounds instead of the five hundred and fifty or so to which he has been used all his life seemed obvious to the commander; but apparently an education, or at least the habit of logical thought, was needed to appreciate that.

Even Dondragmer, who should have known better . . . Barlennan's long body tensed and he almost roared an order before he really took in what was going on two rafts away. The mate had picked this moment, apparently, to check the stays of one of the masts, and had taken advantage of near-weightlessness to rear almost his full length upward from the deck. It was still a fantastic sight to see him towering, balanced precariously on his six rearmost legs, though most of the *Bree*'s crew had become fairly used to such tricks; but that was not what impressed Barlennan. At two pounds' weight, one held onto something or else was blown away by the first breeze; and no one could hold onto anything with six walking legs. When that gale struck—but already no order could be heard, even if the commander were to shriek his loudest. He had actually started to creep across the first buffer space separating him from the scene of action when he saw that the mate had fastened a set of lines to his harness and to the deck, and was almost as securely tied down as the mast he was working on.

Barlennan relaxed once more. He knew why Don had done it—it was a simple act of defiance to whatever was driving this particular storm, and he was deliberately impressing his attitude on the crew. Good fellow, thought Barlennan, and turned his attention once more to the bay.

No witness could have told precisely where the shore line now lay. A blinding whirl of white spray and nearly white sand hid everything more than a hundred yards from the *Bree* in every direction; and now even the ship was growing difficult to see as hard-driven droplets of methane struck bulletlike and smeared themselves over his eye shells. At least the deck under his many feet was still rock-steady; light as it now was, the vessel did not seem prepared to blow away. It shouldn't, the commander thought grimly, as he recalled the scores of cables now holding to deep-struck anchors and to the low trees that dotted the beach. It shouldn't—but this would not be the first ship to disappear while venturing this near the Rim. Maybe his crew's suspicion of the Flyer had some justice. After all, that strange being *had* persuaded him to remain for the winter, and had somehow done it without promising any protection to ship or crew. Still, if the Flyer wanted to destroy them, he could certainly do so more easily and certainly than by arguing them into this trick. If that huge structure he rode should get above the *Bree* even here where weight meant so little, there would be no more to be said. Barlennan turned his mind to other matters; he had in full measure the normal Mesklinite horror of letting himself get even temporarily under anything really solid.

The crew had long since taken shelter under the deck flaps—even the mate ceased work as the storm actually struck. They were all present; Barlennan had counted the humps under the protecting fabric while he could still see the whole ship. There were no hunters out, for no sailor had needed the Flyer's warning that a storm was approaching. None of them had been more than five miles from the security of the ship for the last ten days, and five miles was no distance to travel in this weight.

They had plenty of supplies, of course; Barlennan was no fool himself, and did his best to employ none. Still, fresh food was nice. He wondered how long this particular storm would keep them penned in; that was something the signs did not tell, clearly as they heralded the approach of the disturbance. Perhaps the Flyer knew that. In any case, there was nothing further to be done about the ship; he might as well talk to the strange creature. Barlennan still felt a faint thrill of unbelief whenever he looked at the device the Flyer had given him, and never tired of assuring himself once more of its powers.

It lay, under a small shelter flap of its own, on the poop raft beside him. It was an apparently solid block three inches long and about half as high and wide. A transparent spot in the otherwise blank surface of one end looked like an eye, and apparently functioned as one. The only other feature was a small, round hole in one of the long faces. The block was lying with this face upward, and the "eye" end projecting slightly from under the shelter flap. The flap itself opened downwind, of course, so that its fabric was now plastered tightly against the flat upper surface of the machine.

Barlennan worked an arm under the flap, groped around until he found the hole, and inserted his pincer. There was no moving part, such as a switch or button, inside, but that did not bother him—he had never encountered such devices any more than he had met thermal, photonic, or capacity-activated relays. He knew from experience that the fact of putting anything opaque into that hole was somehow made known to the Flyer, and he knew that there was no point whatever in his attempting to figure out how it was done. It would be, he sometimes reflected ruefully, something like teaching navigation to a ten-day-old child. The intelligence might be there—it was comforting to think so, anyway—but some years of background experience were lacking.

"Charles Lackland here." The machine spoke abruptly, cutting the train of thought. "That you, Barl?"

"This is Barlennan, Charles." The commander spoke the Flyer's language, in which he was gradually becoming proficient.

"Good to hear from you. Were we right about this little breeze?"

"It came at the time you predicted. Just a moment —yes, there is snow with it. I had not noticed. I see no dust as yet, however."

"It will come. That volcano must have fed ten cubic miles of it into the air, and it's been spreading for days."

Barlennan made no direct reply to this. The volcano in question was still a point of contention between them, since it was located in a part of Mesklin which, according to Barlennan's geographical background, did not exist.

"What I really wondered about, Charles, was how long this blow was going to last. I understand your people can see it from above, and should know how big it is."

"Are you in trouble already? The winter's just starting—you have thousands of days before you can get out of here."

"I realize that. We have plenty of food, as far as quantity goes. However, we'd like something fresh occasionally, and it would be nice to know in advance when we can send out a hunting party or two."

"I see. I'm afraid it will take some rather careful timing. I was not here last winter, but I understand that during that season the storms in this area are practically continuous. Have you ever been actually to the equator before?"

"To the what?"

"To the—I guess it's what you mean when you talk of the Rim."

"No, I have never been this close, and don't see how anyone could get much closer. It seems to me that if we went much farther out to sea we'd lose every last bit of our weight and go flying off into nowhere."

"If it's any comfort to you, you are wrong. If you kept going, your weight would start up again. You are on the equator right now—the place where weight is least. That is why I am here. I begin to see why you don't want to believe there is land very much farther north. I thought it might be language trouble when we talked of it before. Perhaps you have time enough to describe to me now your ideas concerning the nature of the world. Or perhaps you have maps?"

"We have a Bowl here on the poop raft, of course. I'm afraid you wouldn't be able to see it now, since the sun has just set and Esstes doesn't give light enough to help through these clouds. When the sun rises I'll show it to you. My flat maps wouldn't be much good, since none of them covers enough territory to give a really good picture."

"Good enough. While we're waiting for sunrise could you give me some sort of verbal idea, though?"

"I'm not sure I know your language well enough yet, but I'll try.

"I was taught in school that Mesklin is a big, hollow

bowl. The part where most people live is near the bottom, where there is decent weight. The philosophers have an idea that weight is caused by the pull of a big, flat plate that Mesklin is sitting on; the farther out we go toward the Rim, the less we weigh, since we're farther from the plate. What the plate is sitting on no one knows; you hear a lot of queer beliefs on that subject from some of the less civilized races."

"I should think if your philosophers were right you'd be climbing uphill whenever you traveled away from the center, and all the oceans would run to the lowest point," interjected Lackland. "Have you ever asked one of your philosophers that?"

"When I was a youngster I saw a picture of the whole thing. The teacher's diagram showed a lot of lines coming up from the plate and bending in to meet right over the middle of Mesklin. They came through the bowl straight rather than slantwise because of the curve; and the teacher said weight operated along the lines instead of straight down toward the plate," returned the commander. "I didn't understand it fully, but it seemed to work. They said the theory was proved because the surveyed distances on maps agreed with what they ought to be according to the theory. That I *can* understand, and it seems a good point. If the shape weren't what they thought it was, the distances would certainly go haywire before you got very far from your standard point."

"Quite right. I see your philosophers are quite well into geometry. What I don't see is why they haven't realized that there are two shapes that would make the distances come out right. After all can't you see that the surface of Mesklin curves *downward?* If your theory were true, the horizon would seem to be above you. How about that?"

"Oh, it is. That's why even the most primitive tribes know the world is bowl-shaped. It's just out here near the Rim that it looks different. I expect it's something to do with the light. After all, the sun rises and sets here even in summer, and it wouldn't be surprising if things looked a little queer. Why, it even looks as though the—horizon, you called it?—was closer to north and south than it is east and west. You can see a ship much farther away to the east or west. It's the light."

"Hmm. I find your point a little difficult to answer at the moment." Barlennan was not sufficiently familiar with the Flyer's speech to detect such a thing as a note of amusement in his voice. "I have never been on the surface far from the—er—Rim—and never can be, personally. I didn't realize that things looked as you describe, and I can't see why they should, at the moment. I hope to see it when you take that radio-vision set on our little errand."

"I shall be delighted to hear your explanation of why our philosophers are wrong," Barlennan answered politely. "When you are prepared to give it, of course. In the meantime, I am still somewhat curious as to whether you might be able to tell me when there will be a break in this storm."

"It will take a few minutes to get a report from the station on Toorey. Suppose I call you back about sunrise. I can give you the weather forecast, and there'll be light enough for you to show me your Bowl. All right?"

"That will be excellent. I will wait." Barlennan crouched where he was beside the radio while the storm shrieked on around him. The pellets of methane that splattered against his armored back failed to bother him—they hit a lot harder in the high latitudes. Occasionally he stirred to push away the fine drift of ammonia that kept accumulating on the raft, but even that was only a minor annoyance—at least, so far. Toward midwinter, in five or six thousand days, the stuff would be melting in full sunlight, and rather shortly thereafter would be freezing again. The main idea was to get the liquid away from the vessel or vice versa before the second freeze, or Barlennan's crew would be chipping a couple of hundred rafts clear of the beach. The *Bree* was no river boat, but a full-sized oceangoing ship.

It took the Flyer only the promised few minutes to get the required information, and his voice sounded once more from the tiny speaker as the clouds over the bay lightened with the rising sun.

"I'm afraid I was right, Barl. There is no letup in sight. Practically the whole northern hemisphere—which doesn't mean a thing to you—is boiling off its icecap. I understand the storms in general last all winter. The fact that they come separately in the higher southern latitudes is because they get broken up into very small cells by Coriolis deflection as they get away from the equator."

"By what?"

"By the same force that makes any projectile you throw swerve so noticeably to the left—at least, while I've never seen it under your conditions, it would practically have to on this planet."

"What is 'throw'?"

"My gosh, we haven't used that word, have we? Well, I've seen you jump—no, by gosh, I haven't either!—when you were up visiting at my shelter. Do you remember that word?"

"No."

"Well, 'throw' is when you take some other object—pick it up—and push it hard away from you so that it travels some distance before striking the ground!"

"We don't do that up in reasonable countries. There are lots of things we can do here which are either impossible or very dangerous there. If I were to 'throw' something at home, it might very well land on someone—probably me."

"Come to think of it, that might be bad. Three G's here at the equator is bad enough; you have nearly seven hundred at the poles. Still, if you could find something small enough so that your muscles could throw it, why couldn't you catch it again, or at least resist its impact?"

"I find the situation hard to picture, but I think I know the answer. There isn't time. If something is let go—thrown or not—it hits the ground before anything can be done about it. Picking up and carrying is one thing; crawling is one thing; throwing and—jumping? —are entirely different matters."

"I see—I guess. We sort of took for granted that

you'd have a reaction time commensurate with your gravity, but I can see that's just man-centered thinking. I guess I get it."

"What I could understand of your talk sounded reasonable. It is certainly evident that we are different; we will probably never fully realize just how different. At least we are enough alike to talk together—and make what I hope will be a mutually profitable agreement."

"I am sure it will be. Incidentally, in furtherance of it you will have to give me an idea of the places you want to go, and I will have to point out on your maps the place where I want you to go. Could we look at that Bowl of yours now? There is light enough for this vision set."

"Certainly. The Bowl is set in the deck and cannot be moved; I will have to move the machine so that you can see it. Wait a moment."

Barlennan inched across the raft to a spot that was covered by a smaller flap, clinging to deck cleats as he went. He pulled back and stowed the flap, exposing a clear spot on the deck; then he returned, made four lines fast about the radio, secured them to strategically placed cleats, removed the radio's cover, and began to work it across the deck. It weighed more than he did by quite a margin, though its linear dimensions were smaller, but he was taking no chances of having it blown away. The storm had not eased in the least, and the deck itself was quivering occasionally. With the eye end of the set almost to the Bowl, he propped the other end up with spars so that the Flyer could look downward. Then he himself moved to the other side of the Bowl and began his exposition.

Lackland had to admit that the map which the Bowl contained was logically constructed and, as far as it went, accurate. Its curvature matched that of the planet quite closely, as he had expected—the major error being that it was concave, in conformity with the natives' ideas about the shape of their world. It was about six inches across and roughly one and a quarter deep at the center. The whole map was protected by a transparent cover—probably of ice, Lackland guessed—set flush with the deck. This interfered somewhat with Barlennan's attempts to point out details, but could not have been removed without letting the Bowl fill with ammonia snow in moments. The stuff was piling up wherever it found shelter from the wind. The beach was staying relatively clear, but both Lackland and Barlennan could imagine what was happening on the other side of the hills that paralleled it on the south. The latter was secretly glad he was a sailor. Land travel in this region would not be fun for some thousands of days.

"I have tried to keep my charts up to date," he said as he settled down opposite the Flyer's proxy. "I haven't attempted to make any changes in the Bowl, though, because the new regions we mapped on the way up were not extensive enough to show. There is actually little I can show you in detail, but you wanted a general idea of where I planned to go when we could get out of here.

"Well, actually I don't care greatly. I can buy and sell anywhere, and at the moment I have little aboard but food. I won't have much of that by the time winter is over, either; so I had planned, since our talk, to cruise for a time around the low-weight areas and pick up plant products which can be obtained here—materials that are valued by the people farther south because of their effect on the taste of food."

"Spices?"

"If that is the word for such products, yes. I have carried them before, and rather like them—you can get good profit from a single shipload, as with most commodities whose value depends less on their actual usefulness than on their rarity."

"I take it, then, that once you have loaded here you don't particularly care where you go?"

"That is right. I understand that your errand will carry us close to the Center, which is fine—the farther south we go, the higher the prices I can get; and the extra length of the journey should not be much more dangerous, since you will be helping us as you agreed."

"Right. That is excellent—though I wish we had been able to find something we could give you in actual payment, so that you would not feel the need to take time in spice-gathering."

"Well, we have to eat. You say your bodies, and hence your foods, are made of very different substances from ours, so we can't use your foodstuffs. Frankly, I can't think of any desirable raw metal or similar material that I couldn't get far more easily in any quantity I wanted. My favorite idea is still that we get some of your machines, but you say that they would have to be built anew to function under our conditions. It seems that the agreement we reached is the best that is possible, under those circumstances."

"True enough. Even this radio was built specifically for this job, and you could not repair it—your people, unless I am greatly mistaken, don't have the tools. However, during the journey we can talk of this again; perhaps the things we learn of each other will open up other and better possibilities."

"I am sure they will," Barlennan answered politely.

He did not, of course, mention the possibility that his own plans might succeed. The Flyer would hardly have approved.

II: THE FLYER

The Flyer's forecast was sound; some four hundred days passed before the storm let up noticeably. Five times during that period the Flyer spoke to Barlennan on the radio, always opening with a brief weather forecast and continuing a more general conversation for a day or two each time. Barlennan had noticed earlier, when he had been learning the strange creature's language and paying personal visits to its outpost in the "Hill" near the bay, that it seemed to have a strangely regular life cycle; he found he could count on finding the Flyer sleeping or eating at quite predictable times, which seemed to have a cycle of about eighty days. Barlennan was no philosopher—he had at least his share of the common tendency to regard them as impractical dreamers—and he simply shrugged this fact off as something pertaining to a weird but admittedly interesting creature. There was nothing in the Mesklinite background that would enable him to deduce the existence of a world that took some eighty times as long as his own to rotate on its axis.

Lackland's fifth call was different from the others, and more welcome for several reasons. The difference was due partly to the fact that it was off schedule; its pleasant nature to the fact that at last there was a favorable weather forecast.

"Barl!" The Flyer did not bother with preliminaries —he knew that the Mesklinite was always within sound of the radio. "The station on Toorey called a few minutes ago. There is a relatively clear area moving toward us. He was not sure just what the winds

12

would be, but he can see the ground through it, so visibility ought to be fair. If your hunters want to go out I should say that they wouldn't be blown away, provided they wait until the clouds have been gone for twenty or thirty days. For a hundred days or so after that we should have very good weather indeed. They'll tell me in plenty of time to get your people back to the ship."

"But how will they get your warning? If I send this radio with them I won't be able to talk to you about our regular business, and if I don't, I don't see—"

"I've been thinking of that," interrupted Lackland. "I think you'd better come up here as soon as the wind drops sufficiently. I can give you another set— perhaps it would be better if you had several. I gather that the journey you will be taking for us will be dangerous, and I know for myself it will be long enough. Thirty-odd thousand miles as the crow flies, and I can't yet guess how far by ship and overland."

Lackland's simile occasioned a delay; Barlennan wanted to know what a crow was, and also flying. The first was the easier to get across. Flying for a living creature, under its own power, was harder for him to imagine than throwing—and the thought was more terrifying. He had regarded Lackland's proven ability to travel through the air as something so alien that it did not really strike home to *him*. Lackland saw this, partly.

"There's another point I want to take up with you," he said. "As soon as it's clear enough to land safely, they're bringing down a crawler. Maybe watching the rocket land will get you a little more used to the whole flying idea."

"Perhaps," Barlennan answered hesitantly. "I'm not sure I want to see your rocket land. I did once before, you know, and—well, I'd not want one of the crew to be there at the time."

"Why not? Do you think they'd be scared too much to be useful?"

"No." The Mesklinite answered quite frankly. "I don't want one of them to see me as scared as I'm likely to be."

"You surprise me, Commander." Lackland tried to give his words in a jocular tone. "However, I understand your feelings, and I assure you that the rocket will not pass above you. If you will wait right next to the wall of my dome I will direct its pilot by radio to make sure of that."

"But how close to overhead will it come?"

"A good distance sideways, I promise. That's for my own safety as well as your comfort. To land on this world, even here at the equator, it will be necessary for him to be using a pretty potent blast. I don't want it hitting my dome, I can assure you."

"All right. I will come. As you say, it would be nice to have more radios. What is this 'crawler' of which you speak?"

"It is a machine which will carry me about on land as your ship does at sea. You will see in a few days, or in a few hours at most."

Barlennan let the new word pass without question, since the remark was clear enough anyway. "I will come, and will see," he agreed.

The Flyer's friends on Mesklin's inner moon had prophesied correctly. The commander, crouched on his poop, counted only ten sunrises before a lightening of the murk and lessening of the wind gave their usual warning of the approaching eye of the storm. From his own experience he was willing to believe, as the Flyer had said, that the calm period would last one or two hundred days.

With a whistle that would have torn Lackland's eardrums had he been able to hear such a high frequency the commander summoned the attention of his crew and began to issue orders.

"There will be two hunting parties made up at once. Dondragmer will head one, Merkoos the other; each will take nine men of his own choosing. I will remain on the ship to coordinate, for the Flyer is going to give us more of his talking machines. I will go to the Flyer's Hill as soon as the sky is clear to get them; they, as well as other things he wants, are being brought down from Above by his friends, therefore all crew members will remain near the ship until I return. Plan for departure thirty days after I leave."

"Sir, is it wise for you to leave the ship so early? The wind will still be high." The mate was too good a friend for the question to be impertinent, though some commanders would have resented any such reflection on their judgment. Barlennan waved his pincers in a manner denoting a smile.

"You are quite right. However, I want to save the time, and the Flyer's Hill is only a mile away."

"But—"

"Furthermore it is downwind. We have many miles of line in the lockers; I will have two bent to my harness, and two of the men—Terblannen and Hars, I think, under your supervision, Don—will pay those lines out through the bitts as I go. I may—probably will—lose my footing, but if the wind were able to get such a grip on me as to break good sea cord, the *Bree* would be miles inland by now."

"But even losing your footing—suppose you were to be lifted into the air—" Dondragmer was still deeply troubled, and the thought he had uttered gave even his commander pause for an instant.

"Falling—yes—but remember that we are near the Edge—at it, the Flyer says, and I can believe him when I look north from the top of his Hill. As some of you have found, a fall means nothing here."

"But you ordered that we should act as though we had normal weight, so that no habits might be formed that would be dangerous when we returned to a livable land."

"Quite true. This will be no habit, since in any reasonable place no wind could pick me up. Anyway, that is what we do. Let Terblannen and Hars check the lines—no, check them yourself. It will take long enough.

"That is all for the present. The watch under shelter may rest. The watch on deck will check anchors and lashings." Dondragmer, who had the latter watch, took the order as a dismissal and proceeded to carry it out in his usual efficient manner. He also set men to work cleaning snow from the spaces between rafts, having seen as clearly as his captain the possible consequences of a thaw followed by a freeze. Barlennan himself relaxed, wondering sadly just which ancestor was responsible for his habit of talking himself into situations that were both unpleasant to face and impossible to back out of gracefully.

For the rope idea was strictly spur-of-the-moment, and it took most of the several days before the clouds vanished for the arguments he had used on his mate to appeal to their inventor. He was not really happy even when he lowered himself onto the snow that had drifted against the lee rafts, cast a last look backward at his two most powerful crew members and the lines they were managing, and set off across the wind-swept beach.

Actually, it was not too bad. There was a slight upward force from the ropes, since the deck was several inches above ground level when he started; but the slope of the beach quickly remedied that. Also, the trees which were serving so nobly as mooring points for the *Bree* grew more and more thickly as he went inland. They were low, flat growths with wide-spreading tentacular limbs and very short, thick trunks, generally similar to those of the lands he knew deep in the southern hemisphere of Mesklin. Here, however, their branches arched sometimes entirely clear of the ground, left relatively free by an effective gravity less than one two-hundredth that of the polar regions. Eventually they grew close enough together to permit the branches to intertwine, a tangle of brown and black cables which furnished excellent hold. Barlennan found it possible, after a time, practically to climb toward the Hill, getting a grip with his front pincers, releasing the hold of his rear ones, and twisting his caterpillarlike body forward so that he progressed almost in inchworm fashion. The cables gave him some trouble, but since both they and the tree limbs were relatively smooth no serious fouling occurred.

The beach was fairly steep after the first two hundred yards; and at half the distance he expected to go, Barlennan was some six feet above the *Bree*'s deck level. From this point the Flyer's Hill could be seen, even by an individual whose eyes were as close to the ground as those of a Mesklinite; and the commander paused to take in the scene as he had many times before.

The remaining half mile was a white, brown, and black tangle, much like that he had just traversed. The vegetation was even denser, and had trapped a good deal more snow, so that there was little or no bare ground visible.

Looming above the tangled plain was the Flyer's Hill. The Mesklinite found it almost impossible to think of it as an artificial structure, partly because of its monstrous size and partly because a roof of any description other than a flap of fabric was completely foreign to his ideas of architecture. It was a glittering metal dome some twenty feet in height and forty in diameter, nearly a perfect hemisphere. It was dotted with large, transparent areas and had two cylindrical extensions containing doors. The Flyer had said that these doors were so constructed that one could pass through them without letting air get from one side to the other. The portals were certainly big enough for the strange creature, gigantic as he was. One of the lower windows had an improvised ramp leading up to it which would permit a creature of Barlennan's size and build to crawl up to the pane and see inside. The commander had spent much time on that ramp while he was first learning to speak and understand the Flyer's language; he had seen much of the strange apparatus and furniture which filled the structure, though he had no idea of the use to which most of it was put. The Flyer himself appeared to be an amphibious creature—at least, he spent much of the time floating in a tank of liquid. This was reasonable enough, considering his size. Barlennan himself knew of no creature native to Mesklin larger than his own race which was not strictly an ocean or lake dweller—though he realized that, as far as weight alone was considered, such things might exist in these vast, nearly unexplored regions near the Rim. He trusted that he would meet none, at least while he himself was ashore. Size meant weight, and a lifetime of conditioning prevented his completely ignoring weight as a menace.

There was nothing near the dome except the ever present vegetation. Evidently the rocket had not yet arrived, and for a moment Barlennan toyed with the idea of waiting where he was until it did. Surely when it came it would descend on the farther side of the Hill—the Flyer would see to that, if Barlennan himself had not arrived. Still, there was nothing to prevent the descending vessel from passing *over* his present position; Lackland could do nothing about that, since he would not know exactly where the Mesklinite was. Few Earthmen can locate a body fifteen inches long and two in diameter crawling horizontally through tangled vegetation at a distance of half a mile. No, he had better go right up to the dome, as the Flyer had advised. The commander resumed his progress, still dragging the ropes behind him.

He made it in good time, though delayed slightly by occasional periods of darkness. As a matter of fact it was night when he reached his goal, though the last part of his journey had been adequately illuminated by light from the windows ahead of him. However, by the time he had made his ropes fast and crawled up to a comfortable station outside the window the sun had lifted above the horizon on his left. The clouds were almost completely gone now, though the wind was still strong, and he could have seen in through the window even had the inside lights been turned out.

Lackland was not in the room from which this window looked, and the Mesklinite pressed the tiny call button which had been mounted on the ramp. Immediately the Flyer's voice sounded from a speaker beside the button.

"Glad you're here, Barl. I've been having Mack hold up until you came. I'll start him down right away, and he should be here by next sunrise."

"Where is he now? On Toorey?"

"No; he's drifting at the inner edge of the ring, only six hundred miles up. He's been there since well before the storm ended, so don't worry about having kept him waiting yourself. While we're waiting for him, I'll bring out the other radios I promised."

"Since I am alone, it might be well to bring only

one radio this time. They are rather awkward things to carry, though light enough, of course."

"Maybe we should wait for the crawler before I bring them out at all. Then I can ride you back to your ship—the crawler is well enough insulated so that riding outside it wouldn't hurt you, I'm sure. How would that be?"

"It sounds excellent. Shall we have more language while we wait, or can you show me more pictures of the place you come from?"

"I have some pictures. It will take a few minutes to load the projector, so it should be dark enough when we're ready. Just a moment—I'll come to the lounge."

The speaker fell silent, and Barlennan kept his eyes on the door which he could see at one side of the room. In a few moments the Flyer appeared, walking upright as usual with the aid of the artificial limbs he called crutches. He approached the window, nodded his massive head at the tiny watcher, and turned to the movie projector. The screen at which the machine was pointed was on the wall directly facing the window; and Barlennan, keeping a couple of eyes on the human being's actions, squatted down more comfortably in a position from which he could watch it easily. He waited silently while the sun arched lazily overhead. It was warm in the full sunlight, pleasantly so, though not warm enough to start a thaw; the perpetual wind from the northern icecap prevented that. He was half dozing while Lackland finished threading the machine, stumped over to his relaxation tank, and lowered himself into it. Barlennan had never noticed the elastic membrane over the surface of the liquid which kept the man's clothes dry; if he had, it might have modified his ideas about the amphibious nature of human beings. From his floating position Lackland reached up to a small panel and snapped two switches. The room lights went out and the projector started to operate. It was a fifteen-minute reel, and had not quite finished when Lackland had to haul himself once more to his feet and crutches with the information that the rocket was landing.

"Do you want to watch Mack, or would you rather

see the end of the reel?" he asked. "He'll probably be on the ground by the time it's done."

Barlennan tore his attention from the screen with some reluctance. "I'd rather watch the picture, but it would probably be better for me to get used to the sight of flying things," he said. "From which side will it come?"

"The east, I should expect. I have given Mack a careful description of the layout here, and he already had photographs; and I know an approach from that direction will be somewhat easier, as he is now set. I'm afraid the sun is interfering at the moment with your line of vision, but he's still about forty miles up —look well above the sun."

Barlennan followed these instructions and waited. For perhaps a minute he saw nothing; his eye was caught by a glint of metal some twenty degrees above the rising sun.

"Altitude ten—horizontal distance about the same," Lackland reported at the same moment. "I have him on the scope here."

The glint grew brighter, holding its direction almost perfectly—the rocket was on a nearly exact course toward the dome. In another minute it was close enough for details to be visible—or would have been, except that everything was now hidden in the glare of the rising sun. Mack hung poised for a moment a mile above the station and as far as to the east; and as Belne moved out of line Barlennan could see the windows and exhaust ports in the cylindrical hull. The storm wind had dropped almost completely, but now a warm breeze laden with a taint of melting ammonia began to blow from the point where the exhaust struck the ground. The drops of semiliquid spattered on Barlennan's eye shells, but he continued to stare at the slowly settling mass of metal. Every muscle in his long body was at maximum tension, his arms held close to his sides, pincers clamped tightly enough to have shorn through steel wire, the hearts in each of his body segments pumping furiously. He would have been holding his breath had he possessed breathing apparatus at all similar to that of a human being. Intellectually he knew that the thing would not fall—he kept telling himself that it could not; but having grown to maturity in an environment where a fall of six inches was usually fatally destructive even to the incredibly tough Mesklinite organism, his emotions were not easy to control. Subconsciously he kept expecting the metal shell to vanish from sight, to reappear on the ground below flattened out of recognizable shape. After all, it was still *hundreds of feet* up . . .

On the ground below the rocket, now swept clear of snow, the black vegetation abruptly burst into flame. Black ash blew from the landing point, and the ground itself glowed briefly. For just an instant this lasted before the glittering cylinder settled lightly into the center of the bare patch. Seconds later the thunder which had mounted to a roar louder than Mesklin's hurricanes died abruptly. Almost painfully, Barlennan relaxed, opening and shutting his pincers to relieve the cramps.

"If you'll stand by a moment, I'll be out with the radios," Lackland said. The commander had not noticed his departure, but the Flyer was no longer in the room. "Mack will drive the crawler over here—you can watch it come while I'm getting into armor."

Actually Barlennan was able to watch only a portion of the drive. He saw the rocket's cargo lock swing open and the vehicle emerge; he got a sufficiently good look at the crawler to understand everything about it —he thought—except what made its caterpillar treads move. It was big, easily big enough to hold several of the Flyer's race unless too much of its interior was full of machinery. Like the dome, it had numerous and large windows; through one of these in the front the commander could see the armored figure of another Flyer, who was apparently controlling it. Whatever drove the machine did not make enough noise to be audible across the mile of space that still separated it from the dome.

It covered very little of that distance before the sun set, and details ceased to be visible. Esstes, the smaller sun, was still in the sky and brighter than the full moon of Earth, but Barlennan's eyes had their limitations.

An intense beam of light projected from the crawler itself along its path, and consequently straight toward the dome, did not help either. Barlennan simply waited. After all, it was still too far for really good examination even by daylight, and would undoubtedly be at the Hill by sunrise.

Even then he might have to wait, of course; the Flyers might object to the sort of examination he really wanted to give their machinery.

III: OFF THE GROUND

The tank's arrival, Lackland's emergence from the dome's main air lock, and the rising of Belne all took place at substantially the same moment. The vehicle stopped only a couple of yards from the platform on which Barlennan was crouched. Its driver also emerged; and the two men stood and talked briefly beside the Mesklinite. The latter rather wondered that they did not return to the inside of the dome to lie down, since both were rather obviously laboring under Mesklin's gravity; but the newcomer refused Lackland's invitation.

"I'd like to be sociable," he said in answer to it, "but honestly, Charlie, would you stay on this ghastly mudball a moment longer than you had to?"

"Well, I could do pretty much the same work from Toorey, or from a ship in a free orbit for that matter," retorted Lackland. "I think personal contact means a good deal. I still want to find out more about Barlennan's people—it seems to me that we're hardly giving him as much as we expect to get, and it would be nice to find out if there were anything more we could do. Furthermore, he's in a rather dangerous situation himself, and having one of us here might make quite a difference—to both of us."

"I don't follow you."

"Barlennan is a tramp captain—a sort of free-lance explorer-trader. He's completely out of the normal areas inhabited and traveled through by his people. He is remaining here during the southern winter, when the evaporating north polar cap makes storms which

23

have to be seen to be believed here in the equatorial regions—storms which are almost as much out of his experience as ours. If anything happens to him, stop and think of our chances of meeting another contact!

"Remember, he normally lives in a gravity field from two hundred to nearly seven hundred times as strong as Earth's. We certainly won't follow him home to meet his relatives! Furthermore, there probably aren't a hundred of his race who are not only in the same business but courageous enough to go so far from their natural homes. Of those hundred, what are our chances of meeting another? Granting that this ocean is the one they frequent most, this little arm of it, from which this bay is an offshoot, is six thousand miles long and a third as wide—with a very crooked shore line. As for spotting one, at sea or ashore, from above— well, Barlennan's *Bree* is about forty feet long and a third as wide, and is one of their biggest oceangoing ships. Scarcely any of it is more than three inches above the water, besides.

"No, Mack, our meeting Barlennan was the wildest of coincidences; and I'm not counting on another. Staying under three gravities for five months or so, until the southern spring, will certainly be worth it. Of course, if you want to gamble our chances of recovering nearly two billion dollars' worth of apparatus on the results of a search over a strip of planet a thousand miles wide and something over a hundred and fifty thousand long—"

"You've made your point," the other human being admitted, "but I'm still glad it's you and not me. Of course, maybe if I knew Barlennan better—" Both men turned to the tiny, caterpillarlike form crouched on the waist-high platform.

"Barl, I trust you will forgive my rudeness in not introducing Wade McLellan," Lackland said. "Wade, this is Barlennan, captain of the *Bree,* and a master shipman of his world—he has not told me that, but the fact that he is here is sufficient evidence."

"I am glad to meet you, Flyer McLellan," the Mesklinite responded. "No apology is necessary, and I assumed that your conversation was meant for my ears as well." He performed the standard pincer-opening gesture of greeting. "I had already appreciated the good fortune for both of us which our meeting represents, and only hope that I can fulfill my part of the bargain as well as I am sure you will yours."

"You speak English remarkably well," commented McLellan. "Have you really been learning it for less than six weeks?"

"I am not sure how long your 'week' is, but it is less than thirty-five hundred days since I met your friend," returned the commander. "I am a good linguist, of course—it is necessary in my business; and the films that Charles showed helped very much."

"It is rather lucky that your voice could make all the sounds of our language. We sometimes have trouble that way."

"That, or something like it, is why I learned your English rather than the other way around. Many of the sounds we use are much too shrill for your vocal cords, I understand." Barlennan carefully refrained from mentioning that much of his normal conversation was also too high-pitched for human ears. After all, Lackland might not have noticed it yet, and the most honest of traders thinks at least twice before revealing all his advantages. "I imagine that Charles has learned some of our language, nevertheless, by watching and listening to us through the radio now on the *Bree*."

"Very little," confessed Lackland. "You seem, from what little I have seen, to have an extremely well-trained crew. A great deal of your regular activity is done without orders, and I can make nothing of the conversations you sometimes have with some of your men, which are not accompanied by any action."

"You mean when I am talking to Dondragmer or Merkoos? They are my first and second officers, and the ones I talk to most."

"I hope you will not feel insulted at this, but I am quite unable to tell one of your people from another. I simply am not familiar enough with your distinguishing characteristics."

Barlennan almost laughed.

"In my case, it is even worse. I am not entirely sure

whether I have seen you without artificial covering or not."

"Well, that is carrying us a long way from business —we've used up a lot of daylight as it is. Mack, I assume you want to get back to the rocket and out where weight means nothing and men are balloons. When you get there, be sure that the receiver-transmitters for each of these four sets are placed close enough together so that one will register on another. I don't suppose it's worth the trouble of tying them in electrically, but these folks are going to use them for a while as contact between separate parties, and the sets are on different frequencies. Barl, I've left the radios by the air lock. Apparently the sensible program would be for me to put you and the radios on top of the crawler, take Mack over to the rocket, and then drive you and the apparatus over to the *Bree*."

Lackland acted on this suggestion, so obviously the right course, before anyone could answer; and Barlennan almost went mad as a result.

The man's armored hand swept out and *picked up* the tiny body of the Mesklinite. For one soul-shaking instant Barlennan felt and saw himself suspended long feet away from the ground; then he was deposited on the flat top of the tank. His pincers scraped desperately and vainly at the smooth metal to supplement the instinctive grips which his dozens of suckerlike feet had taken on the plates; his eyes glared in undiluted horror at the emptiness around the edge of the roof, only a few body lengths away in every direction. For long seconds—perhaps a full minute—he could not find his voice; and when he did speak, he could no longer be heard. He was too far away from the pickup on the platform for intelligible words to carry—he knew that from earlier experience; and even at this extremity of terror he remembered that the sirenlike howl of agonized fear that he wanted to emit would have been heard with equal clarity by everyone on the *Bree,* since there was another radio there.

And the *Bree* would have had a new captain. Respect for his courage was the only thing that had driven that crew into the storm-breeding regions of the

Rim. If that went, he would have no crew and no ship —and, for all practical purpose, no life. A coward was not tolerated on any oceangoing ship in any capacity; and while his homeland was on this same continental mass, the idea of traversing forty thousand miles of coast line on foot was not to be considered.

These thoughts did not cross his conscious mind in detail, but his instinctive knowledge of the facts effectually silenced him while Lackland picked up the radios and, with McLellan, entered the tank below the Mesklinite. The metal under him quivered slightly as the door was closed, and an instant later the vehicle started to move. As it did so, a peculiar thing happened to its non-human passenger.

The fear might have—perhaps should have—driven him mad. His situation can only be dimly approximated by comparing it with that of a human being hanging by one hand from a window ledge forty stories above a paved street.

And yet he did not go mad. At least, he did not go mad in the accepted sense; he continued to reason as well as ever, and none of his friends could have detected a change in his personality. For just a little while, perhaps, an Earthman more familiar with Mesklinites than Lackland had yet become might have suspected that the commander was a little drunk; but even that passed.

And the fear passed with it. Nearly six body lengths above the ground, he found himself crouched almost calmly. He was holding tightly, of course; he even remembered, later, reflecting how lucky it was that the wind had continued to drop, even though the smooth metal offered an unusually good grip for his suckerfeet. It was amazing, the viewpoint that could be enjoyed—yes, he enjoyed it—from such a position. Looking down on things really helped; you could get a remarkably complete picture of so much ground at once. It was like a map; and Barlennan had never before regarded a map as a picture of country seen from above.

An almost intoxicating sense of triumph filled him as the crawler approached the rocket and stopped. The

Mesklinite waved his pincers almost gaily at the emerging McLellan visible in the reflected glare of the tank's lights, and was disproportionately pleased when the man waved back. The tank immediately turned to the left and headed for the beach where the *Bree* lay; Mack, remembering that Barlennan was unprotected, thoughtfully waited until it was nearly a mile away before lifting his own machine into the air. The sight of it, drifting slowly upward apparently without support, threatened for just an instant to revive the old fear; but Barlennan fought the sensation grimly down and deliberately watched the rocket until it faded from view in the light of the lowering sun.

Lackland had been watching too; but when the last glint of metal had disappeared, he lost no further time in driving the tank the short remaining distance to where the *Bree* lay. He stopped a hundred yards from the vessel, but he was quite close enough for the shocked creatures on the decks to see their commander perched on the vehicle's roof. It would have been less disconcerting had Lackland approached bearing Barlennan's head on a pole.

Even Dondragmer, the most intelligent and levelheaded of the *Bree*'s complement—not excepting his captain—was paralyzed for long moments; and his first motion was with eyes only, taking the form of a wistful glance toward the flame-dust tanks and "shakers" on the outer rafts. Fortunately for Barlennan, the crawler was not downwind; for the temperature was, as usual, below the melting point of the chlorine in the tanks. Had the wind permitted, the mate would have sent a cloud of fire about the vehicle without ever thinking that his captain might be alive.

A faint rumble of anger began to arise from the assembled crew as the door of the crawler opened and Lackland's armored figure emerged. Their half-trading, half-piratical way of life had left among them only those most willing to fight without hesitation at the slightest hint of menace to one of their number; the cowards had dropped away long since, and the individualists had died. The only thing that saved Lackland's life as he emerged into their view was habit

—the conditioning that prevented their making the hundred-yard leap that would have cost the weakest of them the barest flick of his body muscles. Crawling as they had done all their lives, they flowed from the rafts like a red and black waterfall and spread over the beach toward the alien machine. Lackland saw them coming, of course, but so completely misunderstood their motivation that he did not even hurry as he reached up to the crawler's roof, picked up Barlennan, and set him on the ground. Then he reached back into the vehicle and brought out the radios he had promised, setting them on the sand beside the commander; and by then it had dawned on the crew that their captain was alive and apparently unharmed. The avalanche stopped in confusion, milling in undecided fashion midway between ship and tank; and a cacophony of voices ranging from deep bass to the highest notes the radio speaker could reproduce gabbled in Lackland's suit phones. Though he had, as Barlennan had intimated, done his best to attach meaning to some of the native conversation he had previously heard, the man understood not a single word from the crew. It was just as well for his peace of mind; he had long been aware that even armor able to withstand Mesklin's eight-atmosphere surface pressure would mean little or nothing to Mesklinite pincers.

Barlennan stopped the babble with a hoot that Lackland could probably have heard directly through the armor, if its reproduction by the radio had not partially deafened him first. The commander knew perfectly well what was going on in the minds of his men, and had no desire to see frozen shreds of Lackland scattered over the beach.

"Calm down!" Actually Barlennan felt a very human warmth at his crew's reaction to his apparent danger, but this was no time to encourage them. "Enough of you have played the fool here at no-weight so that you all should know I was in no danger!"

"But you forbade—"

"We thought—"

"You were *high*—" A chorus of objections answered the captain, who cut them short.

"I know I forbade such actions, and I told you why. When we return to high-weight and decent living we must have no habits that might result in our thoughtlessly doing dangerous things like that—" He waved a pincer-tipped arm upward toward the tank's roof. "You all know what proper weight can do; the Flyer doesn't. He put me up there, as you saw him take me down, without even thinking about it. He comes from a place where there is practically no weight at all; where, I believe, he could fall many times *his* body length without being hurt. You can see that for yourselves: if he felt properly about high places, how could he *fly?*"

Most of Barlennan's listeners had dug their stumpy feet into the sand as though trying to get a better grip on it during this speech. Whether they fully digested, or even fully believed, their commander's words may be doubted; but at least their minds were distracted from the action they had intended toward Lackland. A faint buzz of conversation arose once more among them, but its chief overtones seemed to be of amazement rather than anger. Dondragmer alone, a little apart from the others, was silent; and the captain realized that his mate would have to be given a much more careful and complete story of what had happened. Dondragmer's imagination was heavily backed by intelligence, and he must already be wondering about the effect on Barlennan's nerves of his recent experience. Well, that could be handled in good time; the crew presented a more immediate problem.

"Are the hunting parties ready?" Barlennan's question silenced the babble once more.

"We have not yet eaten," Merkoos replied a little uneasily, "but everything else—nets and weapons—is in readiness."

"Is the food ready?"

"Within a day, sir." Karondrasee, the cook, turned back toward the ship without further orders.

"Don, Merkoos. You will each take one of these *radios*. You have seen me use the one on the ship—all you have to do is talk anywhere near it. You can run a really efficient pincer movement with these, since you won't have to keep it small enough for both leaders to see each other.

"Don, I am not certain that I will direct from the ship, as I originally planned. I have discovered that one can see over remarkable distances from the top of the Flyer's traveling machine; and if he agrees I shall ride with him in the vicinity of your operations."

"But sir!" Dondragmer was aghast. "Won't—won't that thing scare all the game within sight? You can hear it coming a hundred yards away, and see it for I don't know how far in the open. And besides—" He broke off, not quite sure how to state his main objection. Barlennan did it for him.

"Besides, no one could concentrate on hunting with me in sight so far off the ground—is that it?" The mate's pincers silently gestured agreement, and the movement was emulated by most of the waiting crew.

For a moment the commander was tempted to reason with them, but he realized in time the futility of such an attempt. He could not actually recapture the viewpoint he had shared with them until so recently, but he did realize that before that time he would not have listened to what he now considered "reason" either.

"All right, Don. I'll drop that idea—you're probably right. I'll be in radio touch with you, but will stay out of sight."

"But you'll be riding on that thing? Sir, what has happened to you? I know I can *tell* myself that a fall of a few feet really means little here at the Rim, but I could never bring myself to invite such a fall deliberately; and I don't see how anyone else could. I couldn't even picture myself up on top of that thing."

"You were most of a body length up a mast not too long ago, if I remember aright," returned Barlennan dryly. "Or was it someone else I saw checking upper lashings without unshipping the stick?"

"That was different—I had one end on the deck," Dondragmer replied a trifle uncomfortably.

"Your head still had a long way to fall. I've seen

others of you doing that sort of thing too. If you re-member, I had something to say about it when we first sailed into this region."

"Yes, sir, you did. Are those orders still in force, considering—" The mate paused again, but what he wanted to say was even plainer than before. Barlen-nan thought quickly and hard.

"We'll forget the order," he said slowly. "The rea-sons I gave for such things being dangerous are sound enough, but if any of you get in trouble for forgetting when we're back in high-weight it's your own fault. Use your own judgment on such matters from now on. Does anyone want to come with me now?"

Words and gestures combined in a chorus of em-phatic negatives, with Dondragmer just a shade slower than the rest. Barlennan would have grinned had he possessed the physical equipment.

"Get ready for that hunt—I'll be listening to you," he dismissed his audience. They streamed obediently back toward the *Bree,* and their captain turned to give a suitably censored account of the conversation to Lackland. He was a little preoccupied, for the con-versation just completed had given rise to several brand-new ideas in his mind; but they could be worked out when he had more leisure. Just now he wanted another ride on the tank roof.

IV: BREAKDOWN

The bay on the southern shore of which the *Bree* was beached was a tiny estuary some twenty miles long and two in width at its mouth. It opened from the southern shore of a larger gulf of generally similar shape some two hundred fifty miles long, which in turn was an offshoot of a broad sea which extended an indefinite distance into the northern hemisphere—it merged indistinguishably with the permanently frozen polar cap. All three bodies of liquid extended roughly east and west, the smaller ones being separated from the larger on their northern sides by relatively narrow peninsulas. The ship's position was better chosen than Barlennan had known, being protected from the northern storms by both peninsulas. Eighteen miles to the west, however, the protection of the nearer and lower of these points ceased; and Barlennan and Lackland could appreciate what even that narrow neck had saved them. The captain was once more ensconced on the tank, this time with a radio clamped beside him.

To their right was the sea, spreading to the distant horizon beyond the point that guarded the bay. Behind them the beach was similar to that on which the ship lay, a gently sloping strip of sand dotted with the black, rope-branched vegetation that covered so much of Mesklin. Ahead of them, however, the growths vanished almost completely. Here the slope was even flatter and the belt of sand grew ever broader as the eye traveled along it. It was not completely bare, though even the deep-rooted plants were lacking; but scattered here and there on the wave-channeled expanse were dark, motionless relics of the recent storm.

Some were vast, tangled masses of seaweed, or of growths which could claim that name with little strain on the imagination; others were the bodies of marine animals, and some of these were even vaster. Lackland was a trifle startled—not at the size of the creatures, since they presumably were supported in life by the liquid in which they floated, but at the distance they lay from the shore. One monstrous hulk was sprawled over half a mile inland; and the Earthman began to realize just what the winds of Mesklin could do even in this gravity when they had a sixty-mile sweep of open sea in which to build up waves. He would have liked to go to the point where the shore lacked even the protection of the outer peninsula, but that would have involved a further journey of over a hundred miles.

"What would have happened to your ship, Barlennan, if the waves that reached here had struck it?"

"That depends somewhat on the type of wave, and where we were. On the open sea, we would ride over it without trouble; beached as the *Bree* now is, there would have been nothing left. I did not realize just how high waves could get this close to the Rim, of course—now that I think of it, maybe even the biggest would be relatively harmless, because of its lack of weight."

"I'm afraid it's not the weight that counts most; your first impression was probably right."

"I had some such idea in mind when I sheltered behind that point for the winter, of course. I admit I did not have any idea of the actual size the waves could reach here at the Rim. It is not too surprising that explorers tend to disappear with some frequency in these latitudes."

"This is by no means the worst, either. You have that second point, which is rather mountainous, if I recall the photos correctly, protecting this whole stretch."

"Second point? I did not know about that. Do you mean that what I can see beyond the peninsula there is merely another bay?"

"That's right. I forgot you usually stayed in sight of land. You coasted along to this point from the west, then, didn't you?"

"Yes. These seas are almost completely unknown. This particular shore line extends about three thousand miles in a generally westerly direction, as you probably know—I'm just beginning to appreciate what looking at things from above can do for you—and then gradually bends south. It's not too regular; there's one place where you go east again for a couple of thousand miles, but I suppose the actual straight-line distance that would bring you opposite my home port is about sixteen thousand miles to the south—a good deal farther coasting, of course. Then about twelve hundred miles across open sea to the west would bring me home. The waters about there are very well known, of course, and any sailor can cross them without more than the usual risks of the sea."

While they had been talking, the tank had crawled away from the sea, toward the monstrous hulk that lay stranded by the recent storm. Lackland, of course, wanted to examine it in detail, since he had so far seen practically none of Mesklin's animal life; Barlennan, too, was willing. He had seen many of the monsters that thronged the seas he had traveled all his life, but he was not sure of this one.

Its shape was not too surprising for either of them. It might have been an unusually streamlined whale or a remarkably stout sea snake; the Earthman was reminded of the Zeuglodon that had haunted the seas of his own world thirty million years before. However, nothing that had ever lived on Earth and left fossils for men to study had approached the size of this thing. For six hundred feet it lay along the still sandy soil; in life its body had apparently been cylindrical, and over eighty feet in diameter. Now, deprived of the support of the liquid in which it had lived, it bore some resemblance to a wax model that had been left too long in the hot sun. Though its flesh was presumably only about half as dense as that of earthly life, its tonnage was still something to stagger Lackland when he tried to estimate it; and the three-times-earth-normal gravity had done its share.

"Just what do you do when you meet something like this at sea?" he asked Barlennan.

"I haven't the faintest idea," the Mesklinite replied dryly. "I have seen things like this before, but only rarely. They usually stay in the deeper, permanent seas; I have seen one once only on the surface, and about four cast up as is this one. I do not know what they eat, but apparently they find it far below the surface. I have never heard of a ship's being attacked by one."

"You probably wouldn't," Lackland replied pointedly. "I find it hard to imagine any survivors in such a case. If this thing feeds like some of the whales on my own world, it would inhale one of your ships and probably fail to notice it. Let's have a look at its mouth and find out." He started the tank once more, and drove it along to what appeared to be the head end of the vast body.

The thing had a mouth, and a skull of sorts, but the latter was badly crushed by its own weight. There was enough left, however, to permit the correction of Lackland's guess concerning its eating habits; with those teeth, it could only be carnivorous. At first the man did not recognize them as teeth; only the fact that they were located in a peculiar place for ribs finally led him to the truth.

"You'd be safe enough, Barl," he said at last. "That thing wouldn't dream of attacking you. One of your ships would not be worth the effort, as far as its appetite is concerned—I doubt that it would notice anything less than a hundred times the *Bree*'s size."

"There must be a lot of meat swimming around in the deeper seas," replied the Mesklinite thoughtfully. "I don't see that it's doing anyone much good, though."

"True enough. Say, what did you mean a little while ago by that remark about permanent seas? What other kind do you have?"

"I referred to the areas which are still ocean just before the winter storms begin," was the reply. "The ocean level is at its highest in early spring, at the end of the storms, which have filled the ocean beds during the winter. All the rest of the year they shrink again. Here at the Rim, where shore lines are so steep, it doesn't make much difference; but up where weight is decent the shore line may move anywhere from two hundred to two thousand miles between spring and fall." Lackland emitted a low whistle.

"In other words," he said, half to himself, "your oceans evaporate steadily for over four of my years, precipitating frozen methane on the north polar cap, and then get it all back in the five months or so that the northern hemisphere spends going from its spring to autumn. If I was ever surprised at those storms, that ends it." He returned to more immediate matters.

"Barl, I'm going to get out of this tin box. I've been wanting samples of the tissue of Mesklin's animal life ever since we found it existed, and I couldn't very well take a paring from you. Will the flesh of this thing be very badly changed in the length of time it has probably been dead? I suppose you'd have some idea."

"It should still be perfectly edible for us, though from what you have said you could never digest it. Meat usually becomes poisonous after a few hundred days unless it is dried or otherwise preserved, and during all that time its taste gradually changes. I'll sample a bit of this, if you'd like." Without waiting for an answer and without even a guilty glance around to make sure that none of his crew had wandered in this direction, Barlennan launched himself from the roof of the tank toward the vast bulk beside it. He misjudged badly, sailing entirely over the huge body, and for just an instant felt a twinge of normal panic, but he was in full control of himself before he landed on the farther side. He leaped back again, judging his distance better this time, and waited while Lackland opened the door of his vehicle and emerged. There was no air lock on the tank; the man was still wearing pressure armor, and had simply permitted Mesklin's atmosphere to enter after closing his helmet. A faint swirl of white crystals followed him out—ice and carbon dioxide, frozen out of the Earth-type air inside as it cooled to

Mesklin's bitter temperature. Barlennan had no sense of smell, but he felt a burning sensation in his breathing pores as a faint whiff of oxygen reached him, and jumped hastily backward. Lackland guessed correctly at the cause of his action and apologized profusely for not giving proper warning.

"It is nothing," the captain replied. "I should have foreseen it—I got the same sensation once before when you left the Hill where you live, and you certainly told me often enough how the oxygen you breathe differs from our hydrogen—you remember, when I was learning your language."

"I suppose that's true. Still, I could hardly expect a person who hasn't grown up accustomed to the idea of different worlds and different atmospheres to remember the possibility all the time. It was still my fault. However, it seems to have done you no harm; I don't yet know enough about the life chemistry of Mesklin even to guess just what it might do to you. That's why I want samples of this creature's flesh."

Lackland had a number of instruments in a mesh pouch on the outside of his armor, and while he was fumbling among them with his pressure gauntlets Barlennan proceeded to take the first sample. Four sets of pincers shredded a portion of skin and underlying tissue and passed it along to his mouth; for a few moments he chewed reflectively.

"Not at all bad," he remarked at last. "If you don't need all of this thing for your tests, it might be a good idea to call the hunting parties over here. They'd have time to make it before the storm gets going again, I should think, and there'll certainly be more meat than they could reasonably expect to get any other way."

"Good idea," Lackland grunted. He was giving only part of his attention to his companion; most of it was being taken up by the problem of getting the point of a scalpel into the mass before him. Even the suggestion that he might be able to use the entire monstrous body in a laboratory investigation—the Mesklinite did possess a sense of humor—failed to distract him.

He had known, of course, that living tissue on this planet must be extremely tough. Small as Barlennan and his people were, they would have been flattened into senseless pulp under Mesklin's polar gravity had their flesh been of mere Earthly consistency. He had expected some difficulty in getting an instrument through the monster's skin; but he had more or less unthinkingly assumed that, once through, his troubles would be over in that respect. He was now discovering his error; the meat inside seemed to have the consistency of teak. The scalpel was of a superhard alloy which would have been difficult to dull against anything as long as mere muscular strength was employed, but he could not drive it through that mass and finally had to resort to scraping. This produced a few shreds which he sealed in a collecting bottle.

"Is any part of this thing likely to be softer?" he asked the interested Mesklinite as he looked up from this task. "I'm going to need power tools to get enough out of this body to satisfy the boys on Toorey."

"Some parts inside the mouth might be a little more tractable," Barlennan replied. "However, it would be easier for me to nip off pieces for you, if you'll tell me the sizes and parts you want. Will that be all right, or do your scientific procedures demand that the samples be removed with metal instruments for some reason?"

"Not that I know of—thanks a lot; if the big boys don't like it they can come down and do their own carving," returned Lackland. "Go right ahead. Let's follow your other suggestion, too, and get something from the mouth; I'm not really sure I'm through skin here." He waddled painfully around the head of the stranded behemoth to a point where gravity-distorted lips had exposed teeth, gums, and what was presumably a tongue. "Just get bits small enough to go in these bottles without crowding." The Earthman tentatively tried the scalpel once more, finding the tongue somewhat less obdurate than the earlier sample, while Barlennan obediently nipped off fragments of the desired size. An occasional piece found its way to his mouth—he was not really hungry, but this was fresh meat—but in spite of this drain the bottles were soon filled.

Lackland straightened up, stowing the last of the containers as he did so, and cast a covetous glance at the pillarlike teeth. "I suppose it would take blasting gelatine to get one of those out," he remarked rather sadly.

"What is that?" asked Barlennan.

"An explosive—a substance that changes into gas very suddenly, producing loud noise and shock. We use such material for digging, removing undesirable buildings or pieces of landscape, and sometimes in fighting."

"Was that sound an explosive?" Barlennan asked.

For an instant Lackland made no answer. A *boom!* of very respectable intensity, heard on a planet whose natives are ignorant of explosives and where no other member of the human race is present, can be rather disconcerting, especially when it picks such an incredibly apt time to happen; and to say that Lackland was startled would be putting it mildly. He could not judge accurately the distance or size of the explosion, having heard it through Barlennan's radio and his own sound discs at the same time; but a distinctly unpleasant suspicion entered his mind after a second or two.

"It sounded very much like one," he answered the Mesklinite's question somewhat belatedly, even as he started to waddle back around the head of the dead sea monster to where he had left the tank. He rather dreaded what he would find. Barlennan, more curious than ever, followed by his more natural method of travel, crawling.

For an instant, as the tank came in sight, Lackland felt an overwhelming relief; but this changed to an equally profound shock as he reached the door of the vehicle.

What remained of the floor consisted of upcurled scraps of thin metal, some still attached at the bases of the walls and others tangled among the controls and other interior fittings. The driving machinery, which had been under the floor, was almost completely exposed, and a single glance was enough to tell the dismayed Earthman that it was hopelessly wrecked.

Barlennan was intensely interested in the whole phenomenon.

"I take it you were carrying some explosive in your tank," he remarked. "Why did you not use it to get the material you wanted from this animal? And what made it act while it was still in the tank?"

"You have a genius for asking difficult questions," Lackland replied. "The answer to your first one is that I was not carrying any; and to the second, your guess is as good as mine at this point."

"But it must have been something you were carrying," Barlennan pointed out. "Even I can see that whatever it was happened under the floor of your tank, and wanted to get out; and we don't have things that act like that on Mesklin."

"Admitting your logic, there was nothing under that floor that I can imagine blowing up," replied the man. "Electric motors and their accumulators just aren't explosive. A close examination will undoubtedly show traces of whatever it was if it was in any sort of container, since practically none of the fragments seem to have gone outside the tank—but I have a rather worse problem to solve first, Barl."

"What is that?"

"I am eighteen miles from food supplies, other than what is carried in my armor. The tank is ruined; and if there was ever an Earthman born who could walk eighteen miles in eight-atmosphere heated armor under three gravities, I'm certainly not the one. My air will last indefinitely with these algae gills and enough sunlight, but I'd starve to death before I made the station."

"Can't you call your friends on the faster moon, and have them send a rocket to carry you back?"

"I could; probably they already know, if anyone is in the radio room to hear this conversation. The trouble is if I have to get that sort of help Doc Rosten will certainly make me go back to Toorey for the winter; I had trouble enough as it was persuading him to let me stay. He'll have to hear about the tank, but I want to tell him from the station—after getting back there without his help. There just isn't energy around

here to get me back, though; and even if I could get
more food into the containers in this armor without
letting your air in, you couldn't get into the station to
get the food."

"Let's call my crew, anyway," Barlennan remarked.
"They can use the food that's here—or as much of it
as they can carry. I have another idea too, I think."

"We are coming, Captain." Dondragmer's voice
came from the radio, startling Lackland, who had forgotten his arrangement to let each radio hear the others, and startling the commander himself, who had not
realized that his mate had learned so much English.
"We will be with you in a few days at most; we took
the same general direction as the Flyer's machine
when we started." He gave this information in his native language; Barlennan translated for Lackland's
benefit.

"I can see that *you* won't be hungry for quite a
while," the man replied, glancing somewhat ruefully
at the mountain of meat beside them, "but what was
this other idea of yours? Will it help with my problem?"

"A little, I think." The Mesklinite would have smiled
had his mouth been sufficiently flexible. "Will you
please step on me?"

For several seconds Lackland stood rigid with astonishment at the request; after all, Barlennan looked
more like a caterpillar than anything else, and when a
man steps on a caterpillar—then he relaxed, and even
grinned.

"All right, Barl. For a moment I'd forgotten the circumstances." The Mesklinite had crawled over to his
feet during the pause; and without further hesitation
Lackland took the requested step. There proved to be
only one difficulty.

Lackland had a mass of about one hundred sixty
pounds. His armor, an engineering miracle in its own
way, was about as much more. On Mesklin's equator,
then, man and armor *weighed* approximately nine
hundred fifty pounds—he could not have moved a
step without an ingenious servo device in the legs—
and this weight was only about a quarter greater than

that of Barlennan in the polar regions of his planet. There was no difficulty for the Mesklinite in supporting that much weight; what defeated the attempt was simple geometry. Barlennan was, in general, a cylinder a foot and a half long and two inches in diameter; and it proved a physical impossibility for the armored Earthman to balance on him.

The Mesklinite was stumped; this time it was Lackland who thought of a solution. Some of the side plates on the lower part of the tank had been sprung by the blast inside; and under Lackland's direction Barlennan, with considerable effort, was able to wrench one completely free. It was about two feet wide and six long, and with one end bent up slightly by the native's powerful nippers, it made an admirable sledge; but Barlennan, on this part of his planet, weighed about three pounds. He simply did not have the necessary traction to tow the device—and the nearest plant which might have served as an anchor was a quarter of a mile away. Lackland was glad that a red face had no particular meaning to the natives of this world, for the sun happened to be in the sky when this particular fiasco occurred. They had been working both day and night, since the smaller sun and the two moons had furnished ample light in the absence of the storm clouds.

V: MAPPING JOB

The crew's arrival, days later, solved Lackland's problem almost at once.

The mere number of natives, of course, was of little help; twenty-one Mesklinites still did not have traction enough to move the loaded sledge. Barlennan thought of having them carry it, placing a crew member under each corner; and he went to considerable trouble to overcome the normal Mesklinite conditioning against getting under a massive object. When he finally succeeded in this, however, the effort proved futile; the metal plate was not thick enough for that sort of treatment, and buckled under the armored man's weight so that all but the supported corner was still in contact with the ground.

Dondragmer, with no particular comment, spent the time that this test consumed in paying out and attaching together the lines which were normally used with the hunting nets. They proved, in series, more than long enough to reach the nearest plants; and the roots of these growths, normally able to hold against the worst that Mesklin's winds could offer, furnished all the support needed. Four days later a train of sledges, made from all the accessible plates of the tank, started back toward the *Bree* with Lackland and a tremendous load of meat aboard; and at a fairly steady rate of a mile an hour, reached the ship in sixty-one days. Two more days of work, with more crew members assisting, got Lackland's armor through the vegetation growing between the ship and his dome, and delivered him safely at the air lock. It was none too soon; the wind had already picked up to a point where the assisting crew had to use ground lines in getting back to the *Bree,* and clouds were once again whipping across the sky.

Lackland ate, before bothering to report officially what had happened to the tank. He wished he could make the report more complete; he felt somehow that he should know what had actually happened to the vehicle. It was going to be very difficult to accuse someone on Toorey of inadvertently leaving a cake of gelatine under the tank's floor.

He had actually pressed the call button on the station-to-satellite set when the answer struck him; and when Dr. Rosten's lined face appeared on the screen he knew just what to say.

"Doc, there's a spot of trouble with the tank."

"So I understand. Is it electrical or mechanical? Serious?"

"Basically mechanical, though the electrical system had a share. I'm afraid it's a total loss; what's left of it is stranded about eighteen miles from here, west, near the beach."

"Very nice. This planet is costing a good deal of money one way and another. Just what happened—and how did you get back? I don't think you could walk eighteen miles in armor under that gravity."

"I didn't—Barlennan and his crew towed me back. As nearly as I can figure out about the tank, the floor partition between cockpit and engine compartment wasn't airtight. When I got out to do some investigating, Mesklin's atmosphere—high-pressure hydrogen—began leaking in and mixing with the normal air under the floor. It did the same in the cockpit, too, of course, but practically all the oxygen was swept out through the door from there and diluted below danger point before anything happened. Underneath—well, there was a spark before the oxygen went."

"I see. What caused the spark? Did you leave motors running when you went out?"

"Certainly—the steering servos, dynamotors, and so on. I'm glad of it, too; if I hadn't, the blast would probably have occurred after I got back in and turned them on."

"Hmph." The director of the Recovery Force looked a trifle disgruntled. "Did you have to get out at all?" Lackland thanked his stars that Rosten was a biochemist.

"I didn't exactly have to, I suppose. I was getting tissue samples from a six-hundred-foot whale stranded on the beach out there. I thought someone might—"

"Did you bring them back?" snapped Rosten without letting Lackland finish.

"I did. Come down for them when you like—and have we another tank you could bring along?"

"We have. I'll consider letting you have it when winter is over; I think you'll be safer inside the dome until then. What did you preserve the specimens with?"

"Nothing special—hydrogen—the local air. I supposed that any of our regular preservatives would ruin them from your point of view. You'd better come for them fairly soon; Barlennan says that meat turns poisonous after a few hundred days, so I take it they have micro-organisms here."

"Be funny if they hadn't. Stand by; I'll be down there in a couple of hours." Rosten broke the connection without further comment about the wrecked tank, for which Lackland felt reasonably thankful. He went to bed, not having slept for nearly twenty-four hours.

He was awakened—partially—by the arrival of the rocket. Rosten had come down in person, which was not surprising. He did not even get out of his armor; he took the bottles, which Lackland had left in the air lock to minimize the chance of oxygen contamination, took a look at Lackland, realized his condition, and brusquely ordered him back to bed.

"This stuff was probably worth the tank," he said briefly. "Now get some sleep. You have some more problems to solve—I'll talk to you again when there's a chance you'll remember what I say. See you later." The air-lock door closed behind him.

Lackland did not, actually, remember Rosten's parting remarks; but he was reminded, many hours later, when he had slept and eaten once more.

"This winter, when Barlennan can't hope to travel, will last only another three and a half months," the assistant director started almost without preamble. "We have several reams of telephotos up here which are not actually fitted into a map, although they've been collated as far as general location is concerned. We couldn't make a real map because of interpretation difficulties. Your job for the rest of this winter will be to get in a huddle with those photos and your friend Barlennan, turn them into a usable map, and decide on a route which will take him most quickly to the material we want to salvage."

"But Barlennan doesn't want to get there quickly. This is an exploring-trading voyage as far as he's concerned, and we're just an incident. All we've been able to offer him in return for that much help is a running sequence of weather reports, to help in his normal business."

"I realize that. That's why you're down there, if you remember; you're supposed to be a diplomat. I don't expect miracles—none of us do—and we certainly want Barlennan to stay on good terms with us; but there's two billion dollars' worth of special equipment on that rocket that couldn't leave the pole, and recordings that are literally priceless—"

"I know, and I'll do my best," Lackland cut in, "but I could never make the importance of it clear to a native—and I don't mean to belittle Barlennan's intelligence; he just hasn't the background. You keep an eye out for breaks in these winter storms, so he can come up here and study the pictures whenever possible."

"Couldn't you rig some sort of outside shelter next to a window, so he could stay up even during bad weather?"

"I suggested that once, and he won't leave his ship and crew at such times. I see his point."

"I suppose I do too. Well, do the best that you can —you know what it means. We should be able to learn more about gravity from that stuff than anyone since

Einstein." Rosten signed off, and the winter's work began.

The grounded research rocket, which had landed under remote control near Mesklin's south pole and had failed to take off after presumably recording its data, had long since been located by its telemetering transmitters. Choosing a sea and/or land route to it from the vicinity of the *Bree*'s winter quarters, however, was another matter. The ocean travel was not too bad; some forty or forty-five thousand miles of coastal travel, nearly half of it in waters already known to Barlennan's people, would bring the salvage crew as close to the helpless machine as this particular chain of oceans ever got. That, unfortunately, was some four thousand miles; and there simply were no large rivers near that section of coast which would shorten the overland distance significantly.

There was such a stream, easily navigable by a vessel like the *Bree*, passing within fifty miles of the desired spot; but it emptied into an ocean which had no visible connection with that which Barlennan's people sailed. The latter was a long, narrow, highly irregular chain of seas extending from somewhat north of the equator in the general neighborhood of Lackland's station almost to the equator on the opposite side of the planet, passing fairly close to the south pole on the way—fairly close, that is, as distances on Mesklin went. The other sea, into which the river near the rocket emptied, was broader and more regular in outline; the river mouth in question was at about its southernmost point, and it also extended to and past the equator, merging at last with the northern icecap. It lay to the east of the first ocean chain, and appeared to be separated from it by a narrow isthmus extending from pole to equator—narrow, again by Mesklinite standards. As the photographs were gradually pieced together, Lackland decided that the isthmus varied from about two to nearly seven thousand miles in width.

"What we could use, Barl, is a passage from one of these seas into the other," remarked Lackland one day. The Mesklinite, sprawled comfortably on his ledge outside the window, gestured agreement silently. It was past midwinter now, and the greater sun was becoming perceptibly dimmer as it arched on its swift path across the sky to the north. "Are you sure that your people know of none? After all, most of these pictures were taken in the fall, and you say that the ocean level is much higher in the spring."

"We know of none, at any season," replied the captain. "We know something, but not much, of the ocean you speak of; there are too many different nations on the land between for very much contact to take place. A single caravan would be a couple of years on the journey, and as a rule they don't travel that far. Goods pass through many hands on such a trip, and it's a little hard to learn much about their origin by the time our traders see them in the western seaports of the isthmus. If any passage such as we would like exists at all, it must be here near the Rim where the lands are almost completely unexplored. Our map— the one you and I are making—does not go far enough yet. In any case, there is no such passage south of here during the autumn; I have been along the entire coast line as it was then, remember. Perhaps, however, this very coast reaches over to the other sea; we have followed it eastward for several thousand miles, and simply do not know how much farther it goes."

"As I remember, it curves north again a couple of thousand miles past the outer cape, Barl—but of course that was in the autumn, too, when I saw it. It's going to be quite troublesome, this business of making a usable map of your world. It changes too much. I'd be tempted to wait until next autumn so that at least we could use the map we made, but that's four of my years away. I can't stay here that long."

"You could go back to your own world and rest until the time came—though I would be sorry to see you go."

"I'm afraid that would be a rather long journey, Barlennan."

"How far?"

"Well—your units of distance wouldn't help much. Let's see. A ray of light could travel around Mesklin's 'rim' in—ah—four fifths of a second." He demonstrated this time interval with his watch, while the native looked on with interest. "The same ray would take a little over eleven of my years; that's—about two and a quarter of yours, to get from here to my home."

"Then your world is too far to see? You never explained these things to me before."

"I was not sure we had covered the language problem well enough. No, my world cannot be seen, but I will show you my sun when winter is over and we have moved to the right side of yours." The last phrase passed completely over Barlennan's head, but he let it go. The only suns he knew were the bright Belne whose coming and going made day and night, and the fainter Esstes, which was visible in the night sky at this moment. In a little less than half a year, at midsummer, the two would be close together in the sky, and the fainter one hard to see; but Barlennan had never bothered his head about the reason for these motions.

Lackland had put down the photograph he was holding, and seemed immersed in thought. Much of the floor of the room was already covered with loosely fitted pictures; the region best known to Barlennan was already mapped fairly well. However, there was yet a long, long way to go before the area occupied by the human outpost would be included; and the man was already being troubled by the refusal of the photographs to fit together. Had they been of a spherical or nearly spherical world like Earth or Mars, he could have applied the proper projection correction almost automatically on the smaller map which he was constructing, and which covered a table at one side of the chamber; but Mesklin was not even approximately spherical. As Lackland had long ago recognized, the proportions of the Bowl on the *Bree*—Barlennan's equivalent of a terrestrial globe—were approximately right. It was six inches across and one and a quarter deep, and its curvature was smooth but far from uniform.

To add to the difficulty of matching photographs, much of the planet's surface was relatively smooth, without really distinctive topographic feature; and even where mountains and valleys existed, the different shadowing of adjacent photographs made comparison a hard job. The habit of the brighter sun of crossing from horizon to horizon in less than nine minutes had seriously disarranged normal photographic procedure; successive pictures in the same series were often illuminated from almost opposite directions.

"We're not getting anywhere with this, Barl," Lackland said wearily. "It was worth a try as long as there might be short cuts, but you say there are none. You're a sailor, not a caravan master; that four thousand miles overland right where gravity is greatest is going to stump us."

"The knowledge that enables you to fly, then, cannot change weight?"

"It cannot." Lackland smiled. "The instruments which are on that rocket grounded at your south pole should have readings which might teach us just that, in time. That is why the rocket was sent, Barlennan; the poles of your world have the most terrific surface gravity of any spot in the Universe so far accessible to us. There are a number of other worlds even more massive than yours, and closer to home, but they don't spin the way Mesklin does; they're too nearly spherical. We wanted measures in that tremendous gravity field, all sorts of measures. The value of the instruments that were designed and sent on that trip cannot be expressed in numbers we both know; when the rocket failed to respond to its takeoff signal, it rocked the governments of ten planets. We *must* have that data, even if we have to dig a canal to get the *Bree* into the other ocean."

"But what sort of devices were on board this rocket?" Barlennan asked. He regretted the question almost in the same instant; the Flyer might wonder at such specific curiosity, and come to suspect the captain's true intentions. However, Lackland appeared to take the query as natural.

"I'm afraid I can't tell you, Barl. You simply have no background which would give words like 'electron' and 'neutrino' and 'magnetism' and 'quantum' any meaning at all. The drive mechanism of the rocket might mean a little more to you, but I doubt it." In spite of Lackland's apparent freedom from suspicion, Barlennan decided not to pursue the subject.

"Would it not be well," he said, "to seek the pictures that show the shore and inland regions east of here?"

Lackland replied, "There is still some chance, I suppose, that they do meet; I don't pretend to have memorized the whole area. Maybe down next to the icecap—how much cold can you people stand?"

"We are uncomfortable when the sea freezes, but we can stand it—if it does not get too much colder. Why?"

"It's just possible you may have to crowd the northern icecap pretty closely. We'll see, though." The Flyer riffled through the stack of prints, still taller than Barlennan was long, and eventually extracted a thin sheaf. "One of these . . ." His voice trailed off for a few moments. "Here we are. This was taken from the inner edge of the ring, Barl, over six hundred miles up, with a narrow-angle telephoto lens. You can see the main shore line, and the big bay, and here, on the south side of the big one, the little bay where the *Bree* is beached. This was taken before this station was built—though it wouldn't show anyway.

"Now let's start assembling again. The sheet east of this—" He trailed off again, and the Mesklinite watched in fascination as a readable map of the lands he had not yet reached took form below him. For a time it seemed they were to be disappointed, for the shore line gradually curved northward as Lackland had thought; indeed, some twelve hundred miles to the west and four or five hundred north, the ocean seemed to come to an end—the coast curved westward again. A vast river emptied into it at this point, and with some hope at first that this might be a strait leading to the eastern sea, Lackland began fitting the pictures that covered the upper reaches of the mighty stream. He was quickly disabused of this idea, by the discovery of an extensive series of rapids some two hundred and fifty miles upstream; east of these, the great river dwindled rapidly. Numerous smaller streams emptied into it; apparently it was the main artery for the drainage system of a vast area of the planet. Interested by the speed with which it broke up into smaller rivers, Lackland continued building the map eastward, watched with interest by Barlennan.

The main stream, as far as it could be distinguished, had shifted direction slightly, flowing from a more southerly direction. Carrying the mosaic of pictures in this direction, they found a range of very fair-sized mountains, and the Earthman looked up with a rueful shake of his head. Barlennan had come to understand the meaning of this gesture.

"Do not stop yet!" the captain expostulated. "There is a similar range along the center of my country, which is a fairly narrow peninsula. At least build the picture far enough to determine how the streams flow on the other side of the mountains." Lackland, though not optimistic—he recalled the South American continent on his own planet too clearly to assume any symmetry of the sort the Mesklinite seemed to expect —complied with the native's suggestion. The range proved to be fairly narrow, extending roughly east-northeast by west-southwest; and rather to the man's surprise the numerous "water" courses on the opposite side began very quickly to show a tendency to come together in one vast river. This ran roughly parallel with the range for mile after mile, broadening as it went, and hope began to grow once more. It reached a climax five hundred miles downstream, when what was now a vast estuary merged indistinguishably with the "waters" of the eastern ocean. Working feverishly, scarcely stopping for food or even the rest he so badly needed in Mesklin's savage gravity, Lackland worked on; and eventually the floor of the room was covered by a new map—a rectangle representing some two thousand miles in a east-west line and half as far in the other dimension. The great bay and tiny cove where the *Bree* was beached showed clearly at its western end; much of the other was occupied by the featureless surface of the eastern sea. Between lay the land barrier.

It was narrow; at its narrowest, some five hundred

miles north of the equator, it was a scant eight hundred miles from coast to coast, and this distance was lessened considerably if one measured from the highest usable points of the principal rivers. Perhaps three hundred miles, part of it over a mountain range, was all that lay between the *Bree* and a relatively easy path to the distant goal of the Earthmen's efforts. Three hundred miles; a mere step, as distances on Mesklin went.

Unfortunately, it was decidedly more than a step to a Mesklinite sailor. The *Bree* was still in the wrong ocean; Lackland, after staring silently for many minutes at the mosaic about him, said as much to his tiny companion. He expected no answer, or at most a dispirited agreement; his statement was self-evidently true—but the native fooled him.

"Not if you have more of the metal on which we brought you and the meat back!" was Barlennan's instantaneous reply.

VI: THE SLED

For another long moment Lackland stared out the window into the sailor's eyes, while the implications of the little creature's remark sank into his mind; then he stiffened into something as closely approaching an alert attitude as the gravity permitted.

"You mean you would be willing to tow the *Bree* overland on a sledge, as you did me?"

"Not exactly. The ship outweighs us very much, and we would have the same trouble with traction that we did before. What I had in mind was *your* towing, with another tank."

"I see. I—see. It would certainly be possible, unless we hit terrain that the tank couldn't pass. But would you and your crew be willing to make such a journey? Would the extra trouble and distance from your home be repaid by the little we could do for you?"

Barlennan extended his pincers in a smile.

"It would be much better than what we originally planned. There are trading goods that come from the shores of the eastern ocean to our country, by the long caravan routes overland; by the time they reach the ports on our own sea, they are already fabulously expensive, and an honest trader cannot make a decent profit from them. This way, if I picked them up directly—well, it would be certainly very worth while indeed, for me. Of course, you would have to promise to bring us back across the isthmus when we returned."

"That would certainly be fair enough, Barl; I'm sure my people will gladly agree to it. But how about the land travel itself? This is country you know nothing about, as you have said; might not your crew be afraid of unknown land, and high hills over them, and maybe animals larger than can possibly grow in your part of the world?"

"We have faced dangers before," the Mesklinite replied. "I was able to get used to high places—even the top of your tank. As for animals, the *Bree* is armed with fire, and none that walk on land could be as large as some that swim the oceans."

"That's true enough, Barl. Very well. I was not trying to discourage you, goodness knows; but I wanted to be sure you had thought the matter over before you embarked on such a project. It's hardly one that can be backed out of in the middle."

"That I can readily understand, but you need not fear, Charles. I must return to the ship now; the clouds are gathering again. I will tell the crew what we are going to do; and lest the thoughts of fear should come to any of them, I will remind them that the profits of the voyage will be shared according to rank. There is no member of that crew who would put fear in the way of wealth."

"And you?" Lackland chuckled as he asked the question.

"Oh, I'm not afraid." The Mesklinite vanished into the night as he spoke the words, and Lackland was never sure just how he meant them.

Rosten, when he heard the new plan, made a number of caustic remarks to the effect that Lackland could certainly be counted on for ideas that would give him use of a tank.

"It seems as though it should work, though," he admitted grudgingly. "Just what sort of sled are we supposed to build for this ocean liner of your friend's? How big is it, again?"

"The *Bree* is about forty feet long and fifteen across; I suppose it draws five or six inches. It's made of a lot of rafts about three feet long and half as wide, roped together so they can move fairly freely—I can guess why, on this world."

"Hmph. So can I. If a ship that long had its two ends supported by waves while the middle hung free, up near the pole, it would be in pieces before long whether it started that way or not. How is it driven?"

"Sails; there are masts on twenty or thirty of the rafts. I suspect there may be centerboards on some of them too, retractable so the ship can be beached; but I never asked Barlennan. I don't really know how far advanced the art of sailing is on this world, but from the casual way in which he speaks of crossing long stretches of open ocean, I assume they know about beating into a wind."

"Seems reasonable. Well, we'll build something out of light metal here on the moon, and cart it down to you when we finish."

"You'd better not bring it down until winter's over. If you leave it inland it'll get lost under the snow, and if you drop it at the seashore someone may have to dive for it, if the water line goes up the way Barlennan expects."

"If it's going to, why is it waiting so long? The winter is more than half over, and there's been a fantastic amount of precipitation in the parts of the southern hemisphere that we can see."

"Why ask me things like that? There are meteorologists on the staff, I believe, unless they've gone crazy trying to study this planet. I have my own worries. When do I get another tank?"

"When you can use it; after winter is over, as I said. And if you blow that one up it'll be no use howling for another, because there isn't one closer than Earth."

Barlennan, hearing the gist of this conversation at his next visit some hundreds of days later, was perfectly satisfied. His crew was enthusiastic about the proposed trip; they might, as he had implied, be lured by the prospective gain, but there was liberally distributed among them a share of the plain love of adventure which had carried Barlennan so far into unknown territory.

"We will go as soon as the storms break," he said to Lackland. "There will still be much snow on the ground; that will help where the course lies over land different from the loose sand of the beach."

"I don't think it will make much difference to the tank," replied Lackland.

"It will to us," pointed out Barlennan. "I admit it would not be dangerous to be shaken off the deck, but it would be annoying in the middle of a meal. Have you decided what would be the best course to follow across the land?"

"I've been working on it." The man brought out the map that was the result of his efforts. "The shortest route, that we discovered together, has the disadvantage of requiring that I tow you over a mountain range. It might be possible, but I don't like to think of the effects on your crew. I don't know how high those mountains are, but any altitude is too much on this world.

"I've worked out this route, which I've shown by a red line. It follows up the river that empties into the big bay on this side of the point, for about twelve hundred miles—not counting the small curves in the river, which we probably won't have to follow. Then it goes straight across country for another four hundred or so, and reaches the head of another river. You could probably sail down that if you wanted, or have me keep on towing—whichever would be faster or more comfortable for you. Its worst feature is that so much of it runs three or four hundred miles south of the equator—another half gravity or more for me to take. I can handle it, though."

"If you are sure of that, I would say that this is indeed the best way." Barlennan gave his statement after careful study of the map. "Your towing will probably be faster than sailing, at least in the river where there will probably be no room to tack." He had to use his own language for the last word; Lackland received the explanation of its meaning with satisfaction. He had guessed correctly about the extent of nautical progress among Barlennan's people, it seemed.

With the route agreed on, there was little more for Lackland to do while Mesklin drifted along its orbit toward the next equinox. That would not be too long, of course; with the southern hemisphere's midwinter occurring almost exactly at the time the giant world was closest to its sun, orbital motion during fall and winter was extremely rapid. Each of those seasons was a shade over two Earthly months in length—spring and summer, on the other hand, each occupied some eight hundred and thirty Earth days, roughly twenty-six months. There should be plenty of time for the voyage itself.

Lackland's enforced idleness was not shared aboard the *Bree*. Preparations for the overland journey were numerous and complicated by the fact that no member of the crew knew exactly what the ship would have to face. They might have to make the entire journey on stored food; there might be animal life along the way sufficient not only to feed them but to provide trading material if its skins and bones were of the right sort. The trip might be as safe as the sailors avowedly believed all land journeys to be, or they might face dangers from both the terrain and the creatures inhabiting it. About the first they could do little; that was the Flyer's responsibility. Concerning the second, weapons were brought to a high degree of readiness. Bigger clubs than even Hars or Terblannen could swing up in the higher latitudes were manufactured; some of the plants which stored crystals of chlorine in their stems were found, and the flame tanks replenished from them. There were, of course, no projectile weapons; the idea had never developed on a world where none of the inhabitants had ever seen a solid, unsupported object because it fell too fast to be visible. A .50-caliber bullet fired horizontally at Mesklin's pole would drop over one hundred feet in its first hundred yards of travel. Barlennan, since meeting Lackland, had come to have some idea of the "throw" concept and had even considered asking the Flyer about the possibility of weapons based on the principle; but he had decided to stick to more familiar arms. Lackland, on his part, had done a little wondering about the possible results of meeting a race, on their trip across the isthmus, which had developed the bow and arrow. He did a little more than Barlennan with the thought; he outlined the situation to Rosten and asked that the towing tank be equipped with a 40-millimeter gun with thermite and explosive shells. After the usual grumbling Rosten had acquiesced.

The sled was finished easily and quickly; large amounts of sheet metal were available, and the structure was certainly not complicated. Following Lackland's advice, it was not brought to the surface of Mesklin immediately, since the storms were still depositing their loads of ammonia-tainted methane snow. The ocean level had still not risen appreciably near the equator, and the meteorologists had been making unkind remarks at first about Barlennan's truthfulness and linguistic ability; but as sunlight reached farther and farther into the southern hemisphere with the approach of spring, and new photographs were secured and compared with those of the preceding fall, the weather men grew silent and were observed wandering around the station muttering distractedly to themselves. The sea level in the higher latitudes had already risen several hundreds of feet, as the native had predicted, and was still rising visibly as the days went by. The phenomenon of widely differing sea levels at the same time on the same planet was a little outside the experience of Earth-trained meteorologists, and none of the non-human scientists with the expedition could throw any light on the matter, either. The weather men were still racking their brains when the sun's diurnal arc eased southward past the equator and spring officially began in Mesklin's southern hemisphere.

The storms had decreased tremendously both in frequency and intensity long before this time, partly because the planet's extreme flattening had cut down the radiation on the north polar cap very rapidly after midwinter and partly because Mesklin's distance from the sun had increased more than fifty per cent during the same time; Barlennan, when consulted on the matter, proved perfectly willing to start the journey with the astronomical advent of spring, and showed no apparent anxiety about equinoctial gales.

Lackland reported the natives' readiness to the station on the inner moon, and the operation of transferring tank and sled to the surface was started at once; everything had been in readiness for weeks.

Two trips of the cargo rocket were necessary, though the sledge was light and the thrust developed by the hydrogen-iron slugs fantastically high. The sled was brought down first, with the intention of letting the crew of the *Bree* haul it onto the structure while the rocket went back for the tank; but Lackland warned against landing close to the ship, so that the clumsy-looking vehicle was left beside the dome until the tractor arrived to tow it over to the shore. Lackland himself drove the tractor, although the crew of the rocket stood by to satisfy their curiosity and, if needed, lend assistance with the loading procedure.

No human help was needed. The Mesklinites, under a mere three Earth gravities, were perfectly capable physically of lifting their ship and walking off with it; and the insuperable mental conditioning that prevented their getting any part of their bodies underneath such a mass did not prevent their towing it easily across the beach with ropes—each crewman, of course, anchored firmly to a tree with one or both sets of rear pincers. The *Bree,* sails furled and centerboards retracted, slid easily across the sand and onto the gleaming platform of metal. Barlennan's winterlong vigilance to keep her from freezing to the beach had proved adequate; also, in the last couple of weeks, the ocean level had started to rise as it had already done farther south. The advancing liquid, which had already necessitated moving the vessel two hundred yards inland, would certainly have melted her free had that been necessary.

The builders of the sledge, on distant Toorey, had provided eyes and cleats in sufficient numbers to allow the sailors to lash the *Bree* firmly in place. The cordage used appeared remarkably thin to Lackland, but the natives showed full confidence in it. They had some justice, the Earthman reflected; it had held their ship on the beach during storms when he himself would not have cared to walk abroad in full armor. It might, he reflected, be worth while to find out if the cordage and fabric the Mesklinites used could stand terrestrial temperatures.

This train of thought was interrupted by Barlennan's approach with the report that all was ready on the ship and sledge. The latter was already attached to the tank by its tow cable; the tank itself was stocked with sufficient food to last its one-man crew for several days. The plan was to re-supply Lackland by rocket whenever necessary, landing far enough ahead so that the flying rocket would not cause too much perturbation to the natives on the ship. This was not to be done oftener than strictly necessary; after the first accident, Lackland did not intend to open the tank to the outer air oftener than he could possibly help.

"I guess we're ready to go, then, little friend," he said in response to Barlennan's statement. "I won't need sleep for a good many hours yet, and we can get quite a distance upstream in that time. I wish your days were of a decent length; I'm not too happy about driving over a snow field in the dark. I don't think even your crew could pull the tank out of a hole, even if they could find the traction."

"I rather doubt it myself, though my ability to judge weight is very uncertain here at the Rim," the captain replied. "I doubt that the risk is very great, however; the snow isn't sticky enough to do a good job of covering a large hole."

"Unless it drifted in to fill it completely. Well, I'll worry about that if and when it happens. All aboard!" He entered the tank, sealed the door, pumped out the Mesklinite atmosphere, and released the Earthly air that had been compressed into tanks before opening the door earlier. The small tank that held the algae whose job was to keep the air fresh glimmered as the circulators began driving bubbles through it. A tiny spectrometric "sniffer" reported the hydrogen content of the air to be negligible; once assured of this, Lackland started his main motors without further hesitation, and headed the tank and its unwieldy trailer into the east.

The near flatness of the country around the cove

changed gradually. In the forty days or so before
Lackland had to stop for sleep, they had covered some
fifty miles, and were in an area of rolling hills which
reached heights of three or four hundred feet. No
trouble had been encountered, either in pulling the
sledge or in riding it. Barlennan reported on his radio
that the crew were enjoying the experience, and that
the unusual idleness had not bothered anyone yet.
The speed of the tank and its tow was about five miles
an hour, which was a good deal faster than the usual
Mesklinite crawl; but in the negligible—to them—
gravity, some of the crew were going overside and ex-
perimenting with other methods of travel. None had
actually jumped as yet, but it looked as though Barlennan might have companions before long who shared
his newly acquired indifference to falls.

No animal life had been seen so far, but there had
been occasional tiny tracks in the snow which apparently belonged to creatures similar to those the *Bree*'s
crew had hunted for food during the winter. The plant
life was distinctly different; in some places the snow
was almost hidden by grasslike vegetation that had
grown up through it, and on one occasion the crew
was held spellbound at the sight of a growth which
to Lackland resembled a rather stumpy tree. The Mesklinites had never seen anything grow so far from the
ground.

While Lackland slept as comfortably as he could
in his cramped quarters, the crew spread out over the
surrounding country. They were at least partly moti-
vated by a desire for fresh food, but salable cargo was
the goal that really moved them. All were familiar
with a wide variety of the plants which produced what
Lackland had called spices, but none of these grew
anywhere in the neighborhood. There were numerous
growths bearing seeds, and nearly all had leaflike ap-
pendages of one sort or another and roots; the trouble was that there seemed no way of telling whether
these were even safe to eat, to say nothing of being
palatable. None of Barlennan's sailors was rash or
naïve enough to take even a taste of a plant he had
never seen; too much of Mesklin's vegetable life pro-

tected itself with fearsome efficiency with poisons. The usual means of testing in such cases involved trusting to the senses of any of several small animals commonly used by the Mesklinites as pets; what a *parsk* or a *ternee* would eat was safe. Unfortunately, the only such animal aboard the *Bree* had not survived the winter—or rather, the equator; it had blown away in the advance gust of one of the winter storms when its owner failed to lash it down in time.

The sailors did, indeed, bring numerous hopeful-looking specimens back to the ship; but none of them could offer a practical suggestion as to what to do with his find. Dondragmer alone made what might be termed a successful trip; more imaginative than his fellows, he had thought to look *under* objects, and had indeed turned over a great many stones. He had been a little uneasy at first, but his nervousness had finally worn off completely; and a genuine enthusiasm for the new sport had possessed him. There were lots of things to be found under even quite heavy stones, he discovered; and he presently returned to the ship carrying a number of objects which everyone agreed must be eggs. Karondrasee took them in charge—no one was afraid of eating any sort of animal food—and presently the opinion was confirmed. They *were* eggs —very good, too. Only after they had been consumed did anyone think of hatching some of them to learn what sort of animal they might belong to; and with that thought voiced, Dondragmer carried it a step further by suggesting that perhaps they might hatch an animal which could serve in the place of the missing *ternee*. This idea was enthusiastically accepted, and parties sallied forth once more to look for eggs. The *Bree* had become practically an incubator by the time Lackland woke up.

Making sure that all the *Bree*'s crew had returned aboard, he restarted the tank and resumed the eastward journey. The hills grew higher in the next few days, and twice they crossed streams of methane, fortunately so narrow that the sled could actually bridge them. It was well that the rise in the hills was gradual, for there was a little uneasiness among the sailors whenever they had to look down any distance; but that, Bar-lennan reported, was gradually decreasing.

And then, some twenty days after the start of the second lap of the journey, their minds were taken completely off the terrors of height by something which seized and froze the attention of every living being on both vehicles.

VII: STONE DEFENSE

Up to this time, most of the hills had been gentle, smooth slopes, their irregularities long since worn off by weather. There had been no sign of the holes and crevasses which Lackland somewhat feared before starting. The hilltops had been smoothly rounded, so that even had their speed been much higher the crossing of one would hardly have been noticed. Now, however, as they topped such an acclivity and the landscape ahead came into view a difference in the next hill caught every eye at once.

It was longer than most they had crossed, more a ridge across their path than a mound; but the great difference was in the top. Instead of the smooth, wind-worn curve presented by its fellows, it seemed at first glance actually jagged; a closer look showed that it was crowned with a row of boulders spaced with regularity that could only mean intelligent arrangement. The rocks ranged from monstrous things as big as Lackland's tank down to fragments of basketball size; and all, while rough in detail, were generally spherical in shape. Lackland brought his vehicle to an instant halt and seized his glasses—he was in partial armor, but was not wearing the helmet. Barlennan, forgetting the presence of his crew, made a leap over the twenty yards separating the *Bree* from the tank and settled firmly on top of the latter. A radio had been fastened there for his convenience long before, and he was talking almost before he had landed.

"What is it, Charles? Is that a city, such as you were

telling me about on your own world? It doesn't look very much like your pictures."

"I was hoping you could tell me," was the answer. "It certainly is not a city, and the stones are too far apart for the most part to be any sort of wall or fort that I could imagine. Can you see anything moving around them? I can't with these glasses, but I don't know how keen your eyesight is."

"I can just see that the hilltop is irregular; if the things on top are loose stones, I'll have to take your word for it until we're closer. Certainly I can see nothing moving. Anything my size would be impossible to see at that distance anyway, I should think."

"I could see you at that range without these glasses, but I couldn't count your eyes or arms. With them I can say pretty certainly that that hilltop is deserted. Just the same, I'll practically guarantee that those stones didn't get there by accident; we'd better keep eyes open for whoever set them up. Better warn your crew." Lackland mentally noted the fact of Barlennan's poorer eyesight; he was not physicist enough to have predicted it from the size of the native's eyes.

For two or three minutes, while the sun moved far enough to reveal most of the areas previously in shadow, they waited and watched; but nothing except the shadows moved, and finally Lackland started the tank once more. The sun set while they were descending the slope. The tank had only one searchlight, which Lackland kept aiming at the ground in his path; so they could not see what, if anything, went on among the stones above. Sunrise found them just crossing another brook, and tension mounted as they headed uphill once more. For a minute or two nothing was visible, as the sun was directly ahead of the travelers; then it rose far enough to permit clear forward vision. None of the eyes fastened on the hilltop could detect any change from its appearance of the night before. There was a vague impression, which Lackland found was shared by the Mesklinites, that there were now more stones; but since no one had attempted to make a count of them before, this could not be proved. There was still no visible motion.

It took five or six minutes to climb the hill at the tank's five-mile speed, so the sun was definitely behind them when they reached the top. Lackland found that several of the gaps between the larger stones were wide enough for the tank and sled, and he angled toward one of these as he approached the crest of the ridge. He crunched over some of the smaller boulders, and for a moment Dondragmer, on the ship behind, thought one of them must have damaged the tank; for the machine came to an abrupt halt. Barlennan could be seen still on top of the vehicle, all his eyes fixed on the scene below him; the Flyer was not visible, of course, but after a moment the Bree's mate decided that he, too, must be so interested in the valley beyond as to have forgotten about driving.

"Captain! What is it?" Dondragmer hurled the question even as he gestured the weapons crew to the flame tanks. The rest of the crew distributed themselves along the outer rafts, clubs, knives, and spears in readiness, without orders. For a long moment Barlennan gave no answer, and the mate was on the point of ordering a party overboard to cover the tank—he knew nothing of the nature of the jury-rigged quick-firer at Lackland's disposal—when his captain turned, saw what was going on, and gave a reassuring gesture.

"It's all right, I guess," he said. "We can see no one moving, but it looks a little like a town. Just a moment and the Flyer will pull you forward so that you can see without going overboard." He shifted back to English and made this request to Lackland, who promptly complied. This action produced an abrupt change in the situation.

What Lackland had seen at first—and Barlennan less clearly—was a broad, shallow, bowllike valley entirely surrounded by hills of the type they were on. There should, Lackland felt, have been a lake at the bottom; there was no visible means of escape for rain or melted snow. Then he noticed that there was no snow on the inner slopes of the hills; their topography was bare. And strange topography it was.

It could not possibly have been natural. Starting a short distance below the ridges were broad, shallow channels. They were remarkably regular in arrangement; a cross section of the hills taken just below where they started would have suggested a very pretty series of ocean waves. As the channels led on downhill toward the center of the valley they grew narrower and deeper, as though designed to lead rain water toward a central reservoir. Unfortunately for this hypothesis, they did not all meet in the center—they did not even all reach it, though all got as far as the relatively level, small floor of the valley. More interesting than the channels themselves were the elevations separating them. These, naturally also grew more pronounced as the channels grew deeper; on the upper half of the slopes they were smoothly rounded ridges, but as the eye followed them down their sides grew steeper until they attained a perpendicular junction with the channel floors. A few of these little walls extended almost to the center of the valley. They did not all point toward the same spot; there were gentle curves in their courses that gave them the appearance of the flanges of a centrifugal pump rather than the spokes of a wheel. Their tops were too narrow for a man to walk on.

Lackland judged that channels and separating walls alike were some fifteen or twenty feet wide where they broke off. The walls themselves, therefore, were quite thick enough to be lived in, especially for Mesklinites; and the existence of numerous openings scattered over their lower surfaces lent strength to the idea that they actually were dwellings. The glasses showed that those openings not directly at the bottoms of the walls had ramps leading up to them; and before he saw a single living thing, Lackland was sure he was examining a city. Apparently the inhabitants lived in the separating walls, and had developed the entire structure in order to dispose of rain. Why they did not live on the outer slopes of the hills, if they wanted to avoid the liquid, was a question that did not occur to him.

He had reached this point in his thoughts when Barlennan asked him to pull the *Bree* over the brow of the hill before the sun made good seeing impossible. The moment the tank began to move, a score of dark figures appeared in the openings that he had suspected were doorways; no details were visible at that distance, but the objects, whatever they were, were living creatures. Lackland heroically refrained from stopping the tank and snatching up the glasses once more until he had pulled the *Bree* into a good viewing position.

As it turned out, there was no need for him to have hurried. The things remained motionless, apparently watching the newcomers, while the towing maneuver was completed; he was able to spend the remaining minutes before sunset in a careful examination of the beings. Even with the glasses some details were indistinguishable—for one reason, they seemed not to have emerged entirely from their dwellings; but what could be seen suggested strongly that they belonged to the same race as Barlennan's people. The bodies were long and caterpillarlike; several eyes—they were hard to count at that distance—were on the foremost body segment, and limbs very similar to if not identical with Barlennan's pincer-equipped arms were in evidence. The coloration was a mixture of red and black, the latter predominating, as in the *Bree*'s complement.

Barlennan could not see all this, but Lackland relayed the description to him tensely until the city below faded from sight in the dusk. When he stopped talking the captain issued a boiled-down version in his own language to the tensely waiting crew. When that was done Lackland asked:

"Have you ever heard of people living this close to the Rim, Barl? Would they be at all likely to be known to you, or even speak the same language?"

"I doubt it very much. My people become very uncomfortable, as you know, north of what you once called the 'hundred-G line.' I know several languages, but I can't see any likelihood of finding one of them spoken here."

"Then what shall we do? Sneak around this town, or go through it on the chance its people are not belligerent? I'd like to see it more closely, I admit, but we have an important job to do and I don't want to risk its chances of success. You at least know your race better than I possibly can; how do you think they'll react to us?"

"There's no one rule, there. They may be frightened out of their wits at your tank, or my riding on it—though they might not have normal instincts about height, here at the Rim. We've met lots of strange people in our wanderings, and sometimes we've been able to trade and sometimes we've had to fight. In general, I'd say if we kept weapons out of sight and trade goods in evidence, they would at least investigate before getting violent. I'd like to go down. Will the sled fit through the bottom of those channels, do you think?"

Lackland paused. "I hadn't thought of that," he admitted after a moment. "I'd want to measure them more carefully first. Maybe it would be best if the tank went down alone first, with you and anyone else who cared for the ride traveling on top. That way we might look more peaceful, too—they must have seen the weapons your men were carrying, and if we leave them behind—"

"They didn't see any weapons unless their eyes are a great deal better than ours," pointed out Barlennan. "However, I agree that we'd better go down first and measure—or better yet, tow the ship around the valley first and go down afterward as a side trip; I see no need to risk her in those narrow channels."

"That's a thought. Yes, I guess it would be the best idea, at that. Will you tell your crew what we've decided, and ask if any of them want to come down with us afterward?"

Barlennan agreed, and returned to the *Bree* for the purpose—he could speak in a lower tone there, although he did not feel that there was any real danger of being overheard and understood.

The crew in general accepted the advisability of taking the ship around rather than through the city, but from that point on there was a little difficulty. All of them wanted to see the town, but none would even consider riding on the tank, often as they had seen their captain do so without harm. Dondragmer broke the deadlock by suggesting that the crew, except for those left to guard the *Bree,* follow the tank into the town; there was no need to ride, since all could now keep up the speed the vehicle had been using up to this time.

The few minutes this discussion consumed brought the sun once more above the horizon; and at Barlennan's signal the Earthman swung the tank ninety degrees and started around the rim of the valley just below its coping of boulders. He had taken a look at the city before starting, and saw no sign of life; but as the tank and its tow swung into motion heads appeared once more at the small doors—many more of them, this time. Lackland was able to concentrate on his driving, sure now that their owners would still be there when he was free to examine them more closely. He attended to his job for the few days required to get the sled around to the far side of the valley; then the tow cable was cast off, and the nose of the tank pointed downhill.

Practically no steering was required; the vehicle tended to follow the course of the first channel it met, and went by itself toward the space which Lackland had come to regard—wholly without justification—as the market place of the town. Approximately half of the *Bree's* crew followed; the rest, under the second mate, remained as guards on the ship. Barlennan, as usual, rode on the tank's roof with most of the small supply of trade goods piled behind him.

The rising sun was behind them as they approached from this side of the valley, so the seeing was good. There was much to see; some of the town's inhabitants emerged entirely from their dwellings as the strangers approached. Neither Lackland nor Barlennan attached any significance to the fact that all who did this were on the far side of the open space; those closer to the approaching travelers remained well under cover.

As the distance narrowed, one fact became evident; the creatures were not, in spite of initial appearances, of the same race as Barlennan. Similar they were, indeed; body shape, proportions, number of eyes and limbs—all matched; but the city dwellers were over three times the length of the travelers from the far south. Five feet in length they stretched over the stone floors of the channels with body breadth and thickness to match.

Some of the things had reared the front third of their long bodies high into the air, in an evident effort to see better as the tank approached—an act that separated them from Barlennan's people as effectively as their size. These swayed a trifle from side to side as they watched, somewhat like the snakes Lackland had seen in museums on Earth. Except for this barely perceptible motion they did not stir as the strange metal monster crawled steadily down the channel it had chosen, almost disappeared as the walls which formed the homes of the city dwellers rose gradually to its roof on either side, and finally nosed its way out into the open central space of the town through what had become an alley barely wide enough for its bulk. If they spoke, it was too quietly for either Lackland or Barlennan to hear; even the gestures of pincer-bearing arms that took the place of so much verbal conversation with the Mesklinites Lackland knew was missing. The creatures simply waited and watched.

The sailors edged around the tank through the narrow space left—Lackland had just barely completed emerging from the alley—and stared almost as silently as the natives. Dwellings, to them, consisted of three-inch-high walls with fabric roofs for weather protection; the idea of a covering of solid material was utterly strange. If they had not been seeing with their own eyes the giant city dwellers actually inside the weird structures, Barlennan's men would have taken the latter for some new sort of natural formation.

Lackland simply sat at his controls, looked, and speculated. This was a waste of time, really, since he did not have enough data for constructive imagination; but he had the sort of mind that could not remain completely idle. He looked about the city and tried to picture the regular life of its inhabitants, until Barlennan's actions attracted his attention.

The captain did not believe in wasting time; he was going to trade with these people, and, if they wouldn't trade, he would move on. His action, which focused

Lackland's attention on him, was to start tossing the packaged trade goods from the roof beside him, and calling to his men to get busy. This they did, once the packages had stopped falling. Barlennan himself leaped to the ground after the last bundle—an act which did not seem to bother in the least the silently watching giants—and joined in the task of preparing the goods for display. The Earthman watched with interest.

There were bolts of what looked like cloth of various colors, bundles that might have been dried roots or pieces of rope, tiny covered jars and larger empty ones—a good, varied display of objects whose purpose, for the most part, he could only guess at.

With the unveiling of this material the natives began to crowd forward, whether in curiosity or menace Lackland could not tell. None of the sailors showed visible apprehension—he had come to have some ability at recognizing this emotion in their kind. By the time their preparations seemed to be complete an almost solid ring of natives surrounded the tank. The way it had come was the only direction unblocked by their long bodies. The silence among the strange beings persisted, and was beginning to bother Lackland; but Barlennan was either indifferent to it or able to conceal his feelings. He picked an individual out of the crowd, using no particular method of choice that the Earthman could see, and began his selling program.

How he went about it Lackland was utterly unable to understand. The captain had said he did not expect these people to understand his language, yet he spoke; his gestures were meaningless to Lackland, though he used them freely. How any understanding could be transmitted was a complete mystery to the alien watcher; yet apparently Barlennan was having some degree of success. The trouble was, of course, that Lackland in his few months' acquaintance with the strange creatures had not gained more than the tiniest bit of insight into their psychology. He can hardly be blamed; professionals years later were still being puzzled by it. So much of the Mesklinite action and gesticulation is tied in directly with the physical functioning of their bodies that its meaning, seen by another member of the same race, is automatically clear; these giant city dwellers, though not of Barlennan's precise species, were similar enough in make-up so that communication was not the problem Lackland naturally assumed it would be.

In a fairly short time, numbers of the creatures were emerging from their homes with various articles which they apparently wished to trade, and other members of the *Bree*'s crew took active part in the bargaining. This continued as the sun swept across the sky and through the period of darkness—Barlennan asked Lackland to furnish illumination from the tank. If the artificial light bothered or surprised the giants at all, even Barlennan was unable to detect any signs of the fact. They paid perfect attention to the business at hand, and when one had gotten rid of what he had or acquired what he seemed to want, he would retire to his home and leave room for another. The natural result was that very few days passed before Barlennan's remaining trade goods had changed hands, and the articles freshly acquired were being transferred to the roof of the tank.

Most of these things were as strange to Lackland as the original trade materials had been; but two attracted his attention particularly. Both were apparently living animals, though he could not make out their details too well because of their small size. Both appeared to be domesticated; each stayed crouched at the side of the sailor who had purchased it, and evinced no desire to move away. Lackland guessed—correctly, as it turned out—that these were creatures of the sort the sailors had been hoping to raise in order to test possible plant foods.

"Is that all the trading you're going to do?" he called, as the last of the local inhabitants drifted away from the neighborhood of the tank.

"It's all we can do," replied Barlennan. "We have nothing more to trade. Have you any suggestions, or do you want to continue our journey now?"

"I'd like very much to find out what the interiors of those houses are like; but I couldn't possibly get through the doors, even if I could discard my armor. Would you or any of your people be willing to try to get a look inside?" Barlennan was a trifle hesitant.

"I'm not sure whether it would be wise. These people traded peacefully enough, but there's something about them that bothers me, though I can't exactly put a nipper on it. Maybe it's because they didn't argue enough over prices."

"You mean you don't trust them—you think they'll try to get back what they've given, now that you're out of trade goods?"

"I wouldn't say precisely that; as I said, I don't have actual reason for my feeling. I'll put it this way; if the tank gets back to the valley rim and hooked up to the ship so that we're all ready to go, and we've had no trouble from these things in the meantime, I'll come back down and take that look myself. Fair enough?"

Neither Barlennan nor Lackland had paid any attention to the natives during this conversation; but for the first time the city dwellers did not share this indifference. The nearer giants turned and eyed, with every indication of curiosity, the small box from which Lackland's voice was coming. As the talk went on, more and more of them drew near and listened; the spectacle of someone talking to a box too small, they knew, to contain any intelligent creature seemed, for the first time, to break down a wall of reserve that not even the tank had been able to affect. As Lackland's final agreement to Barlennan's suggestion came booming from the tiny speaker, and it became evident that the conversation was over, several of the listeners disappeared hastily into their homes and emerged almost at once with more objects. These they presented, with gestures which the sailors now understood quite well. The giants wanted the radio, and were willing to pay handsomely for it.

Barlennan's refusal seemed to puzzle them. Each in turn offered a higher price than his predecessor. At last Barlennan made an ultimate refusal in the only way he could; he tossed the set onto the roof of the tank, leaped after it, and ordered his men to resume throwing the newly acquired property up to him. For several seconds the giants seemed nonplused; then, as though by signal, they turned away and disappeared into their narrow doorways.

Barlennan felt more uneasy than ever, and kept watch on as many portals as his eyes could cover while he stowed the newly bought goods; but it was not from the dwellings that the danger came. It was the great Hars who saw it, as he half reared himself over his fellows in imitation of the natives to toss a particularly bulky package up to his captain. His eye chanced to rove back up the channel they had descended; and as it did so he gave one of the incredibly loud hoots which never failed to amaze—and startle—Lackland. He followed the shriek with a burst of speech which meant nothing to the Earthman; but Barlennan understood, looked, and said enough in English to get the important part across.

"Charles! Look back uphill! *Move!*"

Lackland looked, and in the instant of looking understood completely the reason for the weird layout of the city. One of the giant boulders, fully half the size of the tank, had become dislodged from its position on the valley rim. It had been located just above the wide mouth of the channel down which the tank had come; the slowly rising walls were guiding it squarely along the path the vehicle had followed. It was still half a mile away and far above; but its downward speed was building up each instant as its tons of mass yielded to the tug of a gravity three times as strong as that of the Earth!

VIII: CURE FOR
ACROPHOBIA

Flesh and blood have their limits as far as speed is
concerned, but Lackland came very close to setting
new ones. He did not stop to solve any differential
equations which would tell him the rock's time of
arrival; he threw power into the motors, turned the
tank ninety degrees in a distance that threatened to
twist off one of its treads, and got out from the mouth
of the channel which was guiding the huge projectile
toward him. Only then did he really come to appreciate the architecture of the city. The channels did not
come straight into the open space, as he had noticed;
instead, they were so arranged that at least two could
guide a rock across any portion of the plaza. His
action was sufficient to dodge the first, but it had been
forseen; and more rocks were already on their way.
For a moment he looked around in all directions, in
a futile search for a position which was not about to
be traversed by one of the terrible projectiles; then he
deliberately swung the nose of the tank into one of the
channels and started uphill. There was a boulder descending this one too; a boulder which to Barlennan
seemed the biggest of the lot—and to be growing bigger each second. The Mesklinite gathered himself for
a leap, wondering if the Flyer had lost his senses;
then a roar that outdid anything his own vocal apparatus could produce sounded beside him. If his
nervous system had reacted like that of most Earthly
animals he would have landed halfway up the hill.
The startled reaction of his race, however, was to
freeze motionless, so for the next few seconds it would

have taken heavy machinery to get him off the tank roof. Four hundred yards away, fifty yards ahead of the plunging rock, a section of the channel erupted into flame and dust—the fuses on Lackland's shells were sensitive enough to react instantly even to such grazing impact. An instant later the rock hurtled into the dust cloud, and the quick-firer roared again, this time emitting half a dozen barks that blended almost indistinguishably with each other. A fair half of the boulder emerged from the dust cloud, no longer even roughly spherical. The energy of the shells had stopped it almost completely; friction took care of the rest long before it reached the tank. It now had too many flat and concave surfaces to roll very well.

There were other boulders in position to roll down this channel, but they did not come. Apparently the giants were able to analyze a new situation with fair speed, and realized that this method was not going to destroy the tank. Lackland had no means of knowing what else they might do, but the most obvious possibility was a direct personal attack. They could certainly, or almost certainly, get to the top of the tank as easily as Barlennan and repossess everything they had sold as well as the radio; it was hard to see how the sailors were to stop them. He put this thought to Barlennan.

"They may try that, indeed," was the answer. "However, if they try to climb up we can strike down at them; if they jump we have our clubs, and I do not see how anyone can dodge a blow while sailing through the air."

"But how can you hold off alone an attack from several directions at once?"

"I am not alone." Once again came the pincer gesture that was the Mesklinite equivalent of a smile.

Lackland could see the roof of his tank only by sticking his head up into a tiny, transparent view dome, and he could not do this with the helmet of his armor on. Consequently he had not seen the results of the brief "battle" as they applied to the sailors who had accompanied him into the city.

These unfortunates had been faced with a situation

as shocking as had their captain when he first found himself on the roof of the tank. They had seen objects —heavy objects—actually *falling* on them, while they themselves were trapped in an area surrounded by vertical walls. To climb was unthinkable, though the sucker-feet which served them so well in Mesklin's hurricanes would have served as adequately in this task; to jump as they had now seen their captain do several times was almost as bad—perhaps worse. It was not, however, physically impossible; and when minds fail, bodies are apt to take over. Every sailor but two jumped; one of the two exceptions climbed— rapidly and well—up the wall of a "house." The other was Hars, who had first seen the danger. Perhaps his superior physical strength made him slower than the others to panic; perhaps he had more than the normal horror of height. Whatever the reason, he was still on the ground when a rock the size of a basketball and almost as perfectly round passed over the spot he was occupying. For practical purposes, it might as well be considered to have struck an equivalent volume of live rubber; the protective "shell" of the Mesklinites was of a material chemically and physically analogous to the chitin of Earthly insects, and had a toughness and elasticity commensurate with the general qualities of Mesklinite life. The rock bounded twenty-five feet into the air against three gravities, hurtling entirely over the wall which would normally have brought it to a stop, struck at an angle the wall of the channel on the other side, rebounded, and went clattering from wall to wall up the new channel until its energy was expended. By the time it had returned, in more leisurely fashion, to the open space the main action was over; Hars was the only sailor still in the plaza. The rest had brought some degree of control into their originally frantic jumps and had either already reached the top of the tank beside their captain or were rapidly getting there; even the climber had changed his method of travel to the more rapid leaping.

Hars, unbelievably tough as he was by terrestrial standards, could not take the sort of punishment he had just received completely without injury. He did not have his breath knocked out, since he lacked lungs, but he was scraped, bruised, and dazed by the impact. Fully a minute passed before he could control his motions sufficiently to make a coordinated attempt to follow the tank; why he was not attacked during that minute neither Lackland, Barlennan, nor Hars himself was ever able to explain satisfactorily. The Earthman thought that the fact that he was able to move at all after such a blow had frightened any such thoughts out of the minds of the city dwellers; Barlennan, with a more accurate idea of Mesklinite physique, thought that they were more interested in stealing than in killing and simply saw no advantage in attacking the lone sailor. Whatever the reason, Hars was permitted to regain his senses in his own time and, eventually, to regain the company of his fellows. Lackland, finally brought up to date on just what had happened, waited for him; when he finally reached the vehicle two of the crew had to descend and practically throw him to the roof, where the rest promptly undertook first-aid measures.

With all his passengers safely aboard, some of them crowded so close to the edge of the roof that their new-found indifference to height was a trifle strained, Lackland headed uphill once more. He had warned the sailors to keep clear of the gun muzzle, and kept the weapon trained ahead of him; but there was no motion on the ridge, and no more rocks fell. Apparently the natives who had launched them had retreated to the tunnels which evidently led up from their city. This, however, was no assurance that they would not come out again; and everyone on and in the tank kept a sharp lookout for any sort of motion.

The channel they were climbing was not the same as the one they had descended, and consequently did not lead directly to the sled; but the *Bree* became visible some distance before they reached the top, owing to the tank's height. The crew members who had been left behind were still there, all looking with evident anxiety down into the city. Dondragmer muttered something in his own language concerning the stupidity of not keeping an all-around watch, which Barlennan repeated in amplified form in English. However, the worry proved fruitless; the tank reached the stranded sled, turned, and was hitched up to its load without further interference. Lackland, once more under way, decided that the giants had overestimated the effectiveness of the gun; an attack from close quarters —emerging, for example, from the concealed tunnel mouths which must shelter the individuals who started the rocks downhill—would leave the weapon completely helpless, since neither high explosive nor thermite shells could be used close to the *Bree* or her crew.

With great reluctance he decided that there could be no more exploration until the *Bree* had reached the waters of the eastern ocean. Barlennan, when this conclusion was offered for his consideration, agreed, though he made some reservations in his own mind. Certainly while the Flyer slept his own crew was going to keep working.

With the expedition once more under way and the tangible results of the interruption rapidly being transferred from tank roof to ship by leaping Mesklinites, Lackland made a call to Toorey, listened humbly to the expected blast when Rosten learned what he had been doing, and silenced him as before with the report that much plant tissue was now available if Rosten would send down containers for it.

By the time the rocket had landed far enough ahead of them to preserve the Mesklinite nervous systems, had waited for their arrival, picked up the new specimens, and waited once more until the tank had traveled safely out of range of its takeoff blast, many more days had passed. These, except for the rocket's visit, were relatively uneventful. Every few miles a boulder-rimmed hilltop was sighted, but they carefully avoided these, and none of the giant natives were seen outside their cities. This fact rather worried Lackland, who could not imagine where or how they obtained food. With nothing but the relatively boring job of driving to occupy his mind, he naturally formed many hypotheses about the strange creatures. These he occasionally outlined to Barlennan, but that worthy was not much help in deciding among them, and Lackland got little of value from their conversations.

One of his own ideas, however, bothered him. He had been wondering just why the giants built their cities in such a fashion. They could hardly have been expecting either the tank or the *Bree*. It seemed a rather impractical way to repel invasion by others of their own kind, who evidently, from the commonness of the custom, could hardly be taken by surprise.

Still, there was a possible reason. It was just a hypothesis; but it would account for the city design, and for the lack of natives in the country outside, and for the absence of anything resembling farm lands in the neighborhood of the cities. It involved a lot of "iffing" on Lackland's part even to think of such an idea in the first place, and he did not mention it to Barlennan. For one thing, it left unexplained the fact that they had come this far unmolested—if the idea were sound; they should by now have used up a great deal more of the quick-firer's ammunition. He said nothing, therefore, and merely kept his own eyes open; but he was not too surprised, one sunrise when they had come perhaps two hundred miles from the city where Hars received his injuries, to see a small hillock ahead of the cavalcade suddenly rear up on a score of stubby, elephantine legs, lift as far as possible a head mounted on a twenty-foot neck, stare for a long moment out of a battery of eyes, and then come lumbering to meet the oncoming tank.

Barlennan for once was not riding in his usual station on the roof, but he responded at once to Lackland's call. The Earthman had stopped the tank, and there were several minutes to decide on a course of action before the beast would reach them at its present rate of speed.

"Barl, I'm willing to bet you've never seen anything like that. Even with tissue as tough as your planet produces, it could never carry its own weight very far from the equator."

"You are quite right; I haven't. I have never heard of it, either, and don't know whether or not it's likely to be dangerous. I'm not sure I want to find out, either. Still, it's meat; maybe . . ."

"If you mean you don't know whether it eats meat or vegetables, I'll bet on the former," replied Lackland. "It would be a very unusual plant-eater that would come toward something even larger than itself immediately upon sighting it—unless it's stupid enough to think the tank is a female of its own species, which I very much doubt. Also, I was thinking that a large flesh-eater was the easiest way to explain why the giants never seem to come out of their cities, and have them built into such efficient traps. They probably lure any of these things that come to their hill-top by showing themselves at the bottom, as they did with us, and then kill them with rocks as they tried on the tank. It's one way of having meat delivered to your front door."

"All that may be true, but is not of present concern," Barlennan replied with some impatience. "Just what should we do with this one? That weapon of yours that broke up the rock would probably kill it, but might not leave enough meat worth collecting; while if we go out with the nets we'll be too close for you to use it safely should we get in trouble."

"You mean you'd consider using your nets on a thing that size?"

"Certainly. They would hold it, I'm sure, if only we could get it into them. The trouble is that its feet are too big to go through the meshes, and our usual method of maneuvering them into its path wouldn't do much good. We'd have to get the nets around its body and limbs somehow, and then pull them tight."

"Have you a method in mind?"

"No—and we wouldn't have time to do much of the sort anyway; he'll be here in a moment."

"Jump down and unhitch the sled. I'll take the tank forward and keep him occupied for a while, if you want. If you decide to take him on, and get in trouble later, you all should be able to jump clear before I use the gun."

Barlennan followed the first part of the suggestion without hesitation or argument, slipping off the rear

of the deck and undoing with a single deft motion the
hitch which held the tow cable to the tank. Giving a
hoot to let Lackland know the job was done, he sprang
aboard the *Bree* and quickly gave his crew the details
of the new situation. They could see for themselves
by the time he had finished, for the Flyer had moved
the tank forward and to one side, clearing their line
of sight to the great animal. For a short time they
watched with much interest, some astonishment, but
no fear to speak of as the tank maneuvered with its
living counterpart.

The creature stopped as the machine resumed its
forward motion. Its head dropped down to a yard or
so from the ground, and the long neck swung as far as
possible first to one side and then the other, while the
multiple eyes took in the situation from all possible
angles. It paid no attention to the *Bree;* either it failed
to notice the small movements of the crew, or regarded
the tank as a more pressing problem. As Lackland
moved toward one flank, it slewed its gigantic body
around to keep facing it squarely. For a moment the
Earthman thought of driving it into a full hundred-and-
eighty-degree turn, so that it would be facing directly
away from the ship; then he remembered that this
would put the *Bree* in his line of fire should he have
to use the gun, and stopped the circling maneuver
when the stranded sled was at the monster's right.
With that eye arrangement, it would be as likely to see
the sailors moving behind it as in front, anyway, he
reflected.

Once more he moved toward the animal. It had
settled down, belly to the ground, when he stopped
circling; now it rose once more to its many legs and
drew its head back almost into its great trunk, in what
was apparently a protective gesture. Lackland stopped
once more, seized a camera, and took several photographs of the creature; then, since it seemed in no
mood to press an attack, he simply looked it over for
a minute or two.

Its body was a trifle larger than that of an Earthly
elephant; on Earth, it might have weighed eight or ten
tons. The weight was distributed about evenly among

the ten pairs of legs, which were short and enormously thick. Lackland doubted that the creature could move much faster than it had already.

After a minute or two of waiting, the creature began to grow restless; its head protruded a little and began to swing back and forth as though looking for other enemies. Lackland, fearing that its attention would become focused on the now helpless *Bree* and her crew, moved the tank forward another couple of feet; his adversary promptly resumed its defensive attitude. This was repeated several times, at intervals which grew progressively shorter. The feinting lasted until the sun sank behind the hill to the west; as the sky grew dark Lackland, not knowing whether the beast would be willing or able to carry on a battle at night, modified the situation by turning on all the tank's lights. This, at least, would presumably prevent the creature from seeing anything in the darkness beyond, even if it were willing to face what to it must be a new and strange situation.

Quite plainly, it did not like the lights. It blinked several times as the main spotlight burned into its eyes, and Lackland could see the great pupils contract; then, with a wailing hiss that was picked up by the roof speaker and clearly transmitted to the man inside, it lumbered a few feet forward and struck.

Lackland had not realized that he was so close—or, more correctly, that the thing could reach so far. The neck, even longer than he had at first estimated, snapped to full length, carrying the massive head forward and a trifle to one side. As it reached full travel, the head tipped a trifle and came slashing sideways. One of the great tusks clanged resoundingly against the tank's armor, and the main light went out in the same instant. Another, shriller hiss suggested to Lackland that the current feeding the light had grounded into the armor through some portion of the monster's head; but he was not taking time out to analyze the possibility. He backed away hastily, cutting the cabin lights as he did so. He did not want one of those tusks striking a cabin port with the force it had just expended on the upper armor. Now only the running lights, mounted low in the front of the vehicle and set well into the armor, were illuminating the scene. The animal, encouraged by Lackland's retreat, lurched forward again and struck at one of these. The Earthman did not dare extinguish it, since it would have left him effectively blind; but he sent a frantic call on the radio.

"Barl! Are you doing anything about your nets? If you're not about ready for action, I'm going to have to use the gun on this thing, meat or no meat. You'll have to stay away if I do; he's so close that high explosive would endanger the tank, and I'll have to use thermite."

"The nets are not ready, but if you'll lead him back a few more yards he'll be downwind of the ship, and we can take care of him another way."

"All right." Lackland did not know what the other way could be, and was more than a little doubtful of its effectiveness, whatever it was; but as long as retreat would suit the captain he was prepared to cooperate. It did not for an instant occur to him that Barlennan's weapon might endanger the tank; and, in all fairness, it probably did not occur to Barlennan either. The Earthman, by dint of repeated and hasty withdrawals, kept the tusks from his plating most of the time; the monster did not seem to have the intelligence to anticipate motion on his part. Two or three minutes of this dodging satisfied Barlennan.

He, too, had been busy in those minutes. On the leeward rafts, toward the dueling monster and machine, were four devices closely resembling bellows, with hoppers mounted above their nozzles. Two sailors were now at each bellows, and at their captain's signal began pumping for all they were worth. At the same time a third operator manipulated the hopper and sent a stream of fine dust flowing into the current from the nozzle. This was picked up by the wind and carried toward the combatants. The darkness made it difficult to estimate its progress; but Barlennan was a good judge of wind, and after a few moments of pumping suddenly snapped out another order.

The hopper crews promptly did something at the nozzle of the bellows each was tending; and as they did so, a roaring sheet of flame spread downwind from the *Bree* to envelop both of the fighters. The ship's crew were already sheltered behind their tarpaulins, even the "gunners" being protected by flaps of fabric that formed part of their weapons; but the vegetation that sprouted through the snow was neither tall nor dense enough to shelter the fighters. Lackland, using words that he had never taught Barlennan, hurled the tank backward out of the flame cloud with a prayer for the quartz in his portholes. His adversary, though evidently as anxious to dodge, seemed to lack the necessary control. It lurched first one way, then the other, seeking escape. The flame died out in seconds, leaving a cloud of dense white smoke which gleamed in the tank's running lights; but either the brief fire had been sufficient or the smoke was equally deadly, for the monster's disorganization grew steadily worse. Its aimless steps grew shorter and feebler as the legs gradually lost the power to support its vast bulk, and presently it stumbled and rolled on one side. The legs kicked frantically for a time, while the long neck alternately retracted, and stretched to full length, lashing the fanged head frantically through the air and against the ground. By sunrise the only remaining motion was an occasional twitch of head or leg; within a minute or two thereafter all activity of the giant creature ceased. The crew of the *Bree* had already swarmed overboard and across the dark patch where the snow had boiled from the ground, bent on acquiring meat. The deadly white cloud was farther downwind now, and gradually settling. Lackland was surprised to note traces of *black* dust on the snow where the cloud had passed.

"Barl, what on Earth—or rather, on Mesklin—was the stuff you used for that fire cloud? And didn't it occur to you that it might crack the windows in this tank?" The captain, who had remained on the ship and was near one of his radios, answered promptly.

"I'm sorry Charles; I didn't know what your windows are made of, and never thought of our flame cloud as a danger to your great machine. I will be more careful next time. The fuel is simply a dust which we obtain from certain plants—it is found as fairly large crystals, which we have to pulverize very carefully and away from all light." Lackland nodded slowly, digesting this information. His chemical knowledge was slight, but it was sufficient to make a good guess at the fuel's nature. Ignited by light—burned in hydrogen with a white cloud—black specks on the snow—it could, as far as he knew, be only one thing. Chlorine is solid at Mesklin's temperature; it combines violently with hydrogen, and hydrogen chloride is white when in fine powder form; methane snow boiled from the ground would also give up its hydrogen to the voracious element and leave carbon. Interesting plant life this world sported! He must make another report to Toorey—or perhaps he had better save this tidbit in case he annoyed Rosten again.

"I am very sorry I endangered your tank." Barlennan still seemed to feel apologetic. "Perhaps we had better let you deal with such creatures with your gun; or perhaps you could teach us to use it. Is it, like the radios, especially built to work on Mesklin?" The captain wondered if he had gone too far with this suggestion, but decided it had been worth it. He could neither see nor interpret Lackland's answering smile.

"No, the gun was not remade or changed for this world, Barl. It works fairly well here, but I'm afraid it would be pretty useless in your country." He picked up a slide rule, and added one more sentence after employing it for a moment. "The farthest this thing could possibly shoot at your pole would be just about one hundred fifty feet."

Barlennan, disappointed, said nothing further. Several days were spent in butchering the dead monster. Lackland salvaged the skull as a further protection from Rosten's ire, and the cavalcade resumed its journey.

Mile after mile, day after day, the tank and its tow inched onward. Still they sighted occasional cities of the rock-rollers; two or three times they picked up food for Lackland which had been left in their path by the rocket; quite frequently they encountered large animals, some like the one Barlennan's fire had slain, others very different in size and build. Twice specimens of

giant herbivores were netted and killed by the crew
to furnish meat, much to Lackland's admiration. The
discrepancy in size was far greater than that existing
between Earthly elephants and the African pygmies
who sometimes hunted them.

The country grew hillier as they progressed, and
with the rising ground the river, which they had followed intermittently for hundreds of miles, shrank and
split into numerous smaller streams. Two of these
tributaries had been rather difficult to cross, requiring
that the *Bree* be unlashed from the sled and floated
across at the end of a towrope while tank and sled
drove below the surface on the river bed. Now, however, the streams had become so narrow that the sled
actually bridged them and no such delays occurred.

At long last, fully twelve hundred miles from where
the *Bree* had wintered and some three hundred south
of the equator, with Lackland bowing under an additional half gravity, the streams began to bear definitely
in the general direction of their travel. Both Lackland
and Barlennan let several days pass before mentioning
it, wishing to be sure, but at last there was no more
doubt that they were in the watershed leading to the
eastern ocean. Morale, which had never been low,
nevertheless improved noticeably; and several sailors
could now always be found on the tank's roof hoping
for the first glimpse of the sea as they reached each
hilltop. Even Lackland, tired sometimes to the point of
nausea, brightened up; and as his relief was the greater,
so proportionately greater was his shock and dismay
when they came, with practically no warning, to the
edge of an escarpment; an almost sheer drop of over
sixty feet, stretching as far as the eye could see at
right angles to their course.

IX: OVER THE EDGE

For long moments nothing was said. Both Lackland and Barlennan, who had worked so carefully over the photographs from which the map of their journey had been prepared, were far too astonished to speak. The crew, though by no means devoid of initiative, decided collectively and at the first glance to leave this problem to their captain and his alien friend.

"How could it have been there?" Barlennan was first to speak. "I can see it's not high, compared to the vessel from which your pictures were taken, but should it not have cast a shadow far across the country below, in the minutes before sunset?"

"It should, Barl, and I can think of only one reason it escaped us. Each picture, you recall, covered many square miles; one alone would include all the land we can see from here, and much more. The picture that does cover this area must have been made between sunrise and noon, when there would have been no shadow."

"Then this cliff does not extend past the boundary of that one picture?"

"Possibly; or, just as possibly, it chanced that two or three adjacent shots were all made in the morning —I don't know just what course the photo rocket flew. If, as I should imagine, it went east and west, it wouldn't be too great a coincidence for it to pass the cliff several times running at about the same time of day.

"Still, there's little point in going through that question. The real problem, since the cliff obviously *does* exist, is how to continue our journey." That question produced another silence, which lasted for some time. It was broken, to the surprise of at least two people, by the first mate.

"Would it not be advisable to have the Flyer's friends far above learn for us just how far this cliff extends to either side? It may be possible to descend an easier slope without too great a detour. It should not be hard for them to make new maps, if this cliff was missed on the first." Barlennan translated this remark, which was made in the mate's own language. Lackland raised his eyebrows.

"Your friend may as well speak English himself, Barl—he appears to know enough to understand our last conversation. Or do you have some means of communicating it to him that I don't know about?"

Barlennan whirled on his mate, startled and, after a moment, confused. He had not reported the conversation to Dondragmer; evidently the Flyer was right— his mate had learned some English. Unfortunately, however, the second guess had also some truth; Barlennan had long been sure that many of the sounds his vocal apparatus could produce were not audible to the Earthman, though he could not guess at the reason. For several seconds he was confused, trying to decide whether it would be better to reveal Dondragmer's ability, the secret of their communication, both together, or, if he could talk fast enough, neither. Barlennan did the best he could.

"Apparently Dondragmer is sharper than I realized. Is it true that you have learned some of the Flyer's language, Don?" This he asked in English, and in a pitch that Lackland could hear. In the shriller tones that his own language employed so much he added, "Tell the truth—I want to cover up as long as possible the fact that we can talk without his hearing. Answer in his own language, if you can." The mate obeyed, thought not even his captain could have guessed at his thoughts.

"I have learned much of your language, Charles Lackland. I did not realize you would object."

"I don't mind at all, Don; I am very pleased and, I

admit, surprised. I would gladly have taught you as well as Barl if you had come to my station. Since you have learned on your own—I suppose from comparing our conversations and your captain's resultant activities—please enter our discussion. The suggestion you made a moment ago was sound; I will call the Toorey station at once."

The operator on the moon answered immediately, since a constant guard was now being maintained on the tank's main transmitter frequency through several relay stations drifting in Mesklin's outer ring. He indicated understanding of the problem, and promised that a survey would be made as quickly as possible.

"As quickly as possible," however, meant quite a number of Mesklin's days; and while waiting the trio endeavored to formulate other plans in case the cliff could not be rounded within a reasonable distance.

One or two of the sailors expressed a willingness to jump down the cliff, to Barlennan's anxiety—he felt that the natural fear of height should not be replaced with *complete* contempt, even though the entire crew now shared his willingness to climb and jump. Lackland was called upon to help dissuade these foolhardy individuals, which he managed to do by computing that the sixty-foot drop of the cliff was about equal to a one-foot fall at the latitude of their home country. This revived enough memory of childhood experience to put a stop to the idea. The captain, thinking over this event afterward, realized that by his own lifelong standards he had a crew composed entirely of lunatics, with himself well to the front in degree of aberration; but he was fairly sure that this paticular form of insanity was going to be useful.

Ideas more practical than these were not forthcoming for some time; and Lackland took the opportunity to catch up on his sleep, which he badly needed. He had had two long sessions in his bunk, interrupted by a hearty meal, when the report of the surveying rocket came in. It was brief and discouraging. The cliff ran into the sea some six hundred miles northeast of their present location, almost exactly on the equator. In the opposite direction it ran for some twelve hundred miles, growing very gradually lower, and disappearing completely at about the five-gravity latitude. It was not perfectly straight, showing a deep bend away from the ocean at one point; the tank had struck it at this point. Two rivers fell over its edge within the limits of the bay, and the tank was neatly caught between them, since in the interests of common sanity the *Bree* could never be towed across either without first going many miles upstream from the tremendous cataracts. One of the falls was about thirty miles away, almost due south; the other approximately a hundred miles distant to the north and east around the curve of the cliff. The rocket had not, of course, been able to examine the entire stretch of escarpment in complete detail from the altitude it had had to maintain, but the interpreter was very doubtful that the tank could scale it at any point. The best bet, however, would be near one of the falls, where erosion was visible and might conceivably have created negotiable paths.

"How in blazes can a cliff like this form?" Lackland asked resentfully when he had heard all this. "Eighteen hundred miles of ridge just high enough to be a nuisance, and we have to run right into it. I bet it's the only thing of its kind on the planet."

"Don't bet too much," the surveyor retorted. "The physiography boys just nodded in pleasure when I told them about it. One of them said he was surprised you hadn't hit one earlier; then another piped up and said actually you'd expect most of them farther from the equator, so it wasn't surprising at all. They were still at it when I left them. I guess you're lucky that your small friend is going to do most of the traveling for you."

"That's a thought." Lackland paused as another idea struck him. "If these faults are so common, you might tell me whether there are any more between here and the sea. Will you have to run another survey?"

"No. I saw the geologists before I started on this one, and looked. If you can get down this step, you're all right—in fact, you could launch your friend's ship in the river at the foot and he could make it alone.

Your only remaining problem is to get that sailboat hoisted over the edge."

"To get—hmm. I know you meant that figuratively, Hank, but you may have something there. Thanks for everything; I may want to talk to you later." Lackland turned away from the set and lay back on his bunk, thinking furiously. He had never seen the *Bree* afloat; she had been beached before he encountered Barlennan, and on the recent occasions when he had towed her across rivers he had himself been below the surface most of the time in the tank. Therefore he did not know how high the vessel floated. Still, to float at all on an ocean of liquid methane she must be extremely light, since methane is less than half as dense as water. Also she was not hollow—did not float, that is, by virtue of a large central air space which lowered her average density, as does a steel ship on Earth. The "wood" of which the *Bree* was made was light enough to float on methane and support the ship's crew and a substantial cargo as well.

An individual raft, therefore, could not weigh more than a few ounces—perhaps a couple of pounds, on this world at this point. At that rate, Lackland himself could stand on the edge of the cliff and let down several rafts at a time; any two sailors could probably lift the ship bodily, if they could be persuaded to get under it. Lackland himself had no rope or cable other than what he was using to tow the sled; but that was one commodity of which the *Bree* herself had an ample supply. The sailors should certainly be able to rig hoisting gear that would take care of the situation— or could they? On Earth it would be elementary seamanship; on Mesklin, with these startling but understandable prejudices against lifting and jumping and throwing and everything else involving any height, the situation might be different. Well, Barlennan's sailors could at least tie knots, and the idea of towing should not be too strange to them now; so undoubtedly the matter could be straightened out. The real, final problem was whether or not the sailors would object to being lowered over the cliff along with their ship. Some men might have laid that question aside as strictly a problem for the ship's captain, but Lackland more than suspected that he would have to contribute to its solution.

Barlennan's opinion, however, was certainly needed at this point; and reaching out a heavy arm, Lackland energized his smaller transmitter and called his tiny friend.

"Barl, I've been wondering. Why couldn't your people lower the ship over the cliff on cables, one raft at a time, and reassemble it at the bottom?"

"How would you get down?"

"I wouldn't. There is a large river about thirty miles south of here that should be navigable all the way to the sea, if Hank Stearman's report is accurate. What I'm suggesting is that I tow you over to the fall, help you any way I can in getting the *Bree* over the edge, watch you launch her in the river, and wish you the best of luck—all we can do for you from then on give weather and navigation information, as we agreed. You have ropes, do you not, which will hold the weight of a raft?"

"Of course; ordinary cordage would take the weight of the entire ship in this neighborhood. We'd have to snub the lines against trees or your tank or something like that; the whole crew together couldn't furnish traction enough for the job. Still, that's no problem. I'd say you had the answer, Charles."

"How about the personnel? Will they like the idea of being lowered down that way?" Barlennan thought for a moment.

"I think it will be all right. I'll send them down on the rafts, with a job to do like fending off from the cliff. That will keep them from looking straight down, and sufficiently occupied so they shouldn't be thinking of the height. Anyway, with this light feeling everyone has"—Lackland groaned silently—"no one's much afraid of a fall anyway; not even as much as they should be. We'll make that part, all right. Had we better start for that cataract right away?"

"All right." Lackland hauled himself to his controls, suddenly very weary. His part of the job was nearly over, sooner than he had expected, and his body shrieked for relief from the endless weight it had dragged around for the last seven months. Perhaps he shouldn't have stayed through the winter, but tired as he was, he could not regret it.

The tank swung to the right and started moving once more, parallel to the cliff edge two hundred yards away. The Mesklinites might be getting over their horror of heights, but Lackland was developing one. Besides, he had never attempted to repair the main spotlight since their first battle with Mesklin's animal life, and he had no intention of driving close to that edge at night with only the running lights to guide him.

They made the cataract in a single lap of about twenty days. Both natives and Earthman heard it long before they arrived, at first a vague trembling in the air that gradually rose through a muted thunder to a roar that put even the Mesklinite vocal equipment to shame. It was day when they came in sight of it, and Lackland stopped involuntarily as they did so. The river was half a mile wide where it reached the brink, and smooth as glass—no rocks or other irregularities appeared to exist in its bed. It simply curled over the edge and spilled downward. The fall had eroded its way for a full mile back from the cliff line; and they had a splendid view of the gorge. The ripple marks gave no clue to the liquid's speed of fall, but the violence with which the spray erupted from the bottom did. Even in this gravity and atmosphere a permanent cloud of mist hid the lower half of the curved sheet, thinning gradually away from its foot to reveal the roiled, eddied surface of the lower river. There was no wind except that created by the fall itself, and the stream grew rapidly calmer as it moved smoothly away toward the ocean.

The crew of the *Bree* had gone overboard the moment the tank stopped; and the way they were strung out along the rim of the gorge indicated that there would not be much morale difficulty during the descent. Now Barlennan called them back to the ship, and work commenced at once. Lackland relaxed once more while cordage was dragged forth and a plumb line dropped over the edge to secure a more precise measure of the cliff's height. Some of the sailors began securing all loose gear about the rafts, though preparations for the original journey had left little to do in this respect; others reached down between the rafts and began unfastening the lashings which held them together and checking at the same time the buffers that held them safely apart. They were fast workers, and raft after raft was dragged away from the main body of the ship.

Barlennan and his first mate, once this work was well under way, went over to the edge to determine the best place for the lowering operation. The gorge itself was rejected at once; the river within its walls was too rough, even if they had wanted to do their reassembling while afloat. It turned out, however, that almost any point on the cliff face would be suitable, so the officers quickly chose one as close as possible to the mouth of the gorge. The reassembled ship or its separate parts would have to be dragged to the river without the tank's help, and there was no point in making the journey any longer than necessary.

A scaffold of masts was arranged at the edge to give a point of suspension far enough out to prevent rope friction, though the masts were not long enough to hold a raft completely away from the cliff face; a block and tackle, which Lackland observed with interest, was attached to the scaffold, and the first raft dragged into position. It was adjusted in a rope sling that would carry it horizontally, the main cable attached to the sling and hitched around a tree, several sailors seized the cable, and the raft was pushed over the edge.

Everything held up, but Dondragmer and his captain inspected each part very, very carefully before the mate and one of the crew crawled aboard the platform that hung somewhat slanted against the rock an inch or so below the edge. For a moment after they had gone aboard everyone watched expectantly; but again nothing happened, and Dondragmer finally gave the signal to lower away. All the crew members who were not on the cable rushed to the edge to watch the descent. Lackland would have liked to watch it himself, but had no intention of venturing either the tank or his armored person close enough to do so. Beside his own uneasiness at the height, the sight of the cordage the Mesklinites were using made him unhappy; it looked as though an Earthly clerk would scorn it for tying a two-pound bag of sugar.

An excited hooting and general withdrawal from the edge indicated the safe arrival of the first raft, and Lackland blinked as the sailors proceeded to stack several more on top of each other while the cable was being drawn up. Apparently no more time than could be helped was to be wasted. Confident as he was in Barlennan's judgment, the Earthman suddenly decided he wanted to watch the stack of rafts make the descent. He was on the point of donning his armor when he remembered that it was not necessary; he relaxed again, called Barlennan, and asked him to arrange one or more of the little communicators so that their "eyes" could cover the desired activity. The captain complied immediately, having a sailor lash one of the sets to the scaffold so that it looked almost straight down and placing another on top of the pile of rafts which had just been secured in their rope sling. Lackland switched from one to the other as the operation proceeded. The first was a trifle more disconcerting than he had expected, since the supporting cable was visible for only a few feet from the pickup lens and the load seemed to be floating down without support; the other gave him a view of the cliff face that would undoubtedly have been highly interesting to a geologist. With the descent half completed, it occured to him to call Toorey to invite the interested parties to watch. The geology department responded and commented freely during the rest of the process.

Load after load went down, with little variety to make the operation more interesting. Toward the end a longer cable was installed and the lowering was done from below, since the greater part of the crew had now descended; and Lackland had a suspicion of the reason when Barlennan finally turned away from the scene of action and leaped toward the tank. The radio which had been used from that position was permanently mounted, and had not been taken down with the others.

"We have only about two more loads, Charles," the captain opened. "There will be a slight problem in connection with the last one. We'd like to keep all our gear, if possible, which means dismantling and sending down the masts used for our lowering tackle. We don't want to throw them down because we're not sure they'd take it—the soil below is very rocky. Would you be willing to get into your armor and lower the final load by hand? I will arrange for it to consist of one raft, those few masts and the associated tackle, and myself." Lackland was startled by the last item.

"You mean you would trust yourself to my strength, knowing that I'm already under three and a half times my normal gravity and will have the weight of my armor as well?"

"Certainly. The armor will easily be heavy enough to serve as anchor, and if you take a turn of the rope about your own body you can pay it out gradually. I don't see any difficulty; the load will be only a few of your pounds."

"Not that way, perhaps, but there's another point. Your rope is very thin indeed, and the handling clamps of my armor are somewhat clumsy when it comes to managing small objects. What if the cord slips out of my grip?" That silenced Barlennan for a moment.

"What is the smallest object you could handle with reasonable security?"

"Oh—one of your masts, I should say."

"There is no trouble, then. We will wind the rope about a mast, and you can use that as a windlass. You can toss mast and rope over afterward; if the stick is broken the loss will not be too great."

Lackland shrugged. "It's your health and property, Barl. I don't have to say I'll be careful; I wouldn't want anything to happen to you, especially through my negligence. I'll be out shortly." The Mesklinite, satisfied, leaped back to the ground and began to give the necessary orders to the few remaining sailors. The second last load went down with all of these; and a few moments later the Earthman emerged from his conveyance.

Barlennan was waiting for him. A single raft now lay at the cliff edge, tied in its sling and ready to go. A radio and the bundled remains of the scaffolding lay upon it, and the captain was dragging the mast which had the line wrapped about it toward Lackland. The man's approach was slow, for the terrible fatigue seemed to grow with every instant; but he finally reached a point about ten feet from the edge, reached over as far as his clumsy garment would permit, and took the mast from the tiny being who had reared up to meet him. Without a word of caution or any other suggestion of doubt in his big friend, Barlennan turned back to the raft, made sure its cargo was lashed securely, pushed it until it was teetering on the edge of the cliff, and climbed aboard.

He turned for a last look at Lackland, and the man could have sworn that he winked. Then, "Hang on, Charles," came the voice over the radio; and the captain stepped deliberately to the outer edge of the precariously balanced raft. His pincers were securely caught in the lashings, which was all that kept him aboard as the platform teetered once and slipped over the rim.

There was enough slack in the line Lackland was holding to permit a couple of feet of fall; and raft and passenger vanished instantly. A sharp jerk told the man that at least the line was still holding, and an instant later Barlennan's voice cheerfully conveyed the same information. "Lower away!" was the concluding phrase; and Lackland obeyed.

It was rather like handling a kite, at least in the form of windlass he was using—simply a cord wound on a stick. It revived childhood memories; but if he lost this kite he would, he knew, be much longer in getting over it. He did not have the best possible grip on the mast, and he slowly pivoted so as to wind the cord about his body before he tried to change holds. Then, satisfied, he paid out slowly.

Barlennan's voice came at intervals, always with something encouraging; it was as though the midget had an idea of the anxiety in Lackland's mind. "Halfway now." "Smooth going." "You know, I don't mind looking down even this far, now." "Almost there—just a little more—that's it; I'm down. Hold onto the tackle for a little, please; I'll tell you when the area is clear and it's all right to throw it down."

Lackland continued to obey. For a keepsake, he tried to break off a foot or two from the end of the cable, but found it impossible even with armored hands. However, the edge of one of the locking snaps on his armor proved sharp enough to cut the stuff, and he wound the souvenir around his arm before starting to carry out the remaining requests of his ally.

"We have things out from underneath, Charles; you can let go your end of the rope and toss the mast over whenever you want." The fine cord slithered instantly out of sight, and the ten-inch twig that was one of the *Bree*'s main booms followed. *Seeing* things fall free in triple gravity, Lackland found, was even worse than thinking about it. Maybe it would be better at the poles—then you couldn't see them at all. Not where an object falls some two miles in the first second! But perhaps the abrupt vanishing would be just as hard on the nerves. Lackland shrugged off these thoughts and turned back to the tank.

For the couple of hours the process took he watched the *Bree*'s reassembly through the vision sets. With just the traces of a wish that he might go along, he saw the cluster of rafts pushed out into the broad stream, and listened to the farewells of Barlennan, Dondragmer, and the crew—he could guess at the meaning of the sounds uttered even by the sailors who spoke no English. Presently the current bore the vessel far enough from the cliff to be seen from the tank's position. Lackland raised a hand silently in farewell, and watched her as she shrank slowly and finally vanished toward the distant sea.

For long minutes he sat silently; then roused himself to call the Toorey base.

"You may as well come and pick me up. I've done all I can on the surface."

X: HOLLOW BOATS

The river, once away from the vicinity of the great fall, was broad and slow. At first the air trapped by the descending "water" furnished a breeze toward the sea, and Barlennan ordered the sails set to take advantage of it; but this presently died out and left the ship at the mercy of the current. This was going in the right direction, however, and no one complained. The land adventure had been interesting and profitable, for several of the plant products collected could certainly be sold at high prices once they reached home; but no one was sorry to be afloat again. Some looked back at the waterfall as long as it could be seen, and once everyone stared into the west to catch a glimpse of the rocket as the muted thunder of its approach reached them; but in general the feeling was one of anticipation.

The banks on either side began to draw more and more attention as they proceeded. During their overland journey they had become accustomed to the sight of an occasional upright growth of the sort that the Flyer had called a "tree," usually seeing one every few days. They had been fascinating objects at first, and had, indeed, proved a source of one of the foods they planned to sell at home. Now the trees were becoming more and more numerous, threatening to replace the more familiar sprawling, rope-branched plants entirely, and Barlennan began to wonder if even a colony planted here might not be able to support itself by trade in what the Flyer had called fir cones.

For a long time, fully fifty miles, no intelligent life

was sighted, though animals in fair numbers were seen along the banks. The river itself teemed with fish, though none appeared large enough to constitute a danger to the *Bree*. Eventually the river on either side became lined with trees, which extended no one could tell how far inland; and Barlennan, spurred by curiosity, ordered the ship steered closer to shore to see what a forest—he had no such word for it, of course —looked like.

It was fairly bright even in the depths of the wood, since the trees did not spread out at the top nearly as much as is common on Earth, but it was strange enough. Drifting along almost in the shadow of the weird plants, many of the crew felt a resurgence of their old terror of having solid objects overhead; and there was a general feeling of relief when the captain silently gestured the helmsman to steer away from the bank once more.

If anyone lived there they were welcome to it. Dondragmer expressed this opinion aloud, and was answered by a general mutter of approval. Unfortunately, his words were either not heard or not understood by listeners on the bank. Perhaps they were not actually afraid that the *Bree*'s crew meant to take their forest away from them, but they decided to take no chances; and once more the visitors from high-weight suffered an experience with projectile weapons.

The armory this time consisted entirely of spears. Six of them flew silently from the top of the bank and stuck quivering in the *Bree*'s deck; two more glanced from the protective shells of sailors and clattered about on the rafts before coming to rest. The sailors who had been hit leaped convulsively from pure reflex, and both landed yards away in the river. They swam back and clambered aboard without assistance, for all eyes were directed toward the source of the mysterious attack. Without orders the helmsman angled more sharply toward the center of the river.

"I wonder who sent those—and if they used a machine like the Flyer's. There wasn't the same noise." Barlennan spoke half aloud, not caring whether he were answered. Terblannén wrenched one of the spears out of the deck and examined its hardwood point; then, experimentally, he threw it back at the receding shore. Since throwing was a completely new art to him, except for experiments such as he had made in getting objects to the top of the tank in the stone-rollers' city, he threw it as a child throws a stick, and it went spinning end over end back to the woods. Barlennan's question was partly answered; short as his crewman's arms were, the weapon reached the bank easily. The invisible attackers at least didn't *need* anything like Lackland's gun, if they were anything like ordinary people physically. There seemed no way to tell what the present attackers were, and the captain had no intention of finding out by direct examination. The *Bree* kept on downstream, while an account of the affair went winging up to Lackland on distant Toorey.

For fully a hundred miles the forest continued while the river widened gradually. The *Bree* kept out in midstream for a time after her single encounter with the forest dwellers, but even that did not keep her completely out of trouble. Only a few days after the arrival of the spears, a small clearing was sighted on the left bank. His viewpoint only a few inches off the surface prevented Barlennan from seeing as well as he would have liked, but there were certainly objects in that clearing worthy of examination. After some hesitation he ordered the ship closer to that bank. The objects looked a little like trees, but were shorter and thicker. Had he been higher he would have seen small openings in them just above ground level which might have been informative; Lackland, watching through one of the vision sets, compared the things at once to pictures he had seen of the huts of African natives, but he said nothing yet. Actually he was more interested in a number of other items lying partly in and partly out of the river in front of what he already assumed to be a village. They might have been logs or crocodiles, for they were not too clearly visible at this distance, but he rather suspected they were canoes. It would be interesting to see how Barlennan reacted to a boat so radically different from his own.

It was quite a while, however, before anyone on the *Bree* realized that the "logs" were canoes or the other mysterious objects dwellings. For a time, in fact, Lackland feared that they would drift on downstream without ever finding out; their recent experience had made Barlennan very cautious indeed. However, there were others besides Lackland who did not want the ship to drift by without stopping, and as she approached the point on her course opposite the village a red and black flood of bodies poured over the bank and proved that the Earthman's conjecture had been correct. The loglike objects were pushed into the stream, each carrying fully a dozen creatures who apparently belonged to the identical species as the *Bree*'s crew. They were certainly alike in shape, size, and coloring; and as they approached the ship they uttered earsplitting hoots precisely like those Lackland had heard on occasion from his small friends.

The canoes were apparently dugouts, hollowed out sufficiently so that only the head end of each crew member could be seen; from their distribution, Lackland suspected that they lay herring-bone fashion inside, with the paddles operated by the foremost sets of pincer-equipped arms.

The *Bree*'s leeward flame throwers were manned, though Barlennan doubted that they would be useful under these conditions. Krendoranic, the munitions officer, was working furiously at one of his storage bins, but no one knew what he was up to; there was no standard procedure for his department in such a situation. Actually, the entire defense routine of the ship was being upset by the lack of wind, something that almost never occurred on the open sea.

Any chance there might have been to make effective use of the flame dust vanished as the fleet of canoes opened out to surround the *Bree*. Two or three yards from her on all sides, they glided to a stop, and for a minute or two there was silence. To Lackland's intense annoyance, the sun set at this point and he was no longer able to see what went on. The next eight minutes he had to spend trying to attach meaning to the weird sounds that came over the set, which was not a very profitable effort since none of them formed words in any language he knew. There was nothing that denoted any violent activity; apparently the two crews were simply speaking to each other in experimental fashion. He judged, however, that they could find no common language, since there appeared to be nothing like a sustained conversation.

With sunrise, however, he discovered that the night had not been wholly uneventful. By rights, the *Bree* should have drifted some distance downstream during the darkness; actually, she was still opposite the village. Furthermore she was no longer far out in the river, but only a few yards from the bank. Lackland was about to ask Barlennan what he meant by taking such a risk, and also how he had managed to maneuver the *Bree*, when it became evident that the captain was just as surprised as he at this turn of events.

Wearing a slightly annoyed expression, Lackland turned to one of the men sitting beside him, with the remark:

"Barl has let himself get into trouble already. I know he's a smart fellow, but with over thirty thousand miles to go I don't like to see him getting held up in the first hundred."

"Aren't you going to help him? There's a couple of billion dollars, not to mention a lot of reputations, riding with him."

"What can I do? All I could give would be advice, and he can size up the situation better than I can. He can see it better, and is dealing with his own sort of people."

"From what I can see, they're almost as much his sort as the South Sea Islanders were Captain Cook's. I grant they appear to be the same species, but if they're, say, cannibals your friend may really be in hot water."

"I still couldn't help him, could I? How do you talk a cannibal out of a square meal when you don't know his language and aren't even facing him in person? What attention would he pay to a little square box that talked to him in a strange language?" The other raised his eyebrows a trifle.

"While I'm not mind reader enough to predict that one in detail, I would suggest that in such a case he might just possibly be scared enough to do almost anything. As an ethnologist I can assure you that there are primitive races on a lot of planets, including our own Earth, who would bow down, hold square dances, and even make sacrifices to a box that talked to them."

Lackland digested that remark in silence for a few moments, nodded thoughtfully, and turned back to the screens.

A number of sailors had seized spare masts and were trying to pole back toward the center of the river, but were having no success. Dondragmer, after a brief investigation around the outer rafts, reported that they were in a cage formed of piles driven into the river bed; only the upstream side was open. It might or might not be coincidence that the cage was just large enough to accommodate the *Bree*. As this report was made, the canoes drifted away from the three closed sides of the cage and congregated on the fourth; and the sailors, who had heard the mate's report and prepared to pole in the upstream direction, looked to Barlennan for instructions. After a moment's thought, he motioned the crew to the far end of the ship and crawled alone to the end facing the assembled canoes. He had long since figured out how his ship had been moved; with the coming of darkness some of the paddlers must have gone quietly overboard, swum beneath the *Bree,* and pushed her where they wanted. There was nothing too surprising in that; he himself could exist for some time beneath the surface of river or ocean, which normally carried a good deal of dissolved hydrogen. What bothered him was just why these people wanted the ship.

As he passed one of the provision lockers he pulled back its cover and extracted a piece of meat. This he carried to the edge of the ship and held out toward the crowd of now silent captors. Presently some unintelligible gabbling sounded among them; then this ceased, as one of the canoes eased slowly forward and a native in the bow reared up and forward toward the offering. Barlennan let him take it. It was tested and commented upon; then the chief, if that was his position, tore off a generous fragment, passed the rest back to his companions, and thoughtfully consumed what he had kept. Barlennan was encouraged; the fact that he hadn't kept it all suggested that these people had some degree of social development. Obtaining another piece, the captain held it out as before; but this time, when the other reached for it, it was withheld. Barlennan put it firmly behind him, crawled to the nearest of the piles that were imprisoning his ship, indicated it, gestured to the *Bree,* and pointed out into the river. He was sure his meaning was plain, as undoubtedly it was; certainly the human watchers far above understood him, though no word of their language had been used. The chief, however, made no move. Barlennan repeated the gestures, and finished by holding out the meat once more.

Any social consciousness the chief possessed must have been strictly in connection with his own society; for as the captain held out the meat a second time a spear licked out like the tongue of a chameleon, impaled the food, jerked it out of Barlennan's grasp, and was withdrawn before any one of the startled sailors could move. An instant later the chief gave a single barking order; and as he did so half the crew of each of the canoes behind him leaped forward.

The sailors were completely unused to aerial assault, and had also relaxed a trifle when their captain began his negotiation; in consequence, there was nothing resembling a fight. The *Bree* was captured in something less than five seconds. A committee headed by the chief began at once to investigate the food lockers, and their satisfaction was evident even through the language barrier. Barlennan watched with dismay as the meat was dragged out on deck in obvious preparation for transferral to a canoe, and for the first time it occurred to him that there was a possible source of advice which he had not yet used.

"Charles!" he called, speaking English for the first

time since the incident had begun. "Have you been watching?" Lackland, with mixed anxiety and amusement, answered at once.

"Yes, Barl; I know what's been going on." He watched the *Bree*'s captors for reaction as he spoke, and had no reason to feel disappointed. The chief, who had been facing away from the point where the radios were lashed, switched ends like a startled rattlesnake and then began looking around for the source of the voice with an unbelievably human air of bewilderment. One of his men who had been facing the radios indicated to him the one whose speaker Lackland had used, but after poking around the impenetrable box with knife and lance the chief obviously rejected this suggestion. This was the moment the Earthman chose for speaking again.

"Do you think there's any chance of getting them scared of the radios, Barl?"

The chief's head was about two inches from the speaker this time, and Lackland had made no effort to reduce the volume. Consequently there was no question where the sound had come from; and the chief began backing away from the noisy box. He was evidently trying to go slowly enough to satisfy his self-respect and fast enough to suit his other emotions, and once again Lackland had trouble in not laughing aloud.

Before Barlennan had a chance to reply Dondragmer moved over to the pile of meat, selected a choice piece, and laid it in front of the radio set with every indication of humility. He had taken a chance on having a pair of knives meet in his body, and knew it; but his guards were too absorbed by the new situation to take offense at his motion. Lackland, understanding how the mate had interpreted his own lead, followed on; he reduced the volume in the hope that his next utterance would seem less like anger to the canoeists, and heartily approved the mate's action.

"Good work, Don. Every time one of you does something like that I'll try to show approval; and I'll bark like nobody's business at anything I don't want our new acquaintances to be doing. You know the appropriate actions better than I, so just do everything in your power to make 'em think these radio boxes are high-powered beings who'll deliver lightning if properly annoyed."

"I understand; we can hold our end," replied the mate. "I thought that was what you had in mind."

The chief, gathering his courage once more, suddenly lunged at the nearest radio with his spear. Lackland remained silent, feeling that the natural result on the wooden point would be impressive enough; the sailors entered with a will into the game outlined by the Flyer. With what Lackland supposed were the equivalent of gasps of pious horror, they turned away from the scene and covered their eyes with their pincers. After a moment, seeing that nothing further was happening, Barlennan offered another piece of meat, at the same time gesturing in a way meant to convey the impression that he was begging for the life of the ignorant stranger. The river people were quite evidently impressed, and the chief drew back a little, gathered his committee, and began to discuss the whole situation with them. Finally one of the chief's counselors, in what was evidently an experiment, picked up a piece of meat and gave it to the nearest radio. Lackland was about to express gentle thanks when Dondragmer's voice came, "Refuse it!" Not knowing why but willing to trust the mate's judgment, Lackland turned up the volume and emitted a lionlike roar. The donor leaped back in genuine and unmistakable terror; then, at a sharp order from the chief, he crawled forward, retrieved the offending bit of food, selected another from the pile on the deck, and presented that.

"All right." It was the mate's voice again, and the Earthman lowered the volume of the speaker.

"What was wrong the other time?" he asked quietly.

"I wouldn't have given that piece to a *ternee* belonging to my worst enemy," replied Dondragmer.

"I keep finding resemblances between your people and mine in the darnedest situations," Lackland remarked. "I hope this business is suspended for the night; I can't see what's going on in the dark. If anything happens that I should react to, for heaven's sake tell me." This remark was prompted by the arrival of sunset once more, and Barlennan assured him that he would be kept informed. The captain had recovered his poise, and was once again more or less in control of the situation—as far as a prisoner could be.

The night was spent by the chief in discussion; his voice, interrupted occasionally by others which must belong to his counselors, came clearly to the Earthmen far above. By dawn he had apparently reached a decision. He had drawn a little apart from his counselors and laid down his weapons; now, as sunlight slanted once more across the deck, he advanced toward Barlennan, waving the latter's guards away as he approached. The captain, already fairly sure in his mind what the other wanted, waited calmly. The chief halted with his head a few inches from Barlennan's, paused impressively for a moment, and began to speak.

His words were still unintelligible to the sailors, naturally enough; but the gestures accompanying them were clear enough to give the speech meaning even to the distant human watchers.

Quite plainly, he wanted a radio. Lackland found himself speculating idly on just what supernatural powers the chief supposed the device to possess. Perhaps he wanted it to protect the village from enemies, or to bring luck to his hunters. That was not really an important question, however; what mattered would be his attitude when the request was refused. That might possibly be rather anti-social, and Lackland was still worrying a trifle.

Barlennan, showing what his human friend felt was rather more courage than sense, answered the speech briefly; a single word and a gesture which Lackland had long since come to recognize comprised the reply. "No" was the first Mesklinite word which Lackland learned beyond doubt, and he learned it for the first time now. Barlennan was very definite.

The chief, to the relief of at least one watcher, did not take a belligerent attitude. Instead, he gave a brief order to his men. Several of these at once laid aside their weapons and began restoring the looted food to the lockers from which it had been taken. If freedom were not enough for one of the magic boxes, he was willing to pay more. Both Barlennan and Lackland more than suspected that the fellow was now afraid to use force, badly as his possessive instincts were aroused.

With half the food returned, the chief repeated his request; when it was refused as before, he gave an amazingly human gesture of resignation and ordered his men to restore the rest. Lackland was getting uneasy.

"What do you think he'll do when you refuse him now, Barl?" he asked softly. The chief looked at the box hopefully; perhaps it was arguing with its owner, ordering him to give his captor what he wanted.

"I'm not sure enough to venture a prediction," the Mesklinite replied. "With luck, he'll bring us more stuff from the village to add to the price; but I'm not sure luck goes that far. If the radio were less important, I'd give it to him now."

"For heaven's sake!" The ethnologist sitting beside Lackland practically exploded at this point. "Have you been going through all this rigmarole and risking your life and those of your men just to hang onto a cheap vision set?"

"Hardly cheap," muttered Lackland. "They were designed to hold up at Mesklin's poles, under Mesklinite atmosphere, and through the handling of Mesklinite natives."

"Don't quibble!" snapped the student of cultures. "What are those sets down there for if not to get information? Give one to that savage! Where could it be better placed? And how could we observe the everyday life of a completely strange race better than through that eye? Charles, sometimes I wonder at you!"

"That will leave three in Barlennan's possession, of which one absolutely *must* get to the south pole. I see your point, but I think we'd better get Rosten's approval before we actually leave one this early on the way."

"Why? What does he have to do with it? He's not risking anything like Barlennan, and doesn't care about watching that society like some of the rest of us. I say leave it; I'm sure Barlennan wants to leave it; and it seems to me that Barlennan has the final say in any case."

The captain, who had of course overheard this, cut in.

"You forget, friend of Charles, that the radios are not my property. Charles let me take them, at my suggestion to be sure, as a safety measure, so that at least one would reach its goal even though unavoidable incidents deprived me of the others. It seems to me that he, not I, is the one whose word should be final." Lackland answered instantly.

"Do as you think best, Barl. You are on the spot; you know your world and its people better than any of us can hope to; and if you do decide to leave one with these people, even that will do some good to my friends, as you have heard."

"Thank you, Charles." The captain's mind was made up in the instant the Flyer finished speaking. Fortunately the chief had listened enthralled to the conversation, making no attempt to further his own interests while it was going on; now Barlennan, keeping up the play to the end, called some of his crew and gave swift orders.

Moving very circumspectly and never touching a radio at any time, the sailors prepared a rope sling. Then they pried the set up from a "safe" distance with spars, and poked and pushed until the sling was in position under and around it. This accomplished, one of the sling handles was given very respectfully to Barlennan. He in turn gestured the chief closer, and with an air of handling something precious and fragile, handed the loop of rope to him. Then he gestured toward the counselors, and indicated that they should take the other handles. Several of them moved forward rather gingerly; the chief hastily designated three for the honor, and the others fell back.

Very slowly and carefully the bearers moved the radio to the edge of the *Bree*'s outermost raft. The chief's canoe glided up—a long, narrow vessel evidently hollowed to a paper-thin shell from the trunk of one of the forest trees. Barlennan viewed it with distrust. He himself had never sailed anything but a raft; hollow vessels of any kind were strange to him. He felt certain that the canoe was too small to carry the weight of the radio, and when the chief ordered the greater part of the crew out of it he barely suppressed the equivalent of a negative headshake. He felt that the lightening thus obtained would be insufficient. He was more than startled when the canoe, upon receiving its new freight, merely settled a trifle. For a few seconds he watched, expecting vessel and cargo to pop suddenly below the surface; but nothing of the sort happened, and it became evident that nothing would.

Barlennan was an opportunist, as had been proved months ago by his unhesitating decision to associate with the visitor from Earth and learn his language. This was something new, and obviously worth learning about; if ships could be made that would carry so much more weight for their size, the knowledge was obviously vastly important to a maritime nation. The logical thing to do was to acquire one of the canoes.

As the chief and his three co-workers entered the craft, Barlennan followed. They delayed shoving off as they saw his approach, wondering what he might want. Barlennan himself knew what he wanted, but was not sure he could get away with what he planned to try. His people, however, had a proverb substantially identical in meaning with Earth's "Nothing venture, nothing gain," and he was no coward.

Very carefully and respectfully he touched the radio, leaning across the half inch of open river surface between ship and canoe to do so. Then he spoke.

"Charles, I'm going to get this little ship if I have to come back and steal it. When I finish talking, please answer—it doesn't matter what you say. I'm going to give these people the idea that the boat which carried the radio is too changed for ordinary use, and must take the radio's place on my deck. All right?"

"I was brought up to disapprove of racketeers—I'll

translate that word for you sometime—but I admire your nerve. Get away with it if you can, Barl, but please don't stick the neck you don't have out too far." He fell silent and watched the Mesklinite turn his few sentences to good account.

As before, he employed practically no spoken language; but his actions were reasonably intelligible even to the human beings, and clear as crystal to his erstwhile captors. First he inspected the canoe thoroughly, and plainly if reluctantly found it worthy. Then he waved away another canoe which had drifted close, and gestured several members of the river tribe who were still on the *Bree*'s deck away to a safe distance. He picked up a spear which one of the counselors had discarded to take up his new position, and made it clear that no one was to come within its length of the canoe.

Then he measured the canoe itself in spear lengths, took the weapon over to where the radio had been, and ostentatiously cleared away a spot large enough to take the craft; at his order, several of his own crew gently rearranged the remaining radios to make room for their new property. More persuasion might have been attempted, but sunset cut the activity short. The river dwellers did not wait out the night; when the sun returned, the canoe with the radio was yards away, already drawn up on shore.

Barlennan watched it with anxiety. Many of the other canoes had also landed, and only a few still drifted near the *Bree*. Many more natives had come to the edge of the bank and were looking over; but to Barlennan's intense satisfaction, none came any closer to the loaded canoe. He had apparently made some impression.

The chief and his helpers carefully unloaded their prize, the tribe maintaining its original distance. This was, incidentally, several times the spear's length demanded by Barlennan. Up the bank the radio went, the crowd opening wide to let it through and disappearing after it; and for long minutes there was no more activity. The *Bree* could easily have pushed out of her cage at this time, the crews of the few canoes remaining on the river showing little interest in what she did, but her captain did not give up that easily. He waited, eyes on the shore; and at long last a number of long black and red bodies appeared over the bank. One of these proceeded toward the canoe; but Barlennan realized it was not the chief, and uttered a warning hoot. The native paused, and a brief discussion ensued, which terminated in a series of modulated calls fully as loud as any that Lackland had heard Barlennan utter. Moments later the chief appeared and went straight to the canoe; it was pushed off by two of the counselors who had helped carry the radio, and started at once toward the *Bree*. Another followed it at a respectful distance.

The chief brought up against the outer rafts at the point where the radio had been loaded, and immediately disembarked. Barlennan had given his orders as soon as the canoe left the bank, and now the little vessel was hauled aboard and dragged to the space reserved for it, still with every evidence of respect. The chief did not wait for this operation to be finished; he embarked on the other canoe and returned to shore, looking back from time to time. Darkness swallowed up the scene as he climbed the bank.

"You win, Barl. I wish I had some of your ability; I'd be a good deal richer than I am now, if I were still alive by some odd chance. Are you going to wait around to get more out of them tomorrow?"

"We are leaving now!" the captain replied without hesitation.

Lackland left his dark screen and went to his quarters for his first sleep in many hours. Sixty-five minutes —rather less than four of Mesklin's days—had passed since the village was sighted.

XI: EYE OF THE STORM

The *Bree* sailed into the eastern ocean so gradually that no one could say exactly when the change was made. The wind had picked up day by day until she had normal open-sea use of her sails; the river widened rod by rod and at last mile by mile until the banks were no longer visible from the deck. It was still "fresh water"—that is, it still lacked the swarming life that stained practically all of the ocean areas in varying tints and helped give the world such a startling appearance from space—but the taste was coming, as sailor after sailor verified to his own great satisfaction.

Their course was still east, for a long peninsula barred their way to the south, according to the Flyers. Weather was good, and there would be plenty of warning of any change from the strange beings that watched them so carefully. There was plenty of food still aboard, enough to last easily until they reached the rich areas of the deep seas. The crew was happy.

The captain was satisfied as well. He had learned, partly from his own examination and experiment and partly from Lackland's casual explanations, how it was that a hollow vessel like the canoe could carry so much more weight for its size than could a raft. He was already deep in plans for the building of a large ship—as big or bigger than the *Bree*—built on the same principle and able to carry the profits of ten voyages in one. Dondragmer's pessimism failed to shake his rosy dream; the mate felt that there must be some reason such vessels were not used by their own people, though he could not say what the reason might be.

"It's too simple," he kept pointing out. "Someone would have thought of it long ago if that's all there was to it." Barlennan would simply point astern, where the canoe now followed gaily at the end of a rope, laden with a good half of their food. The mate could not shake his head after the fashion of an old family coachman looking over the new horseless carriage, but he would certainly have done so if he had possessed a neck.

He brightened up when they finally swung southward, and a new thought struck him.

"Watch it sink as soon as we start to get a little decent weight!" he exclaimed. "It may be all right for the creatures of the Rim, but you need a good solid raft where things are normal."

"The Flyer says not," replied Barlennan. "You know as well as I do that the *Bree* doesn't float any higher here at the Rim than she does at home. The Flyer says it's because the methane weighs less too, which sounds as though it might be reasonable." Dondragmer did not answer; he simply glanced, with an expression equivalent to a complacent smile, at the tough wood spring balance and weight that formed one of the ship's principal navigating instruments. As that weight began to droop, he was sure, something that neither his captain nor the distant Flyer had counted on would happen. He did not know what it would be, but he was certain of the fact.

The canoe, however, continued to float as the weight slowly mounted. It did not, of course, float as high as it would have on Earth, since liquid methane is less than half as dense as water; it's "water" line, loaded as it was, ran approximately halfway up from keel to gunwale, so that fully four inches was invisible below the surface. The remaining four inches of freeboard did not diminish as the days went by, and the mate seemed almost disappointed. Perhaps Barlennan and the Flyer were correct after all.

The spring balance was starting to show a barely visible sag from the zero position—it had been made, of course, for use where weight was scores or hundreds of times Earth-normal—when the monotony was broken. Actual weight was about seven Earths. The usual call from Toorey was a little late, and both the captain and mate were beginning to wonder whether all the remaining radios had failed for some reason when it finally arrived. The caller was not Lackland but a meteorologist the Mesklinites had come to know quite well.

"Barl," the weather man opened without preamble, "I don't know just what sort of storm you consider too bad to be out in—I suppose your standards are pretty high—but there seems to be one coming that I certainly wouldn't want to ride out on a forty-foot raft. It's a tight cyclone, of what I would consider hurricane force even for Mesklin, and on the thousand-mile course I've been observing so far it has been violent enough to stir up material from below and leave a track of contrasting color on the sea."

"That's enough for me," Barlennan replied. "How do I dodge it?"

"That's the catch; I'm not sure. It's still a long way from your position, and I'm not absolutely sure it will cross your course just when you're at the wrong point. There are a couple of ordinary cyclones yet to pass you, and they will change your course some and possibly even that of the storm. I'm telling you now because there is a group of fairly large islands about five hundred miles to the southeast, and I thought you might like to head for them. The storm will certainly strike them, but there seem to be a number of good harbors where you could shelter the *Bree* until it was over."

"Can I get there in time? If there's serious doubt about it I'd prefer to ride it out in the open sea rather than be caught near land of any sort."

"At the rate you've been going, there should be plenty of time to get there and scout around for a good harbor."

"All right. What's my noon bearing?"

The men were keeping close track of the *Bree*'s position by means of the radiation from the vision sets, although it was quite impossible to see the ship from beyond the atmosphere with any telescope, and the meteorologist had no trouble in giving the captain the bearing he wanted. The sails were adjusted accordingly and the *Bree* moved off on the new course.

The weather was still clear, though the wind was strong. The sun arced across the sky time after time without much change in either of these factors; but gradually a high haze began to appear and thicken, so that the sun changed from a golden disc to a rapidly moving patch of pearly light. Shadows became less definite, and finally vanished altogether as the sky became a single, almost uniformly luminous dome. This change occurred slowly, over a period of many days, and while it was going on the miles kept slipping beneath the *Bree*'s rafts.

They were less than a hundred miles from the islands when the minds of the crew were taken off the matter of the approaching storm by a new matter. The color of the sea had shifted again, but that bothered no one; they were as used to seeing it blue as red. No one expected signs of land at this distance, since the currents set generally across their course and the birds which warned Columbus did not exist on Mesklin. Perhaps a tall cumulous cloud, of the sort which so frequently forms over islands, would be visible for a hundred miles or more; but it would hardly show against the haze that covered the sky. Barlennan was sailing by dead reckoning and hope, for the islands were no longer visible to the Earthmen overhead.

Nevertheless, it was in the sky that the strange event occurred.

From far ahead of the *Bree,* moving with a swooping, dipping motion that was utterly strange to the Mesklinites and would have been perfectly familiar to the human beings, there appeared a tiny dark speck. No one saw it at first, and by the time they did it was too near and too high to be in the field of view of the vision sets. The first sailor to notice it gave vent to the usual hoot of surprise, which startled the human watchers on Toorey but was not particularly helpful to them. All they could see as their wandering attentions snapped back to the screens was the crew of the *Bree,* with the front end of every caterpillarlike body curled upward as its owner watched the sky.

"What is it, Barl?" Lackland called instantly.

"I don't know," the captain replied. "I thought for an instant it might be your rocket down looking for the islands to guide us better, but it's smaller and very different in shape."

"But it's something *flying?*"

"Yes. It does not make any noise like your rocket, however. I'd say it was being blown by the wind, except that it's moving too smoothly and regularly and in the wrong direction. I don't know how to describe it; it's wider than it is long, and a little bit like a mast set cross wise on a spar. I can't get closer than that."

"Could you angle one of the vision sets upward so we could get a look at it?"

"We'll try." Lackland immediately put through a call on the station telephone for one of the biologists.

"Lance, it looks as though Barlennan has run into a flying animal of some sort. We're trying to arrange a look at it. Want to come down to the screen room to tell us what we're looking at?"

"I'll be right with you." The biologist's voice faded toward the end of the sentence; he was evidently already on his way out of the room. He arrived before the sailors had the vision set propped up, but dropped into a chair without asking questions. Barlennan was speaking again.

"It's passing back and forth over the ship, sometimes in straight lines and sometimes in circles. Whenever it turns it tips, but nothing else about it changes. It seems to have a little body where the two sticks meet . . ." He went on with his description, but the object was evidently too far outside his normal experience for him to find adequate similes in a strange language.

"If it does come into view, be prepared to squint," the voice of one of the technicians cut in. "I'm covering that screen with a high-speed camera, and will have to jump the brightness a good deal in order to get a decent exposure."

". . . there are smaller sticks set across the long one, and what looks like a very thin sail stretched between them. It's swinging back toward us again, very low now—I think it may come in front of your eye this time. . . ."

The watchers stiffened, and the hand of the photographer tightened on a double-pole switch whose closing would activate his camera and step up the gain on the screen. Ready as he was, the object was well into the field before he reacted, and everyone in the room got a good glimpse before the suddenly bright light made their eyes close involuntarily. They all saw enough.

No one spoke while the cameraman energized the developing-frequency generator, rewound his film through its poles, swung the mounted camera toward the blank wall of the room, and snapped over the projection switch. Everyone had thoughts enough to occupy him for the fifteen seconds the operation required.

The projection was slowed down by a factor of fifty, and everyone could look as long as he pleased. There was no reason for surprise that Barlennan had been unable to describe the thing; he had never dreamed that such a thing as flying was possible until after his meeting with Lackland a few months before, and had no words in his own language for anything connected with the art. Among the few English words of that group he had learned, "fuselage" and "wing" and "empennage" were not included.

The object was not an animal. It had a body—fuselage, as the men thought of it—some three feet long, half the length of the canoe Barlennan had acquired. A slender rod extending several feet rearward held control surfaces at its extremity. The wings spanned a full twenty feet, and their structure of single main spar and numerous ribs was easily seen through the nearly transparent fabric that covered them. Within his natural limitations, Barlennan had done an excellent job of description.

"What drives it?" asked one of the watchers suddenly. "There's no propeller or visible jet, and Barlennan said it was silent."

"It's a sailplane." One of the meteorological staff spoke up. "A glider operated by someone who has all the skill of a terrestrial sea gull at making use of the updrafts from the front side of a wave. It could easily hold a couple of people Barlennan's size, and could stay aloft until they had to come down for food or sleep."

The *Bree*'s crew were becoming a trifle nervous. The complete silence of the flying machine, their inability to see who or what was in it, bothered them; no one likes to be watched constantly by someone he can't see. The glider made no hostile move, but their experience of aerial assault was still fresh enough to leave them uneasy about its presence. One or two had expressed a desire to practice their newly acquired art of throwing, using any hard objects they could find about the deck, but Barlennan had sternly forbidden this. They simply sailed on, wondering, until the hazy dome of the sky darkened with another sunset. No one knew whether to be relieved or worried when the new day revealed no trace of the flying machine. The wind was now stronger, and almost directly across the *Bree*'s course from the northeast; the waves had not yet followed it and were decidedly choppy in consequence. For the first time Barlennan perceived a disadvantage in the canoe; methane that blew or washed inboard stayed there. He found it necessary before the day was over to haul the little vessel up to the outer rafts and place two men aboard to bail—an act for which he had neither a word nor proper equipment.

The days passed without reappearance of the glider, and eventually only the official lookouts kept their eyes turned upward in expectation of its return. The high haze thickened and darkened, however, and presently turned to clouds which lowered until they hung a scant fifty feet above the sea. Barlennan was informed by the Earthmen that this was not good flying weather, and eliminated the watch. Neither he nor the human beings stopped to wonder how the first glider had found its way on a night too hazy for the stars to provide guidance.

The first of the islands to come into view was fairly high, its ground rising quickly from sea level to disappear into the clouds. It lay downwind from the point where they first sighted it; and Barlennan, after consulting the sketch map of the archipelago he had made from the Earthmen's descriptions, kept on course. As he had expected, another island appeared dead ahead before the first had faded from sight, and he altered course to pass to leeward of it. This side, according to observation from above, was quite irregular and should have usable harbors; also, Barlennan had no intention of coasting the windward shore during the several nights which would undoubtedly be required for his search.

This island appeared to be high also; not only did its hilltops reach the clouds, but the wind was in large measure cut off as the *Bree* passed into its lee. The shore line was cut by frequent fiords; Barlennan was intending simply to sail across the mouth of each in the hunt, but Dondragmer insisted that it would be worth while to penetrate to a point well away from the open sea. He claimed that almost any beach far enough up would be adequate shelter. Barlennan was convinced only to the point of wanting to show the mate how wrong he was. Unfortunately for this project, the first fiord examined made a sharp hook-turn half a mile from the ocean and opened into what amounted to a lake, almost perfectly circular and about a hundred yards in diameter. Its walls rose up into the mist except at the mouth where the *Bree* had entered and a smaller opening only a few yards from the first where a stream from the interior fed into the lake. The only beach was between the two openings.

There was plenty of time to secure both vessel and contents, as it happened; the clouds belonged to the second of the two "normal" cyclones the meteorologist had mentioned, rather than to the major storm. Within a few days of the *Bree*'s arrival in the harbor the weather cleared once more, though the wind continued high. Barlennan was able to see that the harbor was actually the bottom of a bowl-shaped valley whose walls were less than a hundred feet in height, and not particularly steep. It was possible to see far inland through the cleft cut by the small river, provided one climbed a short distance up the walls. In doing this, shortly after the weather cleared, Barlennan made a disconcerting discovery: sea shells, seaweeds, and bones of fairly large sea animals were thickly scattered among the land-type vegetation clothing the hillside. This continued, he discovered upon further investigation, quite uniformly around the valley up to a height fully thirty feet above the present sea level. Many of the remains were old, decayed almost to nothing, and partly buried; these might be accounted for by seasonal changes in the ocean level. Others, however, were relatively fresh. The implication was clear—on certain occasions the sea rose far above its present level; and it was possible that the *Bree* was not in as safe a position as her crew believed.

One factor alone limited Mesklin's storms to the point where sea travel was possible: methane vapor is far denser than hydrogen. On Earth, water vapor is lighter than air, and contributes enormously to the development of a hurricane once it starts; on Mesklin, the methane picked up from the ocean by such a storm tends, in a relatively short time, to put a stop to the rising currents which are responsible for its origin. Also the heat it gives up in condensing to form the storm clouds is only about a quarter as great as would be given by a comparable amount of water —and that heat is the fuel for a hurricane, once the sun has given the initial push.

In spite of all this, a Mesklinite hurricane is no joke. Barlennan, Mesklinite though he was, learned this very suddenly. He was seriously considering towing the *Bree* as far upstream as time would permit when the decision was taken out of his hands; the water in the lake receded with appalling suddenness, leaving the ship stranded fully twenty yards from its edge. Moments later the wind shifted ninety degrees and increased to a speed that made the sailors cling for dear life to deck cleats, if they happened to be on board, and to the handiest vegetation if they did not. The captain's shrill hoot ordering those off the ship to return went completely unheard, sheltered as they were in the almost complete circle of the valley walls; but no one needed any order. They picked their way, bush by bush, never holding with less than two sets of pincers, back to where their comrades had already lashed themselves as best they could to the vessel that was threatening every moment to lift into the wind's embrace. Rain—or, more properly, driven spray that had come completely across the island— lashed at them for long minutes; then both it and the wind ceased as though by magic. No one dared release his lashings, but the slowest sailors now made a final dash for the ship. They were none too soon.

The storm cell at sea level was probably three miles or so in diameter; it was traveling at about sixty or seventy miles per hour. The ending of the wind was only temporary; it meant that the center of the cyclone had reached the valley. This was also the low-pressure zone; and as it reached the sea at the mouth of the fiord, the flood came. It rose, gathering speed as it came, and spurted into the valley like the stream from a hose. Around the walls it swirled, picking up the *Bree* on the first circle; higher and higher, as the ship sought the center of the whirlpool—fifteen, then twenty, then twenty-five feet before the wind struck again.

Tough as the wood of the masts was, they had snapped long since. Two crewmen had vanished, their lashing perhaps a little too hastily completed. The new wind seized the ship, bare of masts as she was, and flung her toward the side of the whirlpool; like a chip, both for helplessness and magnitude, she shot along the stream of liquid now pouring up the little river toward the island's interior. Still the wind urged her, now toward the side of the stream; and as the pressure rose once more, the flood receded as rapidly as it had risen—no, not quite; the portion now floating the *Bree* had nowhere to go except back out through the little river-course, and that took time. Had day-light lasted, Barlennan might even in his ship's present condition have guided her back along that stream while she still floated; but the sun chose this moment to set, and in the darkness he ran aground. The few seconds delay was enough; the liquid continued to recede, and when the sun returned it looked upon a helpless collection of rafts some twenty yards from a stream that was too narrow and too shallow to float any one of them.

The sea was completely out of sight beyond the hills; the limp form of a twenty-foot-long sea monster stranded on the other side of the brook gave a graphic picture of the helplessness of the Gravity Expedition.

XII: WIND RIDERS

Much of what had happened had been seen from Toorey; the radio sets, like most of the less prominent articles about the *Bree*'s deck, had remained lashed in position. Not much had been distinguishable, of course, while the vessel had been whirling in the brief maelstrom; but her present situation was painfully clear. None of the people in the screen room could find anything helpful to say.

The Mesklinites could say little, either. They were used to ships on dry land, since that happened fairly often during late summer and fall as the seas receded in their own latitudes; but they were not accustomed to have it happen so suddenly, and to have so much high ground between them and the ocean. Barlennan and the mate, taking stock of the situation, found little to be thankful for.

They still had plenty of food, though that in the canoe had vanished. Dondragmer took occasion to point out the superiority of rafts, neglecting to mention that the supplies in the canoe had been tied down carelessly or not at all owing to a misplaced confidence in the high sides of the boat. The little vessel itself was still at the end of its towline, and still undamaged. The wood of which it had been made shared the springiness of the low-growing plants of the higher latitudes. The *Bree* herself, constructed of similar materials though in much less yielding form, was also intact, though the story might have been different had there been many rocks in the wall of the round valley. She was and had remained right side up, owing to her construction—Barlennan admitted that point without waiting for the mate to bring it up. The complaints were not in any way connected with lack of ship or supplies, but with lack of an ocean to float them on.

"The surest way would be to take her apart, as we did before, and carry her over the hills. They're not very steep, and there still isn't enough weight to matter." Barlennan made this suggestion after long thought.

"You're probably right, Captain; but wouldn't it save time to separate the rafts only lengthwise, so that we have rows the full length of the ship? We could carry or drag those over to the stream, and surely they'd float before we went down very far." Hars, now his former self after his encounter with the rock, made this suggestion.

"That sounds promising. Hars, why don't you find out just how far down that would be? The rest can start unlashing as Hars suggested, and unloading where we have to. Some of the cargo will be in the way of the lashings, I'm afraid."

"I wonder if the weather is still too bad for those flying machines?" Dondragmer asked, of no one in particular. Barlennan glanced upward.

"The clouds are still low and the wind high," he said. "If the Flyers are right—and they ought to know, I should think—the weather is still too bad. However, it won't hurt to look up occasionally. I rather hope we see one again."

"*One* I wouldn't much mind myself," replied the mate dryly. "I suppose you want a glider to add to the canoe. I'll tell you right now that I might, in extremity, get into the canoe, but the day I climb onto one of those flying machines will be a calm winter morning with both suns in the sky." Barlennan did not answer; he had not consciously considered adding a glider to his collection, but the idea rather struck his fancy. As for flying in it—well, changed as he was, there were limits.

The Flyers reported clearing weather, and the clouds obediently thinned over the next few days.

Greatly improved though the flying weather was, few crew members thought to watch the sky. All were too busy. Hars's plan had proved feasible, the stream being deep enough for the rafts only a few hundred yards toward the sea and wide enough for a single raft very little farther down. Barlennan's statement that the additional weight would mean little proved wrong; every component was twice as heavy as it had been where they last saw Lackland, and they were not accustomed to lifting *anything*. Powerful as they were, the new gravity taxed their hoisting abilities to the point where it was necessary to unload the rafts before the rows of little platforms could be partly carried and dragged to the stream. Once they were partly immersed, the going was much simpler; and after a digging squad had widened the banks up to the point nearest the *Bree*'s resting place the job became almost easy. Not too many hundred days passed before the long, narrow string of rafts, reloaded, was being towed once more toward the sea.

The flying machines appeared just after the ship had entered that portion of the stream where its walls were steepest, shortly before it emptied into the lake. Karondrasee saw them first; he was on board at the time, preparing food while the others pulled, and his attention was freer than theirs. His hoot of alarm roused Earthmen and Mesklinites alike, but the former as usual could not see the approaching visitors since the vision sets were not aimed high enough.

Barlennan saw all too clearly, however. There were eight of the gliders, traveling fairly close together but by no means in tight formation. They came straight on, riding the updraft on the leeward side of the little valley until they were almost over the ship; then they changed course to pass in front of her. As each swooped overhead, it released an object, turned, and swung back to the lee side to recover its altitude.

The falling objects were distinct enough; every sailor could see that they were spears, very much like those the river dwellers had used but with much heavier tips. For a moment the old terror of falling objects threatened to send the crew into hysteria; then they saw that the missiles would not strike them, but fall some distance in front. A few seconds later the gliders swooped again, and the sailors cowered in expectation of an improved aim; but the spears fell in about the same place. With the third pass it became evident that their aim was deliberate; and presently their purpose became apparent. Every projectile had fallen in the still narrow stream, and penetrated more than half its length into the firm clay bottom; by the end of the third run, two dozen stakes formed by the spear handles were effectually blocking the ship's passage downstream.

As the *Bree* approached the barricade, the bombardment stopped. Barlennan had thought it might be continued to prevent their approaching and clearing the obstacle away, but when they reached it they found this to be superfluous. The spears were there to stay; they had been dropped from nearly a hundred feet with superlative aim in a field of seven gravities, and nothing short of power machinery was going to extract them. Terblannen and Hars proved that in five minutes of fruitless upward tugging.

"Can't you cut them?" Lackland asked from his distant observation point. "Those pincers of yours are pretty powerful, as I know."

"These are wood, not metal," Barlennan replied. "We would need one of your hard metal saws, which you claimed would attack even our wood—unless you have some machine for pulling them out."

"You must have tools which will cut it; how do you do repair work on your ship? The rafts certainly didn't grow in that shape."

"Our cutting tools are made of animal teeth set in strong frames, and most of them are not very portable. What we have we will use, but I doubt that we'll be given time to do much."

"I should think you could keep attackers away by fire."

"We can, if they come from downwind. I find it hard to imagine their being that stupid." Lackland fell silent, while the crew fell to work on the stakes with such edged tools as they could find. Their personal knives were of hardwood and would make no impression on the spears, but as Barlennan had intimated, there were a few bone and ivory cutters, and these began to chip away at the incredibly tough wood. Digging was also attempted by some of the crew who lacked tools; they took turns in sinking to the bottom of the inches-deep brook, working the clay loose, and letting its particles wash away in the sluggish current. Dondragmer watched these workers for a time, then pointed out that it would probably be easier to dig a canal around the obstruction than to grub out two dozen sticks from a depth of some four feet. This suggestion was eagerly adopted by the members of the crew who had nothing to cut with, and work progressed at a remarkable rate.

The gliders kept circling while all this was going on; apparently they either remained overnight or were replaced by others during the minutes of darkness— no one could tell which. Barlennan kept a sharp watch on the hills to either side of the stream, expecting ground forces to appear at any moment; but for a long time his own crew and the gliders formed the only moving parts of the scenery. The crews of the gliders themselves remained invisible; no one could even tell how many or what sort of creatures rode in the machines, though both human beings and Mesklinites had come to take more or less for granted that they belonged to Barlennan's race. They showed no evident anxiety about the sailors' digging activities, but it became apparent finally that the excavation had not gone unnoticed. The job was about three quarters finished when they took action; another series of bombing runs left the path of the new waterway as completely staked off as the original. As before, pains were apparently taken to avoid transfixing any of the crew. The action, however, was about as discouraging as if it had been a personal assault; quite evidently the digging process was useless, since the work of days could be nullified in a matter of minutes. Some other line of procedure must be devised.

At the Earthmen's advice, Barlennan had long since ordered his men not to gather in large groups; but now he drew them in toward the ship, establishing a loose cordon parallel to the string of rafts on each side of the creek. The men were far enough apart so there was no really tempting target from above, and close enough to support each other in case an attack actually developed. There they stayed; Barlennan wished it made evident that the next move was up to the personnel of the gliders. They failed to make it, however, for several more days.

Then a dozen more of the flimsy craft appeared in the distance, swooped overhead, split into two groups, and landed on the hilltops to either side of the imprisoned ship. The landings were made as the Flyers had foretold, into the wind; the machines skidded to a stop in a few feet from their point of touchdown. Four beings emerged from each, leaped to the wings, and hastily tied the gliders down, using the local bushes as anchors. What had been assumed all along now proved to be a fact; they were identical in form, size, and coloring with the sailors of the *Bree*.

Once the gliders were secured, their crews proceeded to set up a collapsible structure upwind from them, and attach cords equipped with hooks to this. They appeared to be measuring quite carefully the distance from this device to the nearest glider. Only when this task was completed did they pay any attention to the *Bree* or her crew. A single prolonged wail that sounded from one hilltop to the other apparently served as a signal that the work was complete.

Then the glider crews on the leeward hill began to descend the slope. They did not leap, as they had during the action subsequent to landing, but crawled in the caterpillarlike fashion which was the only means of locomotion Barlennan's people had known prior to his exploration of the Rim. In spite of this they made good speed and were within reasonable throwing distance—as several of the more pessimistic sailors regarded it—by sundown. They stopped at that point and waited for the night to pass; there was just enough light from the moons for each party to see that the other did nothing suspicious. With the coming of sunlight the advance was resumed, and eventually terminated with one of the newcomers only a yard or so from the nearest sailor, while his companions hung a few feet farther back. None of the party seemed to be armed, and Barlennan went to meet them, first ordering two sailors to swing one of the vision sets so that it pointed directly at the place of meeting.

The glider pilot wasted no time, but began speaking as soon as Barlennan stopped in front of him. The captain failed to understand a word. After a few sentences the speaker appeared to realize this; he paused and after a moment continued at somewhat slower speed in what Barlennan judged to be a different language. To save the time that a random search through the tongues known to the other would consume, Barlennan this time indicated his lack of comprehension verbally. The other shifted languages once more, and rather to his surprise Barlennan heard his own speech, uttered slowly and badly pronounced, but quite comprehensible.

"It is long since I have heard your tongue spoken," the other said. "I trust I can still be understood when I use it. Do you follow me?"

"I can understand you perfectly well," replied Barlennan.

"Good. I am Reejaaren, linguist for Marreni, who is Officer of the Outer Ports. I am ordered to find out who you are and where you are from, and your purpose in sailing the seas about these islands."

"We are on a trading journey, with no particular destination." Barlennan had no intention of talking about his connection with the creatures of another world. "We did not know of the existence of these islands; we simply were heading away from the Rim, of which we had had enough. If you wish to trade with us we are willing to do business; if not, we ask only to be allowed to continue our journey."

"Our ships and gliders trade on these seas—we have never seen others," replied Reejaaren. "I fail to understand one point. The trader far to the south from whom I learned your language said that he came from a country that lay on the farther side of a sea across the western continent. We know that there is no sea passage from that ocean to this between here and the ice; yet you were sailing from the north when we first sighted you. That would suggest that you were quartering back and forth through these seas in deliberate search of land. How does that square with your story? We do not like spies."

"We came from the north, after crossing the land between this ocean and ours." Barlennan had no time to think up a convincing lie, though he realized that the truth was likely to be unbelievable. Reejaaren's expression showed that he was right.

"Your ship was obviously built with large tools, which you do not have. That means a shipyard, and there is none to the north on this ocean. Do you want me to believe you took her apart and dragged her across that much land?"

"Yes." Barlennan felt that he saw his way out.

"How?"

"How do you fly? Some would find that much harder to believe." The question was not quite as good a one as Barlennan had hoped, judging by the interpreter's reaction.

"I am sure you do not expect me to tell you that. Mere trespassers we may tolerate; but spies receive much harder treatment."

The captain covered up as well as he could. "I did not expect you to tell me. I was simply pointing out as tactfully as possible that perhaps you should not have asked me how we crossed the land barrier."

"Oh, but I should—and must. You do not yet seem to realize your position, stranger. What you think of me is unimportant; but what I think of you counts a great deal. To put it simply, to leave here as you desire you will have to convince me that you are harmless."

"But what harm could we do you—the crew of a single ship? Why should you fear us so?"

"We do not fear you!" The answer was sharp and emphatic. "The damage you could do is obvious—one person, let alone a shipload, could take away information which we do not wish to give. We realize, of course, that the barbarians could not learn the secret of flight unless it were very carefully explained to them; that is why I laughed at your question. Still, you should be more careful."

Barlennan had not heard any laughter, and began to suspect a good deal about the interpreter and his people. A half-truth that seemed like yielding on Barlennan's part would probably be the best move.

"We had much help pulling the ship across the land," he said, putting a little sullenness in his tone.

"From the rock-rollers and river-dwellers? You must have a remarkably persuasive tongue. We have never received anything but missiles from them." To Barlennan's relief, Reejaaren did not pursue the subject any farther. He returned to more immediate matters.

"So you desire to trade with us, now that you are here. What have you to trade? And I suppose you wish to go to one of our cities?" Barlennan sensed the trap, and answered accordingly.

"We will trade here, or anywhere else you desire, though we would rather not go any farther from the sea. All we have to trade at the moment is a load of foods from the isthmus, which you doubtless have in great quantity already because of your flying machines."

"Food can usually be sold," the interpreter replied noncommittally. "Would you be willing to do your trading before you got any closer to the sea?"

"If necessary, as I said, though I don't see why it should be necessary. Your flying machines could catch us before we got very far, if we tried to leave the coast before you wanted, couldn't they?" Reejaaren might have been losing his suspicions up to this point, but the last question restored them in full force.

"Perhaps we could, but that is not for me to say. Marreni will decide, of course, but I suspect you might as well plan on lightening your ship here. There will be port fees, of course, in any case."

"Port fees? This is no port, and I didn't land here; I was washed up."

"Nevertheless, foreign ships must pay port fees. I might point out that the amount is determined by the

Officer of the Outer Ports, and he will get much of his impression of you through me. A little more courtesy might be in order." Barlennan restrained his temper with difficulty, but agreed aloud that the interpreter spoke the clearest truth. He said it at some length, and apparently mollified that individual to some extent. At any rate he departed without further threats, overt or implied.

Two of his fellows accompanied him; the other remained behind. Men from the other gliders hastily seized the two ropes attached to the collapsible framework and pulled. The cords stretched unbelievably, until their hooks were finally fastened to an attachment in the glider's nose. The aircraft was then released and the ropes contracted to their original length, hurling the glider into the air. Barlennan instantly formed a heartfelt desire for some of that stretching rope. He said so, and Dondragmer sympathized. He had heard the entire conversation, and sympathized also with his captain's feelings toward the linguist for the Officer of the Outer Ports.

"You know, Barl, I think we could put that lad in his place. Want to try it?"

"I'd love to, but I don't think we can afford to let him get mad at us until we're good and far away. I don't want him and his friends dropping their spears on the *Bree* now or any other time."

"I don't mean to make him angry, but afraid of us. 'Barbarians'—he'll eat that word if I have to cook it personally for him. It all depends on certain things: do the Flyers know how these gliders work, and will they tell us?"

"They probably know, unless they've had better ones for so long they've forgotten—"

"So much the better, for what I have in mind."

"—but I'm not sure whether they'll tell. I think you know by now what I'm really hoping to get out of this trip; I want to learn everything I possibly can of the Flyers' science. That's why I want to get to that rocket of theirs near the Center; Charles himself said that it contained much of the most advanced scientific equipment they have. When we have that, there won't be a pirate afloat or ashore who'll be able to touch the *Bree,* and we'll have paid our last port dues—we'll be able to write our own menus from then on."

"I guessed as much."

"That's why I wonder whether they'll tell what you want; they may suspect what I'm after."

"I think you're too suspicious yourself. Have you ever *asked* for any of this scientific information you want to steal?"

"Yes; Charles always said it was too difficult to explain."

"Maybe he was right; maybe he doesn't know it himself. I want to ask one of his people about these gliders, anyway; I want to watch that Reejaaren grovel."

"Just what is this idea of yours, anyway?"

Dondragmer told him, at length. The captain was dubious at first, but gradually grew more enthusiastic; and finally they went over to the radios together.

XIII: SLIP OF THE TONGUE

Fortunately Reejaaren did not return for a good many days. His people remained; four to six gliders were always drifting overhead, and several more squatted on the hilltops beside their catapults. The number of aircraft did not change noticeably, but the population of the hilltops increased day by day. The Earthmen above had entered into Dondragmer's plan with enthusiasm and, Barlennan suspected, some little amusement. A few of the sailors were unable to pick up what was needed with sufficient speed, and had to be left out of the main plan in one sense; but even they understood the situation and would, Barlennan was sure, be able to contribute to the desired effect. In the meantime he put them to work repairing the shattered masts, whose rigging had at least kept them with the ship.

The plan was matured and well rehearsed long before the interpreter's return, and the officers found themselves impatient to try it out though Dondragmer had been spending time at the radio meanwhile on yet another project. In fact, after controlling themselves for a few days, the captain and mate strolled one morning up the hill toward the parked gliders with a full determination to make a test of the idea, though neither had said a word to the other about his intention. The weather had completely cleared long since, and there was only the perpetual wind of Mesklin's seas to help or hinder flying. Apparently it wanted to help; the gliders were tugging at their tie-down cables like living creatures, and crewmen were standing by the wings with a secure grip on the surrounding bushes, evidently ready to add their strength if necessary to that of the restraining lines.

Barlennan and Dondragmer approached the machines until they were ordered sharply to halt. They had no idea of the rank or authority of the individual giving the order, since he wore no insignia; but it was not part of their plan to argue such matters. They halted, and looked over the machines casually from a distance of thirty or forty yards, while the crewmen looked back rather belligerently. Apparently Reejaaren's superciliousness was not a rare trait with his nation.

"You look astonished, barbarians," one of them remarked after a brief silence. "If I thought you could learn anything by looking at our machines, I would have to force you to stop. As it is, I can only assure you that you look rather childish." He spoke Barlennan's tongue with an accent not much worse than that of the chief linguist.

"There seems little to learn from your machines. You could save much trouble with the wind in your present situation by warping the front of your wings down; why do you keep so many people busy instead?" He used the English word for "wings," not having one in his own language. The other requested an explanation; receiving it, he was startled out of his superiority for a moment.

"You have seen gliders before? Where?"

"I have never seen *your* type of flying machine in my life," Barlennan answered. His words were truthful, though their emphasis was decidedly misleading. "I have not been this close to the Rim before, and I should imagine that these flimsy structures would collapse from their added weight if you flew them much farther south."

"How—" The guard stopped, realizing that his attitude was not that of a civilized being toward a barbarian. He was silent for a moment, trying to decide just what his attitude should be in this case; then he decided to pass the problem higher in the chain of command. "When Reejaaren returns, he will no doubt be interested in any minor improvements you may be able to suggest. He might even reduce your port fee, if he deems them of sufficient value. Until then, I think you had better stay entirely away from our gliders; you might notice some of their more valuable features, and then we would regretfully have to consider you a spy." Barlennan and his mate retired to the *Bree* without argument, highly satisfied with the effect they had produced, and reported the conversation in its entirety to the Earthmen.

"How do you think he reacted to the implication that you had gliders capable of flying up in the two-hundred-gravity latitudes?" asked Lackland. "Do you think he believed you?"

"I couldn't say; he decided about then either that he was saying too much or hearing too much, and put us in storage until his chief returns. I think we started the right attitude developing, though."

Barlennan may have been right, but the interpreter gave no particular evidence of it when he returned. There was some delay between his actual landing and his descent of the hill to the *Bree,* and it seemed likely that the guard had reported the conversation; but he made no reference to it at first.

"The Officer of the Outer Ports has decided to assume for the moment that your intentions are harmless," he began. "You have of course violated our rules in coming ashore without permission; but he recognized that you were in difficulties at the time, and is inclined to be lenient. He authorizes me to inspect your cargo and evaluate the amount of the necessary port fee and fine."

"The Officer would not care to see our cargo for himself and perhaps accept some token of our gratitude for his kindness?" Barlennan managed to keep sarcasm out of his voice. Reejaaren gave the equivalent of a smile.

"Your attitude is commendable, and I am sure we will get along very well with each other. Unfortunately, he is occupied on one of the other islands, and will be for many days to come. Should you still be here at the end of that time, I am sure he will be delighted to take advantage of your offer. In the meantime we might proceed to business."

Reejaaren lost little if any of his superiority during his examination of the *Bree*'s cargo, but he managed to give Barlennan some information during the process which he would probably have died rather than give consciously. His words, of course, tended to belittle the value of everything he saw; he harped endlessly on the "mercy" of his so far unseen chief Marreni. However, he appropriated as fine a respectable number of the "fir cones" that had been acquired during the journey across the isthmus. Now these should have been fairly easy to obtain here, since the distance could not be too great for the gliders—in fact, the interpreter had made remarks indicating acquaintance with the natives of those regions. If, then, Reejaaren held the fruit as being of value, it meant that the "barbarians" of the isthmus were a little too much for the interpreter's highly cultured people, and the latter were not so close to being the lords of creation as they wanted people to think. That suggested that the mate's plan had a very good chance of success, since the interpreter would probably do almost anything rather than appear inferior to the "barbarian" crew of the *Bree*. Barlennan, reflecting on this, felt his morale rise like the Earthmen's rocket; he was going to be able to lead this Reejaaren around like a pet *ternee*. He bent all his considerable skill to the task, and the crew seconded nobly.

Once the fine was paid, the spectators on the hills descended in swarms; and the conclusion about the value of the fir-cone-like fruit was amply confirmed. Barlennan at first had a slight reluctance to sell all of it, since he had hoped to get really high prices at home; but then he reflected that he would have to go back through the source of supply before reaching his home in any case.

Many of the buyers were evidently professional merchants themselves, and had plentiful supplies of trade goods with them. Some of these were also edibles, but on their captain's orders the crew paid these little attention. This was accepted as natural enough by the merchants; after all, such goods would be of little value to an overseas trader, who could supply his own food from the ocean but could hardly expect to preserve most types of comestibles for a long enough time to sell at home. The "spices" which kept more or less permanently were the principal exception to this rule, and none of these were offered by the local tradesmen.

Some of the merchants, however, did have interesting materials. Both the cord and the fabric in which Barlennan had been interested were offered, rather to his surprise. He personally dealt with one of the salesmen who had a supply of the latter. The captain felt its unbelievably sheer and even more incredibly tough texture for a long time before satisfying himself that it was really the same material as that used in the glider wings. Reejaaren was close beside him, which made a little care necessary. He learned from the merchant that it was a woven fabric in spite of appearances, the fiber being of vegetable origin—the canny salesman refused to be more specific—the cloth being treated after weaving with a liquid which partly dissolved the threads and filled the holes with the material thus obtained.

"Then the cloth is windproof? I think I could sell this easily at home. It is hardly strong enough for practical uses like roofing, but it is certainly ornamental, particularly the colored versions. I will admit, though it is hardly good buying procedure, that this is the most salable material I have yet seen on this island."

"Not strong enough?" It was Reejaaren rather than the merchant who expressed indignation. "This material is made nowhere else, and is the only substance at once strong and light enough to form the wings of our gliders. If you buy it, we will have to give it to you in bolts too small for such a purpose—no one but a fool, of course, would trust a sewn seam in a wing."

"Of course," Barlennan agreed easily. "I suppose such stuff could be used in wings here, where the weight is so small. I assure you that it would be quite useless for the purpose in high latitudes; a wing large enough to lift anyone would tear to pieces at once in any wind strong enough to furnish the lift." This was almost a direct quote from one of his human friends, who had been suggesting why the gliders had never been seen in countries farther south.

"Of course, there is very little load on a glider in these latitudes," Reejaaren agreed. "Naturally there is no point in building them stronger than necessary here; it adds to the weight." Barlennan decided that his tactical adversary was not too bright.

"Naturally," he agreed. "I suppose with the storms you have here your surface ships must be stronger. Do they ever get flung inland the way mine was? I never saw the sea rise in that fashion before."

"We naturally take precautions when a storm is coming. The rising of the sea occurs only in these latitudes of little weight, as far as I have been able to observe. Actually our ships are very much like yours, though we have different armament, I notice. Yours is unfamiliar to me—doubtless our philosophers of war found it inadequate for the storms of these latitudes. Did it suffer seriously in the hurricane that brought you here?"

"Rather badly," Barlennan lied. "How are your own ships armed?" He did not for a second expect the interpreter to answer the question in any way, except perhaps a resumption of his former haughtiness, but Reejaaren for once was both affable and co-operative. He hooted a signal up the hill to some of his party who had remained above, and one of these obediently came down to the scene of bargaining with a peculiar object in his pincers.

Barlennan had never seen a crossbow, of course, or any other missile weapon. He was suitably impressed when Reejaaren sent three quartz-tipped bolts in a row thudding for over half their six-inch length into the hard trunk of a plant some forty yards away. He also lost most of his surprise at the interpreter's helpfulness; such a weapon would be so much dead weight before the *Bree* was a quarter of the way to her home latitudes. More as a test than anything else, Barlennan offered to buy one of the crossbows; the interpreter pressed it on him as a gift, together with a bundle of bolts. That was good enough for the captain; as a trader, he naturally enjoyed being taken for a fool. It was usually profitable.

He secured an incredible quantity of the wing fabric —Reejaaren either forgot to make sure it was in small bolts, or no longer considered it necessary— much of the elastic rope, and enough of the local artifacts to fill the *Bree*'s decks, except for the normal requirements of working space and the area devoted to a reasonable food reserve. He was rid of everything salable that he had brought to the island, with the possible exception of the flame throwers. Reejaaren had not mentioned these since he had been told they were damaged, though he had obviously recognized them as armament of some sort. Barlennan actually thought of giving him one, minus chlorine ammunition, but realized he would have to explain its operation and even demonstrate. This he had no intention of doing; if these people were not familiar with the weapons he did not want them to know the truth of their nature, and if they were he did not want to be caught in a lie. It was much nicer to have Reejaaren in a good humor.

With the selling completed, the crowd of local people gradually melted away; and at last there remained only the gliders and their crews, some of the latter down near the ship and others on the hilltops by their machines. Barlennan found the interpreter among the former group, as usual; he had spent much time talking casually to the sailors. They had reported that he was, as expected, pumping them gently about the flying ability of their people. They had filled their part of the game with noncommittal replies that nevertheless "accidentally" revealed a considerable knowledge of aerodynamics. Naturally, they carefully gave no hint as to how recently the knowledge had been acquired—or its source. Barlennan at this point was reasonably sure that the islanders, or at least their official representative, believed his people capable of flight.

"That seems to be all I can give or take," he said as he secured Reejaaren's attention. "We have, I think, paid all necessary fees. Is there any objection to our departing?"

"Where do you plan to go now?"

"Southward, toward decent weight. We do not know this ocean at all, except by vague reports from some of our merchants who have made the overland journey. I should like to see more of it."

"Very well. You are free to go. Doubtless you will see some of us on your travels—I occasionally go south myself. Watch out for more storms."

The interpreter, apparently the picture of cordiality, turned up the hill. "We may see you at the coast," he added, looking back. "The fiord where you first landed has been suggested as possibly improvable to harbor status, and I want to inspect it." He resumed his journey to the waiting gliders.

Barlennan turned back to the ship, and was about to give orders for immediate resumption of the downstream journey—the goods had been loaded as fast as they were purchased—when he realized that the stakes dropped by the gliders still barred the way. For an instant he thought of calling the islander back and requesting their removal; then he thought better of it. He was in no position to make a demand, and Reejaaren would undoubtedly grow supercilious again if he put it as a request. The *Bree*'s crew would dig out of their own troubles.

On board, he issued an order to this effect, and the cutters were once more picked up; but Dondragmer interrupted.

"I'm glad to see that this work wasn't wasted time," he said.

"What?" asked the captain. "I knew you were at some stunt of your own for the last forty or fifty days, but was too busy to find out what it was. We were able to handle the trading without you. What have you been doing?"

"It was an idea that struck me just after we were first caught here; something you said to the Flyers about a machine to pull out the stakes gave it to me.

I asked them later if there was such a machine that was *not* too complicated for us to understand, and after some thinking one of them said there was. He told me how to make it, and that's what I've been doing. If we rig a tripod by one of the stakes, I'll see how it works."

"But what is the machine? I thought all the Flyer's machines were made of metal, which we couldn't fashion because the kinds that are hard enough need too much heat."

"This." The mate displayed two objects on which he had been working. One was simply a pulley of the most elementary design, quite broad, with a hook attached. The other was rather similar but double, with peglike teeth projecting from the circumference of both wheels. The wheels themselves were carved from a solid block of hardwood, and turned together. Like the first pulley, this was equipped with a hook; in addition there was a strap of leather threaded through the guards of both wheels, with holes punched in it to match the peg teeth, and the ends buckled together so that it formed a continuous double loop. The whole arrangement seemed pointless to the Mesklinites—including Dondragmer, who did not yet understand why the device worked, or even whether it actually would. He took it over in front of one of the radios and spread it out on the deck.

"Is this now assembled correctly?" he asked.

"Yes, it should work if your strap is strong enough," came the answer. "You must attach the hook of the single pulley to the stake you want to extract; I am sure you have methods of doing that with rope. The other pulley must be fastened to the top of the tripod. I've told you what to do from then on."

"Yes, I know. It occurred to me that instead of taking much time to reverse the machine after it was wound up tightly, however, I could unfasten the buckle and rethread it."

"That would work, provided you were not lifting a load that had to be supported in the meantime," replied the Earthman. "Good for you, Don."

The crew immediately headed for the original group

of stakes, but Barlennan called to them to wait.

"There aren't so many blocking the canal we were digging. Don, did the Flyer say how long it would take to pull them out with that contraption?"

"He wasn't sure, since he didn't know how deeply they were buried or how fast we could operate it; but he guessed at a day or so each—faster than we could cut through them."

"But not so fast we wouldn't gain time by having some of us finish that canal while you take however many men you need to pull the stakes in it. Incidentally, did he have any name for the thing?"

"He called it a differential hoist. The second word is plain enough, but I don't see how to translate the first—it's just a noise to me."

"Me too. Differential it is. Let's get to work; your watch to the hoist, and mine to the canal." The crew buckled down with a will.

The canal was finished first, since it quickly became evident that most of the crew would be free to dig; two sailors, taking turns on the hoist at intervals of a few minutes, proved enough to start the spear shafts sliding very slowly out of the hard ground. To Barlennan's satisfaction the heads came with them, so that he had eight very effective-looking spears when the operation was completed. His people did little work in stone, and the quartz heads were extremely valuable in his estimation.

Once through the barrier, the distance to the lake was relatively short; and there they stopped to reassemble the *Bree* in her natural form. This was quickly accomplished—indeed, the crew might now be considered expert at the task—and once more the ship floated in relatively deep water. The Earthmen above heaved a collective sigh of relief. This proved to be premature.

The gliders had been passing back and forth throughout the journey from the trading site. If their crews had been at all surprised at the method used to extract the spears, no evidence had appeared of the fact. Barlennan, of course, hoped they had seen and added the information to the list of his own people's superior accomplishments. He was not too surprised to see a dozen gliders on the beach near the mouth of the fiord, and ordered the helmsman to turn the ship ashore at that point. Perhaps at least the islanders would notice that he had recovered the spears intact.

Reejaaren was the first to greet them as the *Bree* anchored a few yards offshore. "So your ship is seaworthy again, eh? I'd try to meet any more storms a long way from land, if I were you."

"Right," Barlennan agreed. "The difficulty in a sea you don't know is being sure where you stand in that respect. Perhaps you would tell us the disposition of lands in this sea? Or would you, perhaps, have charts you could provide us with? I should have thought to ask before."

"Our charts of these islands, of course, are secret," the interpreter replied. "You should be out of the group in forty or fifty days, however, and then there is no land for some thousands of days' sail to the south. I do not know your ship's speed, so I cannot guess just when you are likely to make it. Such lands as there are are mostly islands at first; then the coast of the land you crossed turns east, and if you keep straight south you will encounter it at about—" He gave an expression which referred to a spring-balance reading, and corresponded to about forty-five Earth gravities of latitude. "I could tell you about many of the countries along that coast, but it would take a long time. I can sum it up by saying that they will probably trade rather than fight—though some will undoubtedly do their best not to pay for what they get."

"Will any of them assume we are spies?" Barlennan asked pleasantly.

"There is that risk, naturally, though few have secrets worth stealing. Actually they will probably try to steal yours, if they know you have any. I should not advise your discussing the matter of flying while there."

"We did not plan to," Barlennan assured him, with glee that he managed to conceal. "We thank you for the advice and information." He gave the order to hoist the anchor, and for the first time Reejaaren noticed the canoe, now trailing once more at the end of its towrope and loaded with food.

"I should have noticed that before," the interpreter said. "Then I would never have doubted your story of coming from the south. How did you get that from the natives?" In the answer to this question Barlennan made his first serious mistake in dealing with the islander.

"Oh, we brought that with us; we frequently use them for carrying extra supplies. You will notice that its shape makes it easy to tow." He had picked up his elementary notions of streamlining from Lackland not too long after acquiring the canoe.

"Oh, you developed that craft in your country too?" the interpreter asked curiously. "That is interesting; I had never seen one in the south. May I examine it, or do you not have time? We have never bothered to use them ourselves." Barlennan hesitated, suspecting this last statement to be a maneuver of the precise sort he himself had been employing; but he saw no harm in complying, since Reejaaren could learn nothing more from a close examination than he could from where he was. After all, it was the canoe's shape that was important, and anyone could see that. He allowed the *Bree* to drift closer inshore, pulled the canoe to him with the towrope, and gave it a push toward the waiting islander. Reejaaren plunged into the bay and swam out to the little vessel when it ran aground, in a few inches of liquid. The front part of his body arched upward to look into the canoe; powerful pincer-tipped arms poked at the sides. These were of ordinary wood, and yielded springily to the pressure; and as they did so the islander gave a hoot of alarm that brought the four gliders in the air swinging toward the *Bree* and the shore forces up to full alertness.

"Spies!" he shrieked. "Bring your ship aground at once, Barlennan—if that is your real name. You are a good liar, but you have lied yourself into prison this time!"

XIV: THE TROUBLE WITH HOLLOW BOATS

Barlennan had been told at various times during his formative years that he was someday pretty sure to talk himself into more trouble than he could talk himself out of. At various later times during his career this prediction had come alarmingly close to fulfillment, and each time he had resolved to be more careful in future with his tongue. He felt the same way now, together with an injured feeling arising from the fact that he did not yet know just what he had said that had betrayed his mendacity to the islander. He did not have time to theorize over it, either; something in the line of action was called for, the quicker the better. Reejaaren had already howled orders to the glider crews to pin the *Bree* to the bottom if she made a move toward the open sea, and the catapults on shore were launching more of the machines to reinforce those already aloft. The wind was coming from the sea at a sufficient angle to be lifted as it struck the far wall of the fiord, so the flyers could remain aloft as long as necessary. Barlennan had learned from the Earthmen that they probably could not climb very high—high enough for effective missile dropping—under the thrust of the updrafts from ocean waves; but he was a long way from the open sea where they would have to depend on such currents. He had already had a chance to observe their accuracy, and dismissed at once any idea of trusting to his dodging ability to save his ship.

As so frequently happened, the action was performed by a crew member while he was debating the best

153

course. Dondragmer snatched up the crossbow that had been given them by Reejaaren, nocked a bolt, and cocked the weapon with a speed that showed he could not have been completely absorbed in his hoist project at all times. Swinging the weapon shoreward, he rested it on its single support leg and covered the interpreter with the point.

"Hold on, Reejaaren; you're moving in the wrong direction." The islander stopped on his way out of the bay, liquid dripping from his long body, and doubled his front half back toward the ship to see what the mate meant. He saw clearly enough, but seemed for a moment undecided about the proper course of action.

"If you want to assume I'll probably miss because I've never handled one of these things, go right ahead. I'd like to find out myself. If you don't start coming this way in an awfully short time, though, it will be just as though you had tried to escape. Move!" The last word was issued in a barking roar that removed much of the interpreter's indecision. He apparently was not quite sure of the mate's incompetence; he continued the doubling movement, re-entered the bay, and swam out to the *Bree*. If he thought of concealing himself by submerging during the process, he evidently lacked the courage to try it. As he well knew, the methane was only a few inches deep even at the ship's location, and would hardly protect him from a bolt hurled with force enough to penetrate three inches of wood after a forty-yard trajectory under seven gravities. He did not think of it in those terms, of course, but he knew very well what those projectiles could do.

He clambered aboard, shaking with rage and fear together.

"Do you think this will save you?" he asked. "You have simply made things worse for yourselves. The gliders will drop in any event if you try to move, whether I am aboard or not."

"You will order them not to."

"They will obey no order I give while I am obviously in your power; you should know that if you have any sort of fighting force."

"I've never had much to do with soldiers," Barlennan replied. He had recovered the initiative, as he usually did once things had started in a definite direction. "However, I'll believe you for the time being. We'll just have to hold you here until some understanding is reached concerning this nonsense about our going ashore—unless we can take care of those gliders of yours in the meantime. It's a pity we didn't bring some more modern armament into this backward area."

"You can stop that nonsense now," returned the captive. "You have nothing more than the rest of the savages of the south. I'll admit you fooled us for a time, but you betrayed yourself a moment ago."

"And what did I say that made you think I'd been lying?"

"I see no reason to tell you. The fact that you don't yet know just proves my point. It would have been better for you if you hadn't fooled us so completely; then we'd have been more careful with secret information, and you wouldn't have learned enough to make your disposal necessary."

"And if you hadn't made that last remark, you might have talked us into surrendering," cut in Dondragmer, "though I admit it's not likely. Captain, I'll bet that what you slipped up on was what I've been telling you all along. It's too late to do anything about that now, though. The question is how to get rid of these pesky gliders; I don't see any surface craft to worry about, and the folks on shore have only the crossbows from the gliders that were on the ground. I imagine they'll leave things to the aircraft for the time being." He shifted to English. "Do you remember anything we heard from the Flyers that would help us get rid of these pesky machines?" Barlennan mentioned their probable altitude limitations over open sea, but neither could see how that helped at the moment.

"We might use the crossbow on them." Barlennan made the suggestion in his own language, and Reejaaren sneered openly. Krendoranic, the munitions officer of the *Bree,* who like the rest of the crew had been listening eagerly, was less contemptuous.

"Let's do that," he cut in sharply. "There's been something I've wanted to try ever since we were at that river village."

"What?"

"I don't think you'd want me to talk about it with our friend listening. We'll show him instead, if you are willing." Barlennan hesitated a moment, then gave consent.

Barlennan looked a trifle worried as Krendoranic opened one of the flame lockers, but the officer knew what he was doing. He removed a small bundle already wrapped in light-proof material, thus giving evidence of at-least some of his occupation during the nights since they had left the village of the river-dwellers.

The bundle was roughly spherical, and evidently designed to be thrown by arm-power; like everyone else, Krendoranic had been greatly impressed by the possibilities of this new art of throwing. Now he was extending his idea even further, however.

He took the bundle and lashed it firmly to one of the crossbow bolts, wrapping a layer of fabric around bundle and shaft and tying it at either end as securely as possible. Then he placed the bolt in the weapon. He had, as a matter of duty, familiarized himself with the weapon during the brief trip downstream and the reassembly of the *Bree,* and had no doubt about his ability to hit a sitting target at a reasonable distance; he was somewhat less sure about moving objects, but at least the gliders could only turn rapidly if they banked sharply, and that would give him warning.

At his order, one of the sailors who formed part of his flame-thrower crew moved up beside him with the igniting device, and waited. Then, to the intense annoyance of the watching Earthmen, he crawled to the nearest of the radios and set the leg of the bow on top of it to steady himself and the weapon in an upward position. This effectively prevented the human beings from seeing what went on, since the radios were set to look outward from a central point and neither of the others commanded a view of the first.

As it happened, the gliders were still making relatively low passes, some fifty feet above the bay, and coming directly over the *Bree* on what could on an instant's notice become bomb runs; so a much less experienced marksman than the munitions officer could hardly have missed. He barked a command to his assistant as one of the machines approached, and began to lead it carefully. The moment he was sure of his aim, he gave a command of execution and the assistant touched the igniter to the bundle on the slowly rising arrow point. As it caught, Krendoranic's pincers tightened on the trigger and a line of smoke marked the trail of the missile from the bow.

Krendoranic and his assistant ducked wildly back to deck level and rolled upwind to get away from the smoke released at the start; sailors to leeward of the release point leaped to either side. By the time they felt safe, the air action was almost over.

The bolt had come as close as possible to missing entirely; the marksman had underestimated his target's speed. It had struck about as far aft on the main fuselage as it could, and the bundle of chlorine powder was blazing furiously. The cloud of flame was spreading to the rear of the glider and leaving a trail of smoke that the following machines made no effort to avoid. The crew of the target ship escaped the effects of the vapor, but in a matter of seconds their tail controls burned away. The glider's nose dropped and it fluttered down to the beach, pilot and crew leaping free just before it touched. The two aircraft which had flown into the smoke also went out of control as the hydrogen chloride fumes incapacitated their personnel, and both settled into the bay. All in all, it was one of the great anti-aircraft shots of history.

Barlennan did not wait for the last of the victims to crash, but ordered the sails set. The wind was very much against him, but there was depth enough for the centerboards, and he began to tack out of the fiord. For a moment it looked as though the shore personnel were about to turn their own crossbows on the ship, but Krendoranic had loaded another of his frightful missiles and aimed it toward the beach, and the mere threat sent them scampering for safety—upwind; they were sensible beings for the most part.

Reejaaren had watched in silence, while his bodily attitude betrayed blank dismay. Gliders were still in the air, and some were climbing as though they might attempt runs from a higher altitude; but he knew perfectly well that the *Bree* was relatively safe from any such attempt, excellent though his aimers were. One of the gliders did make a run at about three hundred feet, but another trail of smoke whizzing past spoiled his aim badly and no further attempts were made. The machines drifted in wide circles well out of range while the *Bree* slipped on down the fiord to the sea.

"What in blazes has been happening, Barl?" Lackland, unable to restrain himself longer, decided it was safe to speak as the crowd on shore dwindled with distance. "I haven't been butting in for fear the radios might spoil some of your plans, but please let us know what you've been doing."

Barlennan gave a brief résumé of the events of the last few hundred days, filling in for the most part the conversations his watchers had been unable to follow. The account lasted through the minutes of darkness, and sunrise found the ship almost at the mouth of the fiord. The interpreter had listened with shocked dismay to the conversation between captain and radio; he assumed, with much justice, that the former was reporting the results of his spying to his superiors, though he could not imagine how it was being done. With the coming of sunrise he asked to be put ashore in a tone completely different from any he had used before; and Barlennan, taking pity on a creature who had probably never asked for a favor in his life from a member of another nation, let him go overboard from the moving vessel fifty yards from the beach. Lackland saw the islander dive into the sea with some relief; he knew Barlennan quite well, but had not been sure just what course of action he would consider proper under the circumstances.

"Barl," he said after a few moments' silence, "do you suppose you could keep out of trouble for a few weeks, until we get our nerves and digestions back up here? Every time the *Bree* is held up, everyone on this moon ages about ten years."

"Just who got me into this trouble?" retorted the Mesklinite. "If I hadn't been advised to seek shelter from a certain storm—which it turned out I could have weathered better on the open sea—I'd certainly never have met these glider makers. I can't say that I'm very sorry I did, myself; I learned a lot, and I know at least some of your friends wouldn't have missed the show for anything. From my point of view this trip has been rather dull so far; the few encounters we have had have all terminated very tamely, and with a surprising amount of profit."

"Just which do you like best, anyway: adventure or cash?"

"Well—I'm not sure. Every now and then I let myself in for something just because it looks interesting; but I'm much happier in the end if I make something out of it."

"Then please concentrate on what you're making out of this trip. If it will help you any to do that, we'll collect a hundred or a thousand shiploads of those spices you just got rid of and store them for you where the *Bree* wintered; it would still pay us, if you'll get that information we need."

"Thanks, I expect to make profit enough. You'd take all the fun out of life."

"I was afraid you'd feel that way. All right, I can't order you around, but please remember what this means to us."

Barlennan agreed, more or less sincerely, and swung his ship once more southward. For some days the island they had left was visible behind them, and often they had to change course to avoid others. Several times they saw gliders skimming the waves on the way from one island to another, but these always gave the ship a wide berth. Evidently news spread rapidly among these people. Eventually the last visible bit of land slipped below the horizon, and the human beings said that there was no more ahead—good fixes could once more be obtained with the weather in its present clear state.

At about forty-gravity latitude they directed the ship on a more southeasterly course to avoid the land mass which, as Reejaaren had said, swung far to the east ahead of her. Actually the ship was following a relatively narrow passage between two major seas, but the strait was far too wide for that fact to be noticeable from shipboard.

One minor accident occurred some distance into the new sea. At around sixty gravities the canoe, still following faithfully at the end of its towrope, began to settle visibly in the sea. While Dondragmer put on his best "I told you so" expression and remained silent, the little vessel was pulled up to the ship's stern and examined. There was quite a bit of methane in the bottom, but when she was unloaded and pulled aboard for examination no leak was visible. Barlennan concluded that spray was responsible, though the liquid was much clearer than the ocean itself. He put the canoe back in the sea and replaced its load, but detailed a sailor to inspect every few days and bail when necessary. This proved adequate for many days; the canoe floated as high as ever when freshly emptied, but the rate of leakage grew constantly greater. Twice more she was pulled aboard for inspection without result; Lackland, consulted by radio, could offer no explanation. He suggested that the wood might be porous, but in that case the leaking should have been present from the beginning.

The situation reached a climax at about two hundred gravities, with more than a third of the sea journey behind them. The minutes of daylight were longer now as spring progressed and the *Bree* moved ever farther from her sun, and the sailors were relaxing accordingly. The individual who had the bailing job was not, therefore, very attentive as he pulled the canoe up the stern rafts and climbed over its gunwale. He was aroused immediately thereafter. The canoe, of course, settled a trifle as he entered; and as it did so, the springy wood of the sides gave a little. As the sides collapsed, it sank a little farther—and the sides yielded more—and it sank yet farther—

Like any feedback reaction, this one went to completion in a remarkably short time. The sailor barely had time to feel the side of the canoe pressing inward when the whole vessel went under and the outside pressure was relieved. Enough of the cargo was denser than methane to keep the canoe sinking, and the sailor found himself swimming where he had expected to be riding. The canoe itself settled to the end of its towrope, slowing the *Bree* with a jerk that brought the entire crew to full alertness.

The sailor climbed back into the *Bree*, explaining what had happened as he did so. All the crew whose duties did not keep them elsewhere rushed to the stern, and presently the rope was hauled in with the swamped canoe at the end of it. With some effort, the canoe and such of its load as had been adequately lashed down were hauled aboard, and one of the sets turned to view it. The object was not very informative; the tremendous resilience of the wood had resulted in its recovering completely even from this flattening, and the canoe had resumed its original shape, still without leaks. This last fact was established after it had once more been unloaded. Lackland, looking it over, shook his head and offered no explanation. "Tell me just what happened—what everyone who saw anything at all did see."

The Mesklinites complied, Barlennan translating the stories of the crewman who had been involved and the few others who had seen the event in any detail. It was the first, of course, that provided the important bit of information.

"Good Earth!" Lackland muttered, half aloud. "What's the use of a high school education if you can't recall it when needed later on? Pressure in a liquid corresponds to the weight of liquid above the point in question—and even methane under a couple of hundred gravities weighs a good deal per vertical inch. That wood's not much thicker than paper, either; a wonder it held so long." Barlennan interrupted this rather uninformative monologue with a request for information.

"I gather you now know what happened," he said. "Could you please make it clear to us?"

Lackland made an honest effort, but was only partly successful. The concept of pressure, in a quantitative sense, defeats a certain number of students in every high school class.

Barlennan did get the idea that the deeper one went into the sea the greater was the crushing force, and that the rate of increase with depth went up along with gravity; but he did not connect this force with others such as wind, or even the distress he himself had experienced when he submerged too rapidly in swimming.

The main point, of course, was that any floating object had to have some part of itself under the surface, and that sooner or later that part was going to be crushed if it was hollow. He avoided Dondragmer's eye as this conclusion was reached in his conversation with Lackland, and was not comforted when the mate pointed out that this was undoubtedly where he had betrayed his falsehood when talking to Reejaaren. Hollow ships used by his own people, indeed! The islanders must have learned the futility of that in the far south long since.

The gear that had been in the canoe was stowed on deck, and the voyage continued. Barlennan could not bring himself to part with the now useless little vessel, though it took up a good deal of space. He disguised its uselessness thinly by packing it with food supplies which could not have been heaped so high without the sides of the canoe to retain them. Dondragmer pointed out that it was reducing the ship's flexibility by extending the length of two rafts, but the captain did not let this fact worry him.

Time passed, as it had before, first hundreds and then thousands of days. To the Mesklinites, long-lived by nature, its passage meant little; to the Earthmen the voyage gradually became a thing of boredom, part of the regular routine of life. They watched and talked to the captain as the line on the globe slowly lengthened; measured and computed to determine his position and best course when he asked them to; taught English to or tried to learn a Mesklinite language from sailors who sometimes also grew bored; in short, waited, worked where possible, and killed time as four Earthly months—nine thousand four hundred and some odd Mesklinite days—passed. Gravity increased from the hundred and ninety or so at the latitude where the canoe had sunk to four hundred, and then to six, and then further, as indicated by the wooden spring balance that was the *Bree*'s latitude gauge. The days grew longer and the nights shorter until at last the sun rode completely around the sky without touching the horizon, though it dipped toward it in the south. The sun itself seemed shrunken to the men who had grown used to it during the brief time of Mesklin's perihelion passage. The horizon, seen from the *Bree*'s deck through the vision sets, was *above* the ship all around, as Barlennan had so patiently explained to Lackland months before; and he listened tolerantly when the men assured him it was an optical illusion. The land that finally appeared ahead was obviously above them too; how could an illusion turn out to be correct? The land was really there. This was proved when they reached it; for reach it they did, at the mouth of a vast bay that stretched on to the south for some two thousand miles, half the remaining distance to the grounded rocket. Up the bay they sailed, more slowly as it finally narrowed to the dimensions of a regular estuary and they had to tack instead of seeking favorable winds with the Flyer's help, and finally to the river at its head. Up this they went too, no longer sailing except at rare, favorable intervals; for the current against the blunt faces of the rafts was more than the sails could usually overcome, broad as the river still was. They towed instead, a watch at a time going ashore with ropes and pulling; for in this gravity even a single Mesklinite had a respectable amount of traction. More weeks, while the Earthmen lost their boredom and tension mounted in the Toorey station. The goal was almost in sight, and hopes ran high.

And they were dashed, as they had been for a moment months before when Lackland's tank reached the end of its journey. The reason was much the same; but this time the *Bree* and its crew were at the bottom of a cliff, not the top. The cliff itself was three hundred feet high, not sixty; and in nearly seven hundred gravities climbing, jumping and other rapid means of travel which had been so freely indulged at the distant Rim were utter impossibilities for the powerful little monsters who manned the ship.

The rocket was fifty miles away in horizontal distance; in vertical, it was the equivalent, for a human being, of a climb of nearly thirty-five—up a sheer rock wall.

XV: HIGH GROUND

The change of mind that had so affected the *Bree*'s crew was not temporary. The unreasoning, conditioned fear of height that had grown with them from birth was gone. They still, however, had normal reasoning power; and in this part of their planet a fall of as much as half a body's length was nearly certain to be fatal even to their tough organisms. Changed as they were, most of them felt uneasy as they moored the *Bree* to the riverbank only a few rods from the towering cliff that barred them from the grounded rocket.

The Earthmen, watching in silence, tried futilely to think of a way up the barrier. No rocket that the expedition possessed could have lifted itself against even a fraction of Mesklin's polar gravity; the only one that had ever been built able to do so was already aground on the planet. Even had the craft been capable, no human or qualified non-human pilot could have lived in the neighborhood; the only beings able to do that could no more be taught to fly a rocket than a Bushman snatched straight from the jungle.

"The journey simply isn't as nearly over as we thought." Rosten, called to the screen room, analyzed the situation rapidly. "There should be some way to the plateau or farther slope—whichever is present— of that cliff. I'll admit there seems to be no way Barlennan and his people can get *up;* but there seems to be nothing preventing their going around." Lackland relayed this suggestion to the captain.

"That is true," the Mesklinite replied. "There are,

165

however, a number of difficulties. It is already getting harder to procure food from the river; we are very far from the sea. Also, we have no longer any idea of how far we may have to travel, and that makes planning for food and all other considerations nearly impossible. Have you prepared, or can you prepare, maps with sufficient detail to let us plan our course intelligently?"

"Good point. I'll see what can be done." Lackland turned from the microphone to encounter several worried frowns. "What's the matter? Can't we make a photographic map as we did of the equatorial regions?"

"Certainly," Rosten replied. "A map can be made, possibly with a lot of detail; but it's going to be difficult. At the equator a rocket could hold above a given point, at circular velocity, only six hundred miles from the surface—right at the inner edge of the ring. Here circular velocity won't be enough, even if we could use it conveniently. We'd have to use a hyperbolic orbit of some sort to get short-range pictures without impossible fuel consumption; and that would mean speeds relative to the surface of several hundred miles a second. You can see what sort of pictures that would mean. It looks as though the shots will have to be taken with long-focus lenses, at extremely long range; and we can only hope that the detail will suffice for Barlennan's needs."

"I hadn't thought of that," admitted Lackland. "We can do it, though; and I don't see any alternative in any case. I suppose Barlennan could explore blind, but it would be asking a lot of him."

"Right. We'll launch one of the rockets and get to work." Lackland gave the substance of this conversation to Barlennan, who replied that he would stay where he was until the information he needed was obtained.

"I could either go on upstream, following the cliff around to the right, or leave the ship and the river and follow to the left. Since I don't know which is best from the point of view of distance, we'll wait. I'd rather go upstream, of course; carrying food and radios will be no joke otherwise."

"All right. How is your food situation? You said something about its being hard to get that far from the ocean."

"It's scarcer, but the place is no desert. We'll get along for a time at least. If we ever have to go overland we may miss you and your gun, though. This crossbow has been nothing but a museum piece for nine tenths of the trip."

"Why do you keep the bow?"

"For just that reason—it's a good museum piece, and museums pay good prices. No one at home has ever seen, or as far as I know even dreamed of, a weapon that works by throwing things. You couldn't spare one of your guns, could you? It needn't work, for that purpose."

Lackland laughed. "I'm afraid not; we have only one. We don't expect to need it, but I don't see how we could explain giving it away." Barlennan gave the equivalent of an understanding nod, and turned back to his own duties. He had much to bring up to date on the bowl that was his equivalent of a globe; the Earthmen, throughout the trip, had been giving him bearing and distance to land in all directions, so he was able to get most of the shores of the two seas he had crossed onto the concave map.

It was also necessary to see to the food question; it was not, as he had told Lackland, really pressing, but more work with the nets was going to be necessary from now on. The river itself, now about two hundred yards wide, appeared to contain fish enough for their present needs, but the land was much less promising. Stony and bare, it ran a few yards from one bank of the stream to end abruptly against the foot of the cliff; from the other, a series of low hills succeeded each other for mile after mile, presumably far beyond the distant horizon. The rock of the escarpment's face was polished glass-smooth, as sometimes happens even on Earth to the rocks at the sliding edges of a fault. Climbing it, even on Earth, would have required the equipment and body weight of a fly (on Mesklin, the fly would have weighed too much). Vegetation was present, but not in any great amount, and in the first fifty days of their stay no member of the *Bree*'s crew saw any trace of land animal life. Occasionally someone thought he saw motion, but each time it turned out to be shadows cast by the whirling sun, now hidden from them only by its periodic trips beyond the cliff. They were so near the south pole that there was no visible change in the sun's altitude during the day.

For the Earthmen, the time was a little more active. Four of the expedition, including Lackland, manned the rocket and dropped planetward from the rapidly moving moon. From their takeoff point the world looked rather like a pie plate with a slight bulge in the center; the ring was simply a line of light, but it stood out against the background of star-studded blackness and exaggerated the flattening of the giant world.

As power was applied both to kill the moon's orbital velocity and bring them out of Mesklin's equatorial plane the picture changed. The ring showed for what it was, but even the fact that it also had two divisions did not make the system resemble that of Saturn. Mesklin's flattening was far too great for it to resemble anything but itself—a polar diameter of less than twenty thousand miles compared to an equatorial one of some forty-eight thousand has to be seen to be appreciated. All the expedition members had seen it often enough now, but they still found it fascinating.

The fall from the satellite's orbit gave the rocket a very high velocity, but, as Rosten had said, it was not high enough. Power had to be used in addition; and although the actual pass across the pole was made some thousands of miles above the surface, it was still necessary for the photographer to work rapidly. Three runs were actually made, each taking between two and three minutes for the photography and many more for the whipping journey around the planet. They made reasonably sure that the world was presenting a different face to the sun each time, so that the height of the cliff could be checked by shadow measurements on all sides; then, with the photographs already fixed and on one of the chart tables, the rocket spent more fuel swinging its hyperbola into a wide arc that intercepted Toorey, and killing speed so that too much acceleration would not be needed when they got there. They could afford the extra time consumed by such a maneuver; the mapping could proceed during the journey.

Results, as usual with things Mesklinite, were interesting if somewhat surprising. In this case, the surprising fact was the size of the fragment of planetary crust that seemed to have been thrust upward en bloc. It was shaped rather like Greenland, some thirty-five hundred miles in length, with the point aimed almost at the sea from which the *Bree* had come. The river leading to it, however, looped widely around and actually contacted its edge at almost the opposite end, in the middle of the broad end of the wedge. Its height at the edges was incredibly uniform; shadow measurements suggested that it might be a trifle higher at the point end than at the *Bree*'s present position, but only slightly.

Except at one point. One picture, and one only, showed a blurring of the shadow that might be a gentler slope. It was also in the broad end of the wedge, perhaps eight hundred miles from where the ship now was. Still better, it was upstream—and the river continued to hug the base of the cliff. It looped outward at the point where the shadow break existed as though detouring around the rubble pile of a collapsed slope, which was very promising indeed. It meant that Barlennan had sixteen or seventeen hundred miles to go instead of fifty, with half of it overland; but even the overland part should not be overwhelmingly difficult. Lackland said so, and was answered with the suggestion that he make a more careful analysis of the surface over which his small friend would have to travel. This, however, he put off until after the landing, since there were better facilities at the base.

Once there, microscopes and densitometers in the hands of professional cartographers were a little less encouraging, for the plateau itself seemed rather rough. There was no evidence of rivers or any other specific cause for the break in the wall that Lackland had detected; but the break itself was amply confirmed. The densitometer indicated that the center of the region was lower than the rim, so that it was actually a gigantic shallow bowl; but its depth could not be determined accurately, since there were no distinct shadows across the inner portion. The analysts were quite sure, however, that its deepest part was still well above the terrain beyond the cliffs.

Rosten looked over the final results of the work, and sniffed.

"I'm afraid that's the best we can do for him," he said at last. "Personally, I wouldn't have that country on a bet even if I could live in it. Charlie, you may have to figure out some way to give moral support; I don't see how anyone can give physical."

"I've been doing my best all along. It's a nuisance having this crop up when we were so close to home plate. I just hope he doesn't give us up as a bad job this close to the end; he still doesn't believe everything we say, you know. I wish someone could explain that high-horizon illusion to his—and my—satisfaction; that might shake him out of the notion that his world is a bowl, and our claim to come from another is at least fifty per cent superstition on our part."

"You mean you don't understand why it looks higher?" one of the meteorologists exclaimed in a shocked tone.

"Not in detail, though I realize the air density has something to do with it."

"But it's simple enough—"

"Not for me."

"It's simple for anyone. You know how the layer of hot air just above a road on a sunny day bends sky light back upward at a slight angle, since the hot air is less dense and the light travels faster in it; you see the sky reflection and tend to interpret it as water. You get more extensive mirages sometimes even on Earth, but they're all based on the same thing—a 'lens' or 'prism' of colder or hotter air refracts the light. It's the same here, except the gravity is responsible; even hydrogen decreases rapidly in density as you go up from

Mesklin's surface. The low temperature helps, of course."

"All right if you say so; I'm not a—" Lackland got no chance to finish his remark; Rosten cut in abruptly and grimly.

"Just how fast does this density drop off with altitude?" The meteorologist drew a slide rule from his pocket and manipulated it silently for a moment.

"Very roughly, assuming a mean temperature of minus one-sixty, it would drop to about one per cent of its surface density at around fifteen or sixteen hundred feet." A general stunned silence followed his words.

"And—how far would it have dropped at—say— *three hundred feet?*" Rosten finally managed to get the question out. The answer came after a moment of silent lip movement.

"Again very roughly, seventy or eighty per cent— probably rather more."

Rosten drummed his fingers on the table for a minute or two, his eyes following their motions; then he looked around at the other faces. All were looking back at him silently.

"I suppose no one can suggest a bright way out of this one; or does someone really hope that Barlennan's people can live and work under an air pressure that compares to their normal one about as that at forty or fifty thousand feet does to ours?"

"I'm not sure." Lackland frowned in concentration, and Rosten brightened a trifle. "There was some reference a long time ago to his staying under water—excuse me, under methane—for quite a while, and swimming considerable distances. You remember those river-dwellers must have moved the *Bree* by doing just that. If it's the equivalent of holding breath or a storage system such as our whales use, it won't do us any good; but if he can actually get a fair part of the hydrogen he needs from what's in solution in Mesklin's rivers and seas, there might be some hope." Rosten thought for a moment longer.

"All right. Get your little friend on the radio and find out all he knows himself about this ability of his. Rick, look up or find out somehow the solubility of hydrogen in methane at eight atmospheres pressure and temperatures between minus one forty-five and one eighty-five Centigrade. Dave, put that slide rule back in your pocket and get to a calculator; get as precise a value of the hydrogen density on that clifftop as physics, chemistry, math, and the gods of good weather men will let you. Incidentally, didn't you say there was a drop of as much as three atmospheres in the center of some of those tropical hurricanes? Charlie, find out from Barlennan whether and how much he and his men felt that. Let's go." The conference broke up, its members scattering to their various tasks. Rosten remained in the screen room with Lackland, listening to his conversation with the Mesklinite far below.

Barlennan agreed that he could swim below the surface for long periods without trouble; but he had no idea how he did it. He did not breathe anyway, and did not experience any feeling comparable to the human sense of strangulation when he submerged. If he stayed too long and was too active the effect was rather similar to sleepiness, as nearly as he could describe it; if he actually lost consciousness, however, it stopped there; he could be pulled out and revived as much later as anyone cared as long as he didn't starve in the meantime. Evidently there was enough hydrogen in solution in Mesklin's seas to keep him alive, but not for normal activity. Rosten brightened visibly.

"There is no discomfort of the sort you suggest in the middle of the worst storms I have ever experienced," the captain went on. "Certainly no one was too weak to hold on during that one which cast us on the island of the gliders—though we were in its center for only two or three minutes, of course. What is your trouble? I do not understand what all these questions are leading to." Lackland looked to his chief for permission, and received a silent nod of affirmation.

"We have found that the air on top of this cliff, where our rocket is standing, is very much thinner than at the bottom. We doubt seriously that it will be dense enough to keep you and your people going."

"But that is only three hundred feet; why should it change that much in such a short distance?"

"It's that gravity of yours; I'm afraid it would take too long to explain why, but on any world the air gets thinner as you go higher, and the more the gravity the faster that change. On your world the conditions are a trifle extreme."

"But where is the air at what you would call normal for this world?"

"We assume at sea level; all our measures are usually made from that reference."

Barlennan was thoughtful for a little while. "That seems silly; I should think you'd want a level that stayed put to measure from. Our seas go up and down hundreds of feet each year—and I've never noticed any particular change in the air."

"I don't suppose you would, for several reasons; the principal one is that you would be at sea level as long as you were aboard the *Bree,* and therefore at the bottom of the atmosphere in any case. Perhaps it would help you to think of this as a question of what weight of air is above you and what weight below."

"Then there is still a catch," the captain replied. "Our cities do not follow the seas down; they are usually on the seacoast in spring and anywhere from two hundred miles to two thousand inland by fall. The slope of the land is very gentle, of course, but I am sure they are fully three hundred feet above sea level at that time." Lackland and Rosten stared silently at each other for a moment; then the latter spoke.

"But you're a lot farther from the pole in your country—but no, that's quibbling. Even if gravity were only a third as great you'd be experiencing tremendous pressure changes. Maybe we've been taking nova precautions for a red dwarf." He paused for a moment, but the Mesklinite made no answer. "Would you be willing, then, Barlennan, to make at least an attempt to get up to the plateau? We certainly will not insist on your going on if it proves too hard on your physical make-up, but you already know its importance to us."

"Of course I will; we've come this far, and have no real reason to suppose what's coming will be any worse than what's past. Also, I want . . ." He paused briefly, and went on in another vein. "Have you yet found any way of getting up there, or is your question still hypothetical?" Lackland resumed the human end of the conversation.

"We have found what looks like a way, about eight hundred miles upstream from your present position. We can't be sure you can climb it; it resembles a rock fall of very moderate slope, but we can't tell from our distance how big the rocks may be. If you can't get up there, though, I'm afraid you just can't get up at all. The cliff seems to be vertical all around the plateau except for that one point."

"Very well, we will head upstream. I don't like the idea of climbing even small rocks here, but we'll do our best. Perhaps you will be able to give suggestions when you can see the way through the vision sets."

"It will take you a long time to get there, I'm afraid."

"Not too long; for some reason there is a wind along the cliff in the direction we wish to go. It has not changed in direction or strength since we arrived several score days ago. It is not as strong as the usual sea wind, but it will certainly pull the *Bree* against the current—if the river does not grow too much swifter."

"This one does not grow too much narrower, at any rate, as far as you will be going. If it speeds up, it must be because it grows shallower. All we can say to that is that there was no sign of rapids on any of the pictures."

"Very well, Charles. We will start when the hunting parties are all in."

One by one the parties came back to the ship, all with some food but none with anything interesting to report. The rolling country extended as far in all directions as anyone had gone; animals were small, streams scarce, and vegetation sparse except around the few springs. Morale was a trifle low, but it improved with the news that the *Bree* was about to travel again. The few articles of equipment that had been disembarked were quickly reloaded on the rafts, and the ship pushed out into the stream. For a moment she drifted seaward, while the sails were being set; then they filled with the strangely steady wind and she bore up against the current, forging slowly but steadily into unknown areas of the hugest planet man had yet attempted to explore.

XVI: VALLEY OF WIND

Barlennan rather expected the riverbanks to become more barren as his ship ascended the stream, but if anything, the reverse was the case. Clumps of sprawling, octopuslike growths hugged the ground at either bank, except where the cliff on his left crowded the river too closely to leave them room. After the first hundred miles from the point where they had waited several streams were seen emptying into the main course; and a number of crewmen swore they saw animals slinking among the plants. The captain was tempted to land a hunting party and await its return, but two considerations decided him against it. One was the wind, which still blew steadily the way he wanted to go; the other was his desire to reach the end of the journey and examine the miraculous machine the Flyers had set down and lost on the polar wastes of his world.

As the journey progressed, the captain grew more and more astonished at the wind; he had never before known it to blow steadily for more than a couple of hundred days in any direction. Now it was not merely maintaining direction but was turning to follow the curve of the cliff, so that it was always practically dead astern. He did not actually let the watch on deck relax completely, but he did not object when a man turned his attention away from his section of rigging for a day or so. He himself had lost count of the number of days since it had been necessary to trim sails.

The river retained its width, as the Flyers had foretold; as they had also intimated was possible, it grew shallower and swifter. This should have slowed the

Bree down, and actually did so; but not as much as it might have, for the wind began also to increase. Mile after mile went by, and day after day; and the meteorologists became frantic. Imperceptibly the sun crept higher in its circles about the sky, but much too slowly to convince those scientists that it was responsible for the increased wind force. It became evident to human beings and Mesklinites alike that something about the local physiography must be responsible; and at long last Barlennan became confident enough to stop briefly and land an exploring and hunting party, sure that the wind would still be there when he re-embarked.

It was, and the miles flowed once more under the *Bree*'s rafts. Eight hundred miles, the Flyers had said. The current of the river made the log indication much more than that, but at last the break that had been foretold appeared in the wall of rock, far ahead of them.

For a time the river flowed straight away from it, and they could see it in profile—a nearly straight slope, angling up at about twenty degrees, projecting from the bottom fifty feet of the cliff. As they approached, the course of the stream bent out away from the wall at last, and they could see that the slope was actually a fan-shaped spill radiating from a cleft less than fifty yards wide. The slope grew steeper within the cut, but might still be climbable; no one could tell until they were close enough to see what sort of debris composed the spill itself. The first near view was encouraging; where the river touched the foot of the slope, it could be seen to be composed of pebbles small even by the personal standards of the crew members. If they were not too loose, climbing should be easy.

Now they were swinging around to a point directly in front of the opening, and as they did so the wind at last began to change. It angled *outward* from the cliff, and its speed increased unbelievably. A roar that had sounded as a faint murmur for the last several days in the ears of crewmen and Earthmen alike now began to swell sharply, and as the *Bree* came directly opposite the opening in the rock the source of the sound became apparent.

A blast of wind struck the vessel, threatening to split

the tough fabric of her sails and sending her angling across the stream away from the wall of rock. At the same instant the roar increased to almost explosive violence, and in the space of less than a minute the ship was struggling in a storm that vied with any she had encountered since leaving the equator. It lasted only moments; the sails had already been set to catch a quartering wind, and they put enough upstream motion into the ship's path to carry her across the worst of the wind before she could run aground. Once out of it, Barlennan hastily turned his vessel to starboard and ran her across the short remaining distance to shore while he collected his wits. This accomplished, he did what was becoming a habit in unfamiliar situations; he called the Earthmen and asked for an explanation. They did not disappoint him; the voice of one of the weather men answered promptly, vibrant with the overtones the captain had learned to associate with human pleasure.

"That accounts for it, Barl! It's the bowl shape of that plateau! I should say that you'd find it easier to get along up there than we had believed. I can't see why we didn't think of it before!"

"Think of what?" The Mesklinite did not actually snarl, but his puzzlement showed clearly to the crew members who heard him.

"Think what a place like that could do in your gravity, climate, and atmosphere. Look: winter in the part of Mesklin you know—the southern hemisphere—coincides with the world's passage of its closest point to the sun. That's summer in the north, and the icecap boils off—that's why you have such terrific and continual storms at that season. We already knew that. The condensing moisture—methane—whatever you want to call it—gives up its heat and warms the air in your hemisphere, even though you don't see the sun for three or four months. The temperature probably goes up nearly to the boiling point of methane—around minus one forty-five at your surface pressure. Isn't that so? Don't you get a good deal warmer in winter?"

"Yes," admitted Barlennan.

"Very well, then. The higher temperature means

that your air *doesn't* get thin so rapidly with altitude—
you might say the whole atmosphere expands. It expands, and pours over the edge into that bowl you're
beside like water into a sinking soup plate. Then you
pass the vernal equinox, the storms die out, and
Mesklin starts moving away from the sun. You cool off
—right?—and the atmosphere shrinks again; but the
bowl has a lot caught inside, with its surface pressure
now higher than at the corresponding level outside the
bowl. A lot of it spills over, of course, and tends to flow
away from the cliff at the bottom—but gets deflected to
the left by the planet's spin. That's most of the wind
that helped you along. The rest is this blast you just
crossed, pouring out of the bowl at the only place it
can, creating a partial vacuum on either side of the
cleft, so that the wind tends to rush toward it from the
sides. It's simple!"

"Did you think of all that while I was crossing the
wind belt?" asked Barlennan dryly.

"Sure—came to me in a flash. That's why I'm sure
the air up there must be denser than we expected.
See?"

"Frankly, no. However, if you are satisfied I'll accept it for now. I'm gradually coming to trust the
knowledge of you Flyers. However, theory or no theory, what does this mean to us practically? Climbing
the slope in the teeth of that wind is not going to be any
joke."

"I'm afraid you'll have to. It will probably die down
eventually, but I imagine it will be some months before
the bowl empties—perhaps a couple of Earthly years.
I think, if it's at all possible for you, Barl, it would be
worth attempting the climb without waiting."

Barlennan thought. At the Rim, of course, such a
hurricane would pick up a Mesklinite bodily and drive
him out of sight in seconds; but at the Rim such a wind
could never form, since the air caught in the bowl
would have only a tiny fraction of its present weight.
That much even Barlennan now had clear.

"We'll go now," he said abruptly to the radio, and
turned to give orders to the crew.

The *Bree* was guided across the stream—Barlennan

had landed her on the side away from the plateau. There she was dragged well out of the river and her tie lines secured to stakes—there were no plants capable of taking the desired load growing this close to the landslide. Five sailors were selected to remain with the ship; the rest harnessed themselves, secured the drag-lines of their packs to the harness, and started at once for the slope.

For some time they were not bothered by the wind; Barlennan had made the obvious approach, coming up the side of the fan of rubble. Its farthest parts, as they had already seen, were composed of relatively fine particles—sand and very small pebbles; as they climbed, the rock fragments grew constantly larger. All could understand the reason for this; the wind could carry the smallest pieces farthest, and all began to worry a trifle about the size of the rocks they would have to climb over in the cut itself.

Only a few days were consumed in reaching the side of the wall's opening. The wind was a little fresher here; a few yards on, it issued from behind the corner with a roar that made conversation ever harder as they approached. Occasional eddies struck them, giving a tiny taste of what was to come; but Barlennan halted for only a moment. Then, making sure that his pack was close behind him and securely attached to his harness, he gathered himself together and crawled into the full blast of the wind. The others followed without hesitation.

Their worst fears failed to materialize; climbing individual boulders was not necessary. Such huge fragments were present, indeed, but the downhill side of each was nearly covered by a ramp of finer material that had been swept into the relatively sheltered area by the everlasting wind. The ramps overlapped to a great extent, and where they did not it was always possible to travel across the wind from one to another. Their way was tortuous, but they slowly climbed.

They had to modify the original idea that the wind was not really dangerous. One sailor became hungry, paused in what he thought was shelter, and attempted to take a piece of food from his pack; an eddy around his sheltering rock, caused probably by his very presence which disturbed the equilibrium attained after months and years of steady wind, caught in the open container. It acted like a parachute, snatched its unfortunate owner out of his shelter and down the slope. He was gone from sight in a cloud of freshly disturbed sand in moments, and his fellows looked away. A six-inch fall under this gravity could kill; there would be many such falls before their comrade reached the bottom. If by chance there were not, his own hundreds of pounds of weight would be scraped against the rocks hard enough and fast enough to accomplish the same end. The survivors dug their feet in a little farther, and gave up all thought of eating before they reached the top.

Time after time the sun crossed ahead of them, shining down the cleft. Time after time it appeared behind, blazing into the opening from the opposite direction. Each time the rocks about them lighted up under its direct impact they were a little farther up the long hill; each time, they began at last to feel, the wind was just a little less furious as it roared past their long bodies. The cleft was visibly wider, and the slope gentler. Now they could see the cliff opening out forward and to each side; at last the way ahead of them became practically horizontal and they could see the broad regions of the upper plateau ahead. The wind was still strong, but no longer deadly; and as Barlennan led the way to the left it decreased still further. It was not sharply defined here as it was below; it fed into the cleft from all directions, but from that very fact its strength decreased rapidly as they left the cut behind them. At long last they felt safe in stopping, and all immediately opened their packs and enjoyed a meal for the first time in some three hundred days—a long fast even for Mesklinites.

With hunger attended to, Barlennan began to look over the country ahead. He had stopped his group to one side of the cut, almost at the edge of the plateau, and the ground sloped down away from him around nearly half the compass. It was discouraging ground. The rocks were larger, and would have to be traveled around—climbing any of them was unthinkable. Even keeping to one direction among them would be impossible; no one could see more than a few yards in any direction once the rocks surrounded him, and the sun was utterly useless as a means of guidance. It would be necessary to keep close to the edge (but not too close; Barlennan repressed an inward shudder). The problem of finding the rocket when they reached its neighborhood would have to be solved on the spot; the Flyers would surely be able to help there.

The next problem was food. There was enough in the packs for a long time—probably for the eight hundred miles back to the point above the *Bree*'s old halting place; but there would have to be some means of replenishing the supply, for it would never last the round trip or maintain them at the rocket for any length of time. For a moment Barlennan could not see his way through this problem; then a solution slowly grew on him. He thought it over from every angle and finally decided it was the best that could be managed. Once settled on details, he called Dondragmer.

The mate had brought up the rear on the arduous climb, taking without complaint the bits of sand loosened by the others which had been hurled cruelly against him by the wind. He seemed none the worse for the experience, however; he could have matched the great Hars for endurance, if not for strength. He listened now to the captain's orders without any show of emotion, though they must have disappointed him deeply in at least one way. With his duties clear, he called together the members of his watch who were present, and added to them half the sailors of the captain's watch. Packs were redistributed; all the food was given to the relatively small group remaining with Barlennan, and all the rope except for a single piece long enough to loop through the harnesses of Dondragmer's entire company. They had learned from experience—experience they had no intention of repeating.

These preliminaries attended to, the mate wasted no time; he turned and led his group toward the slope they had just ascended with such effort, and presently the tail of the roped-together procession vanished into the dip that led to the cleft. Barlennan turned to the others.

"We will have to ration food strictly from now on. We will not attempt to travel rapidly; it would do us no good. The *Bree* should get back to the old stopping place well before us, but they will have some preparations to make before they can help us. You two who have radios, don't let anything happen to them; they're the only things that will let us find out when we're near the ship—unless someone wants to volunteer to look over the edge every so often. Incidentally, that may be necessary anyway; but I'll do it if it is."

"Shall we start right away, Captain?"

"No. We will wait here until we know that Dondragmer is back to the ship. If he runs into trouble we will have to use some other plan, which would probably require us to go back down ourselves; in that case it would be a waste of time and effort to have traveled any distance, and would cost time that might be valuable in getting back."

Meanwhile, Dondragmer and his group reached the slope without difficulty. They stopped just long enough for the mate to make sure that all harnesses were securely fastened at regular intervals along the rope he had brought; then he attached his own at the rear, and gave the order to start down.

The rope proved a good idea; it was harder even for the many feet of the Mesklinites to keep their traction while heading downward than it had been on the way up. The wind showed no tendency to pick anyone up this time, since they had no packs on which it could get a grip, but the going was still awkward. As before, everyone lost all track of time, and all were correspondingly relieved when the way opened ahead and they were able to swing to the left out of the wind's path. They still found themselves looking *down,* of course, which was extremely hard on Mesklinite nerves; but the worst of the descent was over. Only three or four days were consumed in getting down the rest of the way and aboard the still waiting *Bree.* The sailors with the ship had seen them coming long enough in advance to develop a number of theories, mostly tragic in tone, concerning the fate of the rest of the party. They were quickly reassured, and the mate reported his arrival to the men on Toorey so that they could relay the information to Barlennan on the plateau. Then the ship was dragged back to the river—a real task, with a quarter of the crew missing and the full power of polar gravity to plaster the rafts to the beach, but it was finally accomplished. Twice the vessel hung up on small pebbles that had not quite stopped her going the other way; the differential hoist was put to effective use. With the *Bree* once more afloat, Dondragmer spent much of the time on the downstream trip examining the hoist. He already knew its principles of construction well enough to have made one without help; but he could not quite figure out just *why* it worked. Several Earthmen watched him with amusement, but none was discourteous enough to show the fact—and none dreamed of spoiling the Mesklinite's chance of solving the problem by himself. Even Lackland, fond as he was of Barlennan, had long since come to the conclusion that the mate was considerably his captain's superior in general intelligence, and rather expected that he would be regaling them with a sound mechanical explanation before the *Bree* reached her former stopping place; but he was wrong.

The position of the grounded rocket was known with great accuracy; the uncertainty was less than half a dozen miles. Its telemetering transmitters—not all the instruments had been of permanent-record type—had continued to operate for more than an Earth year after the failure to answer takeoff signals; in that time an astronomical number of fixes had been taken on the location of the transmitters. Mesklin's atmosphere did not interfere appreciably with radio.

The *Bree* could also be located by radio, as could Barlennan's party; it would be the job of the Earthmen to guide the two groups together and, eventually, lead them to the grounded research projectile. The difficulty was in obtaining fixes from Toorey; all three targets were on the "edge" of the disc as seen from the moon. Still worse, the shape of the planet meant that a tiny error in the determination of signal direction could mean a discrepancy of some thousands of miles on the world's surface; the line of the antenna just about grazed the flattest part of the planet. To remedy this, the rocket that had photographed the planet so much was launched once more, and set into a circular orbit that crossed the poles at regular intervals.

From this orbit, once it was accurately set up, fixes could be taken with sufficient precision on the tiny transmitters that the Mesklinites were carrying with them.

The problem became even simpler when Dondragmer finally brought the *Bree* to its former halting place and established a camp. There was now a fixed transmitter on the planet, and this made it possible to tell Barlennan how much farther he had to go within a minute or two of any time he chose to ask. The trip settled down to routine once more—from above.

XVII: ELEVATOR

For Barlennan himself it was hardly routine. The upper plateau was as it had seemed from the beginning: arid, stony, lifeless, and confusing. He did not dare go far from the edge; once among those boulders, direction would quickly vanish. There were no hills of any size to serve as land marks, or at least none which could be seen from the ground. The thickly scattered rocks hid everything more than a few yards away, towering into the line of sight in every direction except toward the edge of the cliff.

Travel itself was not too difficult. The ground was level, except for the stones; these merely had to be avoided. Eight hundred miles is a long walk for a man, and a longer one for a creature only fifteen inches long who has to "walk" by rippling forward caterpillar style; and the endless detours made the actual distance covered much more than eight hundred miles. True, Barlennan's people could travel with considerable speed, all things considered; but much had to be considered.

The captain actually began to worry somewhat about the food supply before the trip was over. He had felt that he was allowing a generous safety margin when he first conceived the project; this idea had to be sharply modified. Time and again he anxiously asked the human beings far above how much farther he had to go; sometimes he received an answer—always discouraging—and sometimes the rocket was on the other side of the planet and his answer came from Toorey, telling him to wait a short time for a fix. The relay stations were still functioning, but they could not be used to take a directional reading on his radio.

It did not occur to him until the long walk was nearly over that he could have cut across among the stones after all. The sun by itself, of course, could not have served him as a directional guide; it circled the horizon completely in less than eighteen minutes, and a very accurate clock would be necessary to calculate the actual desired course from its apparent direction. However, the observers in the rocket could have told him at any time whether the sun was in front of him, behind him, or to a particular side with respect to his desired direction of travel. By the time this occurred to anyone, the remaining distance could be covered about as easily by keeping the edge in sight; the cliff was nearly straight between where Barlennan then was and the rendezvous point.

There were still a little food, but not too much, when they finally reached a position, where the Earthmen could find no significant difference in the positions of the radios. Theoretically, the first thing to do should have been to proceed with the next phase of Barlennan's plan in order to replenish the supply of eatables; but actually there was a serious step to be taken first. Barlennan had mentioned it before the march began, but no one had really considered the matter with any care. Now it stared them in the eye.

The Earthmen had said they were about as close to the *Bree* as they could get. There should be, then, food only a hundred yards below them; but before they could take any steps toward getting it, someone—and probably several people—must *look over the edge*. They must *see* just where they were in relation to the ship; they must rig up lifting tackle to bring the food up; in short, they must look fully three hundred feet straight down—and they had excellent depth perception.

Still, it had to be done; and eventually it was done. Barlennan, as befitted his position, set the example.

He went—not too rapidly, it must be admitted—to the three-foot limit and fixed his eyes on the low hills and other terrain features visible between him and the distant horizon. Slowly he let his gaze wander downward to closer and closer objects, until it was blocked by the lip of rock directly ahead of him. Without haste, he looked back and forth, getting used to seeing things that he could tell already were below him. Then, almost imperceptibly, he inched forward to take in more and more of the landscape near the foot of the cliff. For a long time it looked generally the same, but he managed to keep his attention principally on the new details he could see rather than on the fearful thing he was doing. At last, however, the river became visible, and he moved forward almost rapidly. The far bank was there, the spot where most of the hunting parties had landed after swimming across; from above, even the branching and rebranching trails they had left—he had never realized that such things showed so plainly from overhead.

Now the near bank could be seen, and the mark where the *Bree* had been drawn up before; a little farther—and the *Bree* herself was there, not a bit changed, sailors sprawled on her rafts or moving slowly about the bank in the neighborhood. For just an instant Barlennan forgot all about height and moved forward another body loop to call out to them. That loop put his head over the edge.

And he looked straight down the cliff.

He had thought that being lifted to the roof of the tank was the most hideous experience—at first—that he had ever undergone. He was never sure, after this, whether or not the cliff was worse. Barlennan did not know just how he got back from the cliff face, and he never asked his men whether he had needed help. When he fully realized his surroundings once more he was a good, safe two yards from the edge, still shaking and uncertain of himself. It took days for his normal personality and thinking ability to resume course.

He finally decided what could—and must—be done. He had been all right merely looking at the ship; the trouble had occurred when his eyes actually had a line to follow between his own position and that remote lower level. The Earthmen suggested this point, and after thought Barlennan agreed. That meant it was possible to do all that was necessary; they could signal the sailors below, and do any rope-pulling needed, as long as they did not actually look down the cliff face itself. Keeping heads a safe couple of inches back from the rim was the key to sanity—and life.

Dondragmer had not seen his captain's head on its brief appearance, but he knew that the other party had arrived at the cliff top. He, too, had been kept informed of its progress by the Flyers. Now he and his crew began examining the edge of the rock wall above them with extreme care while those above pushed a pack to the extreme verge and moved it back and forth. It was finally seen from below, almost exactly above the ship; Barlennan had noticed before giddiness overwhelmed him that they were not exactly in the right spot, and the error had been corrected in showing the signal.

"All right, we have you." Dondragmer made the call in English, and it was relayed by one of the men in the rocket.

The sailor above thankfully stopped waving the empty pack, set it down projecting slightly over the edge so it could still be seen, and moved back to a safe distance from the verge. Meanwhile the rope that had been brought along was broken out. One end was bent firmly around a small boulder, Barlennan taking extreme pains with this operation; if the rope were lost, everyone on the plateau would almost certainly starve to death.

Satisfied at last on this matter, he had the rest of the cable carried close to the edge; and two sailors began carefully paying it over. Dondragmer was informed of their state of progress, but did not station anyone underneath to take the end as it came down. If anyone slipped above and the whole coil went over, the point immediately below could be rather uncomfortable, light as the cable was. He waited until Barlennan reported the line as completely paid out; then he and the rest of the crew went over to the foot of the cliff to find it.

The extra rope had fallen into a tight bundle on the hard ground. Dondragmer's first act was to cut off the excess, straighten it out, and measure it. He had a very accurate idea now of the height of the cliff, for during the long wait he had had time to do much careful checking of shadow lengths.

The excess rope proved to be insufficiently long to reach again the full height of the cliff; so the mate obtained another length from the *Bree,* made sure it was long enough, attached it to the section hanging from the cliff top, and informed the Earthmen that Barlennan could start pulling up.

It was a hard job, but not too hard for the powerful beings at the upper end; and in a relatively short time the second rope was at the top of the cliff and the worst fears of the captain were eased. Now if a cable were dropped they at least had a spare.

The second load was very different from the first, as far as ease of hoisting went. It was a pack loaded with food, weighing about as much as one of the sailors. Normally a single Mesklinite could not lift such a weight anywhere near this part of the planet, and the relatively small crew with Barlennan had their work cut out for them. Only by snagging the rope around a convenient boulder and taking frequent rests did they finally manage to get the load up to and over the edge, and when it was done the rope showed distinct signs of wear all along its length from contact with the boulder as well as the cliff edge itself. Something obviously had to be done, and while he and his group were celebrating the end of the strict food rationing Barlennan decided what it would have to be. He gave the appropriate orders to the mate after the feast.

The next several loads, in accordance with Barlennan's instructions, consisted of several masts and spars, more rope, and a number of pulleys of the sort they had used previously in lowering the *Bree* over the cliff at the distant equator. These were used to construct a tripod and hoist arrangement similar to what they had used before—very gingerly, since the pieces had to be lifted into position for lashing and the old prejudice against having solid objects overhead was present in full force. Since the Mesklinites could not reach far from the ground now anyway, most of the lashing was done with the pieces involved lying flat; the assembly was then pried up into position with other spars as levers and boulders which had been laboriously rolled to convenient locations as fulcrums. A similar team of men, working under their natural conditions, could have done a corresponding job in an hour; it took the Mesklinites many times as long—and none of the watching Earthmen could blame them.

The tripod was assembled and erected well back from the edge, then inched laboriously into position as close to that point as could be managed and its legs propped in place with small boulders which the watching men classed mentally as pebbles. The heaviest of the pulleys was attached to the end of a mast as firmly as possible, the rope threaded through it, and the mast levered into position so that about a quarter of its length projected over the abyss past the supporting tripod. Its inner end was also weighted in place with the small stones. Much time was consumed in this work, but it proved worth while. Only a single pulley was used at first, so the hoisting crew still had their load's full weight to handle; but the friction was largely eliminated, and a cleat attached to the inner end of the mast simplified the holding problem while the crew rested.

Load after load of supplies came up, while the crew below hunted and fished endlessly to keep the stream flowing. The area around the hoisting tackle began to take on a settled appearance; indeed, most of the sailors found time between spells at the rope to erect inch-high walls of pebbles around selected areas of their own so that the neighborhood came gradually to resemble more than slightly one of the cities of their own land. No fabric was available for roofs—or rather, Barlennan wasted no effort bringing any up from below—but in other respects the enclosures were almost homelike.

The supplies on hand were already more than one person could conveniently carry; Barlennan planned to establish caches along the route to the rocket. The journey was not expected to be as long as from the cleft they had climbed, but their stay at the site of the crippled machine would be long, and every provision to make it safe was to be taken. Actually, Barlennan would have liked a few more men on the plateau, so that he could leave some at the hoist and take others with him; but there were certain practical difficulties connected with that. For another group to travel up to the cleft, climb it, and come back to their present station seemed too lengthy a job; nobody liked to think of the alternative. Barlennan, of course, did; but an experiment on the part of one of the crew made it a difficult subject to broach.

That individual, after getting his captain's approval —Barlennan regretted giving it later—and having the crewmen below warned away, had rolled a bullet-sized pebble to the edge of the cliff and given it a final shove. The results had been interesting, to both Mesklinites and Earthmen. The latter could see nothing, since the only view set at the foot of the cliff was still aboard the *Bree* and too distant from the point of impact to get a distinct view; but they heard as well as the natives. As a matter of fact, they saw almost as well; for even to Mesklinite vision the pebble simply vanished. There was a short note like a breaking violin string as it clove the air, followed a split second later by a sharp report as it struck the ground below.

Fortunately it landed on hard, slightly moist ground rather than on another stone; in the latter case, there would have been a distinct chance of someone's being killed by flying splinters. The impact, at a speed of approximately a mile a second, sent the ground splashing outward in a wave too fast for any eye to see while it was in motion, but which froze after a fraction of a second, leaving a rimmed crater surrounding the deeper hole the missile had drilled in the soil. Slowly the sailors gathered around, eying the gently steaming grounds; then with one accord they moved a few yards away from the foot of the cliff. It took some time to shake off the mood that experiment engendered.

Nevertheless, Barlennan wanted more men at the top; and he was not the individual to give up a project for fear it might not work. He came out with the proposal of an elevator one day, met the expected flat silence, but continued to revert to the subject at regular intervals as the work went on. As Lackland had long since noted, the captain was a persuasive individual. It was a pity that the present job of persuasion was done in the native language, for the men would greatly have enjoyed hearing Barlennan's remarkably varied and original approaches and seeing his listeners go from utter refusal to consideration, through unsympathetic listening, to grudging consent. They never became enthusiastic partisans of the idea, but Barlennan did not expect miracles anyway. Actually, it is very likely that his success was not entirely due to his own efforts. Dondragmer badly wanted to be among those present when the rocket was reached; he had been extremely unhappy at being ordered back down with the group that returned to the ship, though his ingrained dislike of people who argued against orders had prevented his allowing his feelings to show. Now that there seemed to be a chance to get back to the active group, as he looked on it, he found it much easier than might otherwise have been the case to persuade himself that being pulled up a cliff on the end of a rope really wasn't so bad. In any case, he reflected, if the rope broke he'd never know it. He therefore became a disciple of the captain's views among the sailors at the bottom of the cliff; and as they realized that their senior officer intended to go first, and actually seemed to *want* to go, much of their natural sales resistance disappeared. The automatic relays had now been completed, and Barlennan could talk directly to the other group, so his full strength of personality could also come into play.

The upshot was that a small wooden platform was constructed with a low, solid railing—Dondragmer's invention—that would prevent anyone from seeing down once he was inside. The whole arrangement was supported in a rope sling that would hold it in a horizontal position; this was a relic of the previous hoisting experience at the equator.

The platform, all ropes and knots carefully tested by a tug of war that greatly interested the human spectators, was dragged over beneath the hoist and attached to the main rope. At the request of the mate, some slack was given from above and the last knot tested in the same fashion as the others; satisfied that all was secure, Dondragmer promptly climbed onto the platform, put the last section of railing in place, and gave the signal to hoist. The radio had been dragged over from the ship; Barlennan heard the mate directly. He joined his crew at the rope.

There was practically no swinging, anyway; Dondragmer remembered how uncomfortable that had been the last time he had been on such a device. Here the wind, though still blowing steadily along the cliff, was unable to budge perceptibly the pendulum of which he was a part; its cord was too narrow to furnish a grip for air currents, and the weight of its bob too enormous to be easily shifted by them. This was fortunate not merely from the point of view of comfort; if a swing had started from any cause, its period would have been around half a second at the start, decreasing as he ascended to a value that would have amounted to nearly sonic vibration and almost certainly pulled the structure at the top from its foundations.

Dondragmer was a being of straightforward, practical intelligence, and he made no attempt to do any sightseeing as he ascended. On the contrary, he kept his eyes carefully closed, and was not ashamed to do so. The trip seemed endless, of course; in actual fact, it took about six days. Barlennan periodically stopped proceedings while he inspected the hoist and its anchorage, but these were always sound.

At long last the platform appeared above the edge of the cliff and its supporting sling reached the pulley, preventing any further elevation. The edge of the elevator was only an inch or so from the cliff; it was long and narrow, to accommodate the Mesklinite form, and a push on one end with a spar sent the other swinging over solid ground. Dondragmer, who had opened his eyes at the sound of voices, crawled thankfully off and away from the edge.

The watching Lackland announced his safety even before Barlennan could do so to the waiting sailors below, and his words were at once translated by one who knew some English. They were relieved, to put it mildly; they had seen the platform arrive, but could not tell the condition of its passenger. Barlennan took advantage of their feelings, sending the lift down as fast as possible and starting another passenger up.

The whole operation was completed without accident; ten times in all the elevator made its trip before Barlennan decided that there could be no more taken from below without making the supply job of those who remained too difficult.

The tension was over now, however, and once again a feeling that they were in the final stages of the mission spread through Earthmen and natives alike.

"If you'll wait about two minutes, Barl," Lackland relayed the information given him by one of the computers, "the sun will be exactly on the direction line you should follow. We've warned you that we can't pin the rocket down closer than about six miles; we'll guide you into the middle of the area that we're sure contains it, and you'll have to work out your own search from there. If the terrain is at all similar to what you have where you are now, that will be rather difficult, I fear."

"You are probably right, Charles; we have had no experience with such matters. Still, I am sure we will solve that problem; we have solved all others—frequently with your help, I confess. Is the sun in line yet?"

"Just a moment—there! Is there any landmark even reasonably distant which you can use to hold your line until the sun comes around again?"

"None, I fear. We will have to do the best we can, and take your corrections each day."

"That's a bit like dead reckoning where you don't know the winds or currents, but it will have to do. We'll correct our own figures every time we can get a fix on you. Good luck!"

XVIII: MOUND BUILDERS

Direction was a problem, as all concerned found out at once. It was physically impossible to maintain a straight line of travel; every few yards the party had to detour around a boulder that was too high to see or climb over. The physical structure of the Mesklinites aggravated the situation, since their eyes were so close to the ground. Barlennan tried to make his detours in alternate directions, but he had no means of checking accurately the amount of each one. It was a rare day when the direction check from the rocket did not show them to be twenty or thirty degrees off.

About every fifty days a check was made on the position of the transmitter—there was only one moving now; another had been left with the group at the hoist —and a new direction computed. High-precision work was required, and occasionally some doubt was felt about the accuracy of a given fix. When this happened Barlennan was always warned, and left to his own discretion. Sometimes, if the Earthmen did not sound too doubtful of their own work, he would go on; at others, he would wait for a few days to give them a chance for a better fix. While waiting he would consolidate his position, redistributing pack loads and modifying the food rations when it seemed necessary. He had hit upon the idea of trail blazing almost before starting, and a solid line of pebbles marked their path from the edge. He had the idea of eventually clearing all the stones from a path and heaping them on each side, thus making a regular road; but this would be later, when trips back and forth between the grounded rocket and the supply base became regular.

The fifty miles passed slowly under their many feet, but pass it finally did. The men, as Lackland said, had done all they could; to the best of their ability to measure, Barlennan should now be standing beside the stranded machine. Both the vision set and the captain's voice clearly informed him that no such state of affairs existed, which did not surprise him at all.

"That's the best we can do, Barl. I'll swear, knowing our math boys, that you're within six miles of that gadget, and probably a good deal less. You can organize your men better than I for a search. Anything we can do we certainly will, but I can't imagine what it might be at this point. How do you plan to arrange matters?"

Barlennan paused before answering. A six-mile circle is an appalling area to search when visibility averages three or four yards. He could cover territory most rapidly, of course, by spreading out his men; but that raised to the point of near certainty the chance of losing some of them. He put this point up to Lackland.

"The rocket itself is about twenty feet tall," the man pointed out. "For practical purposes your vision circle is therefore larger than you say. If you could only get up on one of those larger boulders you'd probably see the ship from where you are—that's what's so annoying about the whole situation."

"Of course; but we can't do that. The large rocks are six or eight of your feet in height; even if we could climb their nearly vertical sides, I would certainly never again look down a straight wall, and will not risk having my men do so."

"Yet you climbed that cleft up to the plateau."

"That was different. We were never beside an abrupt drop."

"Then if a similar slope led up to one of these boulders, you wouldn't mind getting that far from the ground?"

"No, but—hmmm. I think I see what you're driving at. Just a moment." The captain looked at his surroundings more carefully. Several of the great rocks were nearby; the highest, as he had said, protruded some six feet from the hard ground. Around and between them were the ever present pebbles that seemed to floor the whole plateau. Possibly if Barlennan had ever been exposed to solid geometry he would not have made the decision he did; but having no real idea of the volume of building material he was undertaking to handle, he decided that Lackland's idea was sound.

"We'll do it, Charles. There's enough small rock and dirt here to build anything we want." He turned from the radio and outlined the plan to the sailors. If Dondragmer had any doubts about its feasibility he kept them to himself; and presently the entire group was rolling stones. Those closest to the selected rock were moved close against it, and others against these, until a circle of bare ground began to spread outward from the scene of operations. Periodically a quantity of the hard soil was loosened by harder pincers and spread onto the layer of small rocks; it was easier to carry and filled more space—until the next layer of stone tamped it down.

Progress was slow but steady. Some indication of the time it took may be gained from the fact that at one point part of the group had to be sent back along the blazed trail for further food supplies—a thing which had been unnecessary in the eight-hundred-mile walk from the cleft; but at last the relatively flat top of the boulder felt the tread of feet, probably for the first time since the inner energies of Mesklin had pushed the plateau to its present elevation. The ramp spread down and to each side from the point of access; no one approached the other side of the boulder, where the drop was still sheer.

From the new vantage point Lackland's prediction was fulfilled—after months of travel and danger, the goal of the expedition was in sight. Barlennan actually had the vision set hauled up the ramp so the Earthmen could see it too; and for the first time in over an Earth year, Rosten's face lost its habitual grim expression. It was not much to see; perhaps one of the Egyptian pyramids, plated with metal and placed far enough away, would have looked somewhat like the blunt cone that lifted above the intervening stones. It did not resemble the rocket Barlennan had seen before—in fact, it did not greatly resemble any rocket previously built within twenty light-years of Earth; but it was obviously something that did not belong to Mesklin's normal landscape and even the expedition members who had not spent months on the monstrous planet's surface seemed to feel weight roll from their shoulders.

Barlennan, though pleased, did not share the abandon that was approaching party intensity on Toorey. He was better able than those whose view depended on television to judge just what lay between his present position and the rocket. This appeared no worse than what they had already crossed, but it was certainly no better. There would no longer be the Earthmen's guidance, either; and even with the present vantage point, he could not quite see how the party was to maintain its line of march for the mile and a half that they would have to travel. The men did not actually know the direction now, so their method would not work—or would it? He could *tell* them when the sun lay in the right direction; after that they could call him each time it passed through the same bearing. For that matter, one man could stay here and give the same information without bothering the Flyers—but wait; he had only one radio now. It could not be in both places at once; for the first time Barlennan really missed the set that had been left with the river-dwellers.

Then it occurred to him that he might not need a radio. True, the air did not carry sound so well here—it was the only aspect of the thinner atmosphere of the plateau that the sailors had noticed at all—but the Mesklinite voice, as Lackland had remarked, was something that had to be heard to be believed. The captain decided to try it; he would leave one man here on the lookout platform, whose duty would consist of hooting with all the energy the muscles around his swimming-siphon could muster each time the sun passed straight above the gleaming cone that was their goal. The trail would be blazed as before so that he could follow when the others arrived.

Barlennan outlined this idea to the group. Don-dragmer pointed out that on the basis of past experience they might even so go too far to one side, since there would be no way of making fixes as the Earthmen had done to correct cumulative errors; the fact that the watcher's voice did not sound from directly opposite the sun at any time would mean nothing in this echo-rich neighborhood. He admitted, however, that it was the best idea so far, and did stand a good chance of bringing them within sight of the rocket. A sailor was chosen, therefore, to man the observation post, and the trip was resumed in the new direction.

For a short distance the post itself remained in sight, and it was possible to judge the error that had crept into their course each time the sailor's voice was heard. Presently, however, the rock on which he was standing was lost behind others of equal size, and navigation settled down to the task of making sure they were heading as closely as possible toward the sun each time the echoing hoot sounded in their ears. The sound grew weaker as the days passed, but with no other sounds on the lifeless plateau to cover it there was never any doubt of what they heard.

None of them even yet considered themselves experienced enough in land travel to estimate accurately the distance covered, and all were used to arriving much later than original hopes called for; so the group was pleasantly surprised when finally the monotony of the desert of stone was broken by a change in the landscape. It was not exactly the change that had been expected, but it attracted attention for all that.

It was almost directly ahead of them, and for a moment several of the group wondered whether they had in some incomprehensible way traveled in a circle. A long slope of mixed dirt and pebbles showed between the boulders. It was about as high as the one they had built to the observation station; but as they approached they saw it extended much farther to each side—as far, in fact, as anyone could see. It lapped around large boulders like an ocean wave frozen in mid-motion; even the Mesklinites, totally unused to explosion or meteor craters, could see that the material had been hurled outward from some point beyond the slope. Barlennan, who had seen rockets from Toorey land more than once, had a pretty good idea of the cause and of what he was going to see even before the party topped the rise. He was right in general, if not in detail.

The rocket stood in the center of the bowl-shaped indentation that had been blasted by the fierce wash of her supporting jets. Barlennan could remember the way snow had swirled out of the way when the cargo rocket landed near Lackland's "Hill." He could appreciate the fact that the lifting power used here must have been far mightier in order to ease the bulk of this machine down, smaller though it was. There were no large boulders near it, though a few reared up near the sides of the bowl. The ground inside was bare of pebbles; the soil itself had been scooped out so that only four or five of the projectile's twenty feet of height rose above the general run of rocks covering the plain.

Its base diameter was almost as great as its height, and remained so for perhaps a third of the way upward. This, Lackland explained when the vision set had been brought to bear on the interior of the blast crater, was the part housing the driving power.

The upper part of the machine narrowed rapidly to a blunt point, and this housed the apparatus which represented such a tremendous investment in time, intellectual effort, and money on the part of so many worlds. A number of openings existed in this part, as no effort had been made to render the compartments airtight. Such apparatus as required either vacuum or special atmosphere in which to function was individually sealed.

"You said once, after the explosion in your tank that wrecked it so completely, that something of the sort must have happened here," Barlennan said. "I see no signs of it; and if the holes I see were open when you landed it, how could enough of your oxygen still be there to cause an explosion? You told me that beyond and between worlds there was no air, and what you had would leak out through any opening."

Rosten cut in before Lackland could answer. He and

the rest of the group had been examining the rocket on their own screen.

"Barl is quite right. Whatever caused the trouble was not an oxygen blast. I don't know what it was. We'll just have to keep our eyes open when we go inside, in the hope of finding the trouble—not that it will matter much by then, except to people who want to build another of these things. I'd say we might as well get to work; I have a horde of physicists on my neck simply quivering for information. It's lucky they put a biologist in charge of this expedition; from now on there won't be a physicist fit to approach."

"Your scientists will have to contain themselves a little longer," Barlennan interjected. "You seem to have overlooked something."

"What?"

"Not one of the instruments you want me to put before the lens of your vision set is within seven feet of the ground; and all are inside metal walls which I suspect would be rather hard for us to remove by brute force, soft as your metals seem to be."

"Blast it, you're right, of course. The second part is easy; most of the surface skin is composed of quick-remove access plates that we can show you how to handle without much trouble. For the rest—hmm. You have nothing like ladders, and couldn't use them if you had. Your elevator has the slight disadvantage of needing at least an installation crew at the top of its travel before you can use it. Offhand, I'm afraid I'm stuck for the moment. We'll think of something, though; we've come too far to be stumped now."

"I would suggest that you spend from now until my sailor gets here from the lookout in thought. If by that time you have no better idea, we will use mine."

"What? You have an idea?"

"Certainly. We got to the top of that boulder from which we saw your rocket; what is wrong with using the same method here?" Rosten was silent for fully half a minute; Lackland suspected he has kicking himself mentally.

"I can only see one point," he said at last. "You will have a much larger job of rock-piling than you did before. The rocket is more than three times as high as the boulder where you built the ramp, and you'll have to build up all around it instead of on one side, I suspect."

"Why can we not simply make a ramp on one side up to the lowest level containing the machines you are interested in? It should then be possible to get up the rest of the way inside, as you do in the other rockets."

"For two principal reasons. The more important one is that you won't be able to climb around inside; the rocket was not built to carry living crews, and has no communication between decks. All the machinery was built to be reached from outside the hull, at the appropriate level. The other point is that you cannot start at the lower levels; granted that you could get the access covers off, I seriously doubt that you could lift them back in place when you finished with a particular section. That would mean that you'd have the covers off all around the hull before you built up to the next level; and I'm rather afraid that such a situation would not leave enough metal in place below to support the sections above. The top of the cone would—or at least might—collapse. Those access ports occupy the greater part of the skin, and are thick enough to take a lot of vertical load. Maybe it was bad design, but remember we expected to open them only in space, with no weight at all.

"What you will have to do, I fear, is bury the rocket completely to the *highest* level containing apparatus and then dig your way down, level by level. It may even be advisable to remove the machinery from each section as you finish with it; that will bring the load to an absolute minimum. After all, there'll only be a rather frail-looking skeleton when you have all those plates off, and I don't like to picture what would happen to it with a full equipment load times seven hundred, nearly."

"I see." Barlennan took his turn at a spell of silent thought. "You yourself can think of no alternative to this plan? It involves, as you rightly point out, much labor."

"None so far. We will follow your recommendation, and think until your other man comes from the observation point. I suspect we work under a grave disadvantage, though—we are unlikely to think of any solution which does not involve machinery we couldn't get to you."

"That I had long since noticed."

The sun continued to circle the sky at a shade better than twenty degrees a minute. A call had long since gone echoing out to the observation platform to let the guide know his work was done; he was presumably on the way in. The sailors did nothing except rest and amuse themselves; all, at one time or another, descended the easy slope of the pit the blasts had dug to examine the rocket at close quarters. All of them were too intelligent to put its operation down to magic, but it awed them nonetheless. They understood nothing of its principle of operation, though that could easily have been made clear if Lackland had stopped to wonder how a race that did not breathe could nevertheless speak aloud. The Mesklinites possessed in well-developed form the siphon arrangement, similar to that of Earthly cephalopods, which their amphibious ancestors had used for high-speed swimming; they used it as the bellows for a very Earthly set of vocal cords, but were still able to put it to its original function. They were well suited by nature to understand the rocket principle.

Their lack of understanding was not all that aroused the sailors' respect. Their race built cities, and they had regarded themselves as good engineers; but the highest walls they ever constructed reached perhaps three inches from the ground. Multi-storied buildings, even roofs other than a flap of fabric, conflicted too violently with their almost instinctive fear of solid material overhead. The experiences of this group had done something to change the attitude from one of unreasoning fear to one of intelligent respect for weight, but the habit clung nevertheless. The rocket was some eighty times the height of any artificial structure their race had ever produced; awe at the sight of such a thing was inevitable.

The arrival of the lookout sent Barlennan back to the radio, but there was no better idea than his own to be had. This did not surprise him at all. He brushed Rosten's apologies aside, and set to work along with his crew. Not even then did any of the watchers above think of the possibility of their agent's having ideas of his own about the rocket. Curiously enough, such a suspicion by then would have come much too late—too late to have any foundation.

Strangely, the work was not as hard or long as everyone had expected. The reason was simple; the rock and earth blown out by the jets was relatively loose, since there was no weather in the thin air of the plateau to pack it down as it had been before. A human being, of course wearing the gravity nullifier the scientists hoped to develop from the knowledge concealed in the rocket, could not have pushed a shovel into it, for the gravity was a pretty good packing agent; it was loose only by Mesklinite standards. Loads of it were being pushed down the gentle inner slope of the pit to the growing pile around the tubes; pebbles were being worked clear of the soil and set rolling the same way, with a hooted warning beforehand. The warning was needed; once free and started, they moved too fast for the human eye to follow, and usually buried themselves completely in the pile of freshly moved earth.

Even the most pessimistic of the watchers began to feel that no more setbacks could possibly occur, in spite of the number of times they had started to unpack shelved apparatus and then had to put it away again. They watched now with mounting glee as the shining metal of the research projectile sank lower and lower in the heap of rock and earth, and finally vanished entirely except for a foot-high cone that marked the highest level in which machinery had been installed.

At this point the Mesklinites ceased work, and most of them retreated from the mound. The vision set had been brought up and was now facing the projecting tip of metal, where part of the thin line marking an access port could be seen. Barlennan sprawled alone in front of the entrace, apparently waiting for instructions on the method of opening it; and Rosten, watching as tensely as everyone else, explained to him. There were four quick-disconnect fasteners, one on each corner of the trapezoidal plate. The upper two were about on a level with Barlennan's eyes; the others some six inches below the present level of the mound. Normally they were released by pushing in and making a quarter turn with a broad-bladed screwdriver; it seemed likely that Mesklinite pincers could perform the same function. Barlennan, turning to the plate, found that they could. The broad, slotted heads turned with little effort and popped outward, but the plate did not move otherwise.

"You had better fasten ropes to one or both of those heads, so you can pull the plate outward from a safe distance when you've dug down to the others and unfastened them," Rosten pointed out. "You don't want that piece of hardware falling on top of anyone; it's a quarter of an inch thick. The lower ones are a darned sight thicker, I might add."

The suggestion was followed, and the earth scraped rapidly away until the lower edge of the plate was uncovered. The fasteners here proved no more troublesome than their fellows, and moments later a hard pull on the ropes unseated the plate from its place in the rocket's skin. For the first fraction of an inch of its outward motion it could be seen; then it vanished abruptly, and reappeared lying horizontally while an almost riflelike report reached the ears of the watchers. The sun, shining into the newly opened hull, showed clearly the single piece of apparatus inside; and a cheer went up from the men in the screen room and the observing rocket.

"That did it, Barl! We owe you more than we can say. If you'll stand back and let us photograph that as it is, we'll start giving you directions for taking out the record and getting it to the lens." Barlennan did not answer at once; his actions spoke some time before he did.

He did not get out of the way of the eye. Instead he crawled toward it and pushed the entire set around until it no longer covered the nose of the rocket.

"There are some matters we must discuss first," he said quietly.

XIX: NEW BARGAIN

Dead silence reigned in the screen room. The head of the tiny Mesklinite filled the screen, but no one could interpret the expression on the completely unhuman "face." No one could think of anything to say; asking Barlennan what he meant would be a waste of words, since he obviously planned to tell anyway. He waited for long moments before resuming his speech; and when he did, he used better English than even Lackland realized he had acquired.

"Dr. Rosten, a few moments ago you said that you owed us more than you could hope to repay. I realize that your words were perfectly sincere in one way—I do not doubt the actuality of your gratitude for a moment—but in another they were merely rhetorical. You had no intention of giving us any more than you had already agreed to supply—weather information, guidance across new seas, possibly the material aid Charles mentioned some time ago in the matter of spice collecting. I realize fully that by your moral code I am entitled to no more; I made an agreement and should adhere to it, particularly since your side of the bargain has largely been fulfilled already.

"However, I want more; and since I have come to value the opinions of some, at least, of your people I want to explain why I am doing this—I want to justify myself, if possible. I tell you now, though, that whether I succeed in gaining your sympathy or not, I will do exactly as I planned.

"I am a merchant, as you well know, primarily interested in exchanging goods for what profit I can get. You recognized that fact, offering me every material you could think of in return for my help; it was not your fault that none of it was of use to me. Your machines, you said, would not function in the gravity and pressure of my world; your metals I cannot use, and would not need if I could; they lie free on the surface in many parts of Mesklin. Some people use them for ornaments; but I know from talk with Charles that they cannot be fashioned into really intricate forms without great machines, or at least more heat than we can easily produce. We do know the thing you call fire, by the way, in ways more manageable than the flame cloud; I am sorry to have deceived Charles in that matter, but it seemed best to me at the time.

"To return to the original subject, I refused all but the guidance and weather information of the things you were willing to give. I thought some of you might be suspicious of that, but I have heard no sign of it in your words. Nevertheless, I agreed to make a voyage longer than any that has been made in recorded history to help solve your problem. You had told me how badly you needed the knowledge; none of you appeared to think that I might want the same thing, though I asked time and again for just that when I saw one or another of your machines. You refused answers to those questions, making the same excuse every time. I felt, therefore, that any way in which I could pick up some of the knowledge you people possess was legitimate. You have said, at one time or another, much about the value of what you call 'science,' and always implied was the fact that my people did not have it. I cannot see why, if it is good and valuable to your people, it would not be equally so to mine.

"You can see what I am leading up to. I came on this voyage with exactly the same objective in my mind that was in yours when you sent me; I came to learn. I want to know the things by which you perform such remarkable acts. You, Charles, lived all winter in a place that should have killed you at once, by the aid of that science; it could make as much difference in the lives of my people, I am sure you will agree.

"Therefore I offer you a new bargain. I realize that my failure to live up to the letter of the old one may make you reluctant to conclude another with me. That will be simply too bad; I make no bones about pointing out that you can do nothing else. You are not here; you cannot come here; granting that you might drop some of your explosives down here in anger, you will not do so as long as I am near this machine of yours. The agreement is simple: knowledge for knowledge. You teach me, or Dondragmer, or anyone else in my crew who has the time and ability to learn the material, all the time we are working to take this machine apart for you and transmit the knowledge it contains."

"Just a—"

"Wait, Chief." Lackland cut short Rosten's expostulation. "I know Barl better than you do. Let me talk." He and Rosten could see each other in their respective screens, and for a moment the expedition's leader simply glared. Then he realized the situation and subsided.

"Right, Charlie. Tell him."

"Barl, you seemed to have some contempt in your tone when you referred to our excuse for not explaining our machines to you. Believe me, we were not trying to fool you. They are complicated; so complicated that the men who design and build them spend nearly half their lives first learning the laws that make them operate and the arts of their actual manufacture. We did not mean to belittle the knowledge of your people, either; it is true that we know more, but it is only because we have had longer in which to learn.

"Now, as I understand it, you want to learn about the machines in this rocket as you take it apart. Please, Barl, take my word as the sincerest truth when I tell you first that I for one could not do it, since I do not understand a single one of them; and second, that not one would do you the least good if you did comprehend it. The best I can say right now is that they are machines for measuring things that cannot be seen or heard or felt or tasted—things you would have to see in operation in other ways for a long time before you could even begin to understand. That is not meant as insult; what I say is almost as true for me, and I have grown up from childhood surrounded by and even using those forces. I do not understand them. I do not expect to understand them before I die; the science we have covers so much knowledge that no one man can even begin to learn all of it, and I must be satisfied with the field I do know—and perhaps add to it what little one man may in a lifetime.

"We cannot accept your bargain, Barl, because it is physically impossible to carry out our side of it."

Barlennan could not smile in the human sense, and he carefully refrained from giving his own version of one. He answered as gravely as Lackland had spoken.

"You can do your part, Charles, though you do not know it.

"When I first started this trip, all the things you have just said were true, and more. I fully intended to find this rocket with your help, and then place the radios where you could see nothing and proceed to dismantle the machine itself, learning all your science in the process.

"Slowly I came to realize that all you have said is true. I learned that you were *not* keeping knowledge from me deliberately when you taught us so quickly and carefully about the laws and techniques used by the glider-makers on that island. I learned it still more surely when you helped Dondragmer make the differential pulley. I was expecting you to bring up those points in your speech just now; why didn't you? They were good ones.

"It was actually when you were teaching us about the gliders that I began to have a slight understanding of what was meant by your term 'science.' I realized, before the end of that episode, that a device so simple you people had long since ceased to use it actually called for an understanding of more of the universe's laws than any of my people realized existed. You said specifically at one point, while apologizing for a lack of exact information, that gliders of that sort had been used by your people more than two hundred years ago. I can guess how much more you know now—guess just enough to let me realize what I can't know.

"But you can still do what I want. You have done a little already, in showing us the differential hoist. I do not understand it, and neither does Dondragmer, who spent much more time with it; but we are both sure it is some sort of relative to the levers we have been using all our lives. We want to start *at the beginning,* knowing fully that we cannot learn all you know in our lifetimes. We do hope to learn enough to understand how you have found these things out. Even I can see it is not just guesswork, or even philosophizing like the learned ones who tell us that Mesklin is a bowl. I am willing at this point to admit you are right; but I would like to know how you found out the same fact for your own world. I am sure you knew before you left its surface and could see it all at once. I want to know why the *Bree* floats, and why the canoe did the same, for a while. I want to know what crushed the canoe. I want to know why the wind blows down the cleft all the time—no, I didn't understand your explanation. I want to know why we are warmest in winter when we can't see the sun for the longest time. I want to know why a fire glows, and why flame dust kills. I want my children or theirs, if I ever have any, to know what makes this radio work, and your tank, and someday this rocket. I want to know much— more than I can learn, no doubt; but if I can start my people learning for themselves, the way you must have—well, I'd be willing to stop selling at a profit." Neither Lackland nor Rosten found anything to say for a long moment. Rosten broke the silence.

"Barlennan, if you learned what you want, and began to teach your people, would you tell them where the knowledge came from? Do you think it would be good for them to know?"

"For some, yes; they would want to know about other worlds, and people who had used the same way to knowledge they were starting on. Others—well, we have a lot of people who let the rest pull the load for them. If they knew, they wouldn't bother to do any learning themselves; they'd just ask for anything particular they wanted to know—as I did at first; and they'd never realize you weren't telling them because you couldn't. They'd think you were trying to cheat them. I suppose if I told anyone, that sort would find out sooner or later, and—well, I guess it would be better to let them think I'm the genius. Or Don; they'd be more likely to believe it of him."

Rosten's answer was brief and to the point.

"You've made a deal."

XX: FLIGHT OF THE BREE

A gleaming skeleton of metal rose eight feet above a flat-topped mound of rock and earth. Mesklinites were busily attacking another row of plates whose upper fastenings had just been laid bare. Others were pushing the freshly removed dirt and pebbles to the edge of the mound. Still others moved back and forth along a well-marked road that led off into the desert, those who approached dragging flat, wheeled carts loaded with supplies, those departing usually hauling similar carts empty. The scene was one of activity; practically everyone seemed to have a definite purpose. There were two radio sets in evidence now, one on the mound where an Earthman was directing the dismantling from his distant vantage point and the other some distance away.

Dondragmer was in front of the second set, engaged in animated conversation with the distant being he could not see. The sun still circled endlessly, but was very gradually descending now and swelling very, very slowly.

"I am afraid," the mate said, "that we will have serious trouble checking on what you tell us about the bending of light. Reflection I can understand; the mirrors I made from metal plates of your rocket made that very clear. It is too bad that the device from which you let us take the lens was dropped in the process; we have nothing like your glass, I am afraid."

"Even a reasonably large piece of the lens will do, Don," the voice came from the speaker. It was not Lackland's voice; he was an expert teacher, he had

212

found, but sometimes yielded the microphone to a specialist. "Any piece will bend the light, and even make an image—but wait; that comes later. Try to find what's left of that hunk of glass, Don, if your gravity didn't powder it when the set landed." Dondragmer turned from the set with a word of agreement; then turned back as he thought of another point.

"Perhaps you could tell what this 'glass' is made of, and whether it takes very much heat? We have good hot fires, you know. Also there is the material set over the Bowl—ice, I think Charles called it. Would that do?"

"Yes, I know about your fires, though I'm darned if I see how you do burn plants in a hydrogen atmosphere, even with a little meat thrown in. For the rest, ice should certainly do, if you can find any. I don't know what the sand of your river is made of, but you can try melting it in one of your hottest fires and see what comes out. I certainly don't guarantee anything, though; I simply say that on Earth and the rest of the worlds I know ordinary sand will make a sort of glass, which is greatly improved with other ingredients. I'm darned if I can see either how to describe those ingredients to you or suggest where they might be found, though."

"Thank you; I will have someone try the fire. In the meantime, I will search for a piece of lens, though I fear the blow when it struck left little usable. We should not have tried to take the device apart near the edge of the mound; the thing you called a 'barrel' rolled much too easily."

Once more the mate left the radio, and immediately encountered Barlennan.

"It's about time for your watch to get on the plates," the captain said. "I'm going down to the river. Is there anything your work needs?"

Dondragmer mentioned the suggestion about sand.

"You can carry up the little bit I'll need, I should think, without getting the fire too hot; or did you plan on a full load of other things?"

"No plans; I'm taking the trip mainly for fun. Now

that the spring wind has died out and we get breezes in every old direction, a little navigation practice might be useful. What good is a captain who can't steer his ship?"

"Fair enough. Did the Flyers tell you what this deck of machines was for?"

"They did pretty well, but if I were really convinced about this space-bending business I'd have swallowed it more easily. They finished up with the old line about words not really being enough to describe it. What else beside words can you use, in the name of the Suns?"

"I've been wondering myself; I think it's another aspect of this quantity-code they call mathematics. I like mechanics best myself; you can do something with it from the very beginning." He waved an arm toward one of the carts and another toward the place where the differential pulley was lying.

"It would certainly seem so. We'll have a lot to take home—and some, I guess, we'd better not be too hasty in spreading about." He gestured at what he meant, and the mate agreed soberly. "Nothing to keep us from playing with it now, though." The captain went his way, and Dondragmer looked after him with a mixture of seriousness and amusement. He rather wished that Reejaaren were around; he had never liked the islander, and perhaps now he would be a little less convinced that the *Bree*'s crew was composed exclusively of liars.

That sort of reflection was a waste of time, however. He had work to do. Pulling plates off the metal monster was less fun than being told how to do experiments, but his half of the bargain had to be fulfilled. He started up the mound, calling his watch after him.

Barlennan went on to the *Bree*. She was already prepared for the trip, two sailors aboard and her fire hot. The great expanse of shimmering, nearly transparent fabric amused him; like the mate, he was thinking of Reejaaren, though in this case it was of what the interpreter's reaction would be if he saw the use to which his material was being put. Not possible to trust sewn seams, indeed! Barlennan's own people knew a thing or two, even without friendly Flyers to tell them. He had patched sails with the stuff before they were ten thousand miles from the island where it had been obtained, and his seams had held even in front of the valley of wind.

He slipped through the opening in the rail, made sure it was secured behind him, and glanced into the fire pit, which was lined with metal foil from a condenser the Flyers had donated. All the cordage seemed sound and taut; he nodded to the crewmen. One heaped another few sticks on the glowing, flameless fire in the pit; the other released the moorings.

Gently, her forty-foot sphere of fabric bulging with hot air, the new *Bree* lifted from the plateau and drifted riverward on the light breeze.

AUTHOR'S AFTERWORD
Whirligig World *

Writing a science fiction story is fun, not work. If it were work I wouldn't be writing this article, which would then constitute a chapter for a textbook. I don't plan to write such a text, since if the subject is teachable I'd be creating competition and if it isn't I'd be wasting time.

The fun, and the material for this article, lies in treating the whole thing as a game. I've been playing the game since I was a child, so the rules must be quite simple. They are; for the reader of a science-fiction story, they consist of finding as many as possible of the author's statements or implications which conflict with the facts as science currently understands them. For the author, the rule is to make as few such slips as he possibly can.

Certain exceptions are made by both sides, of course. For example, it is commonly considered fair to ignore certain of Dr. Einstein's theories, if the story background requires interstellar travel. Sometimes a passing reference is made to travel through a "hyperspace" in which light can travel faster or distances are shorter, but in essence we ignore the speed-of-light rule since we can—so far—see no way around it. The author asssumes that problem, or perhaps others equally beyond our present ability to solve, to be answered, and goes ahead from there. In such a case, of course, fair play demands that all such matters be mentioned as early as possible in the story,

* This article originally appeared in *Astounding Science Fiction*'s June 1953 issue.

so that the reader has a chance to let his imagination grow into the new background.

I always feel cheated when the problem which has been developed in a story is solved by the discovery in the last chapter of antigravity, time travel, or a method of reviving the dead; such things *must* be at least near full development and known to the reader long enough in advance to give him a chance to foresee the ending. I have always assumed, perhaps wrongly, that others felt as I do; I try to write accordingly.

In "Mission of Gravity" I've been playing this game as fairly as I could.

The author has one disadvantage, of course; all his moves must be completed first. Once the story is in print, the other side can take all the time in the world to search out the mistakes; they can check with reference libraries or write letters to universities, if they play the game that seriously. Sooner or later the mistakes will come out; there is no further chance to correct them. If "Mission of Gravity" contains such errors, they're out of my hands now. I did my best to avoid them, but you still have a good chance to win. As I said, my moves were fun, not work.

The basic idea for the story came nearly ten years ago. In 1943 Dr. K. Aa. Strand published the results of some incredibly—to anyone but an astronomer —painstaking work on the orbit of the binary star 61 Cygni, a star otherwise moderately famous for being the first to have its parallax, and hence its distance, measured. In solving such a problem, the data normally consist of long series of measurements of the apparent direction and distance of one star from the other; if the stars are actually moving around each other, and the observations cover a sufficient fraction of a revolution, it is ordinarily possible if not easy to compute the actual relative orbit of the system— that is, the path of one assuming that the other is stationary. Dr. Strand's work differed from the more usual exercises of this type in that his measures were made from photographs. This eliminated some of the difficulties usually encountered in visual observation,

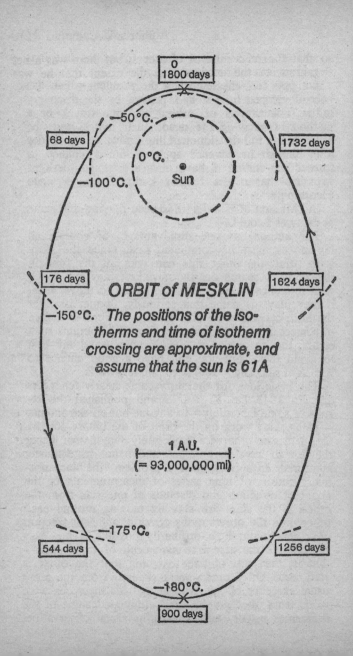

ORBIT of MESKLIN. The positions of the isotherms and time of isotherm crossing are approximate, and assume that the sun is 61A

1 A.U.
(= 93,000,000 mi)

and supplied a number of others; but there was a net gain in overall accuracy, to the extent that he was not only able to publish a more accurate set of orbital elements than had previously been available, but to show that the orbital motion was not regular.

The fainter star, it seemed, did *not* move around the brighter in a smooth ellipse at a rate predictable by the straightforward application of Kepler's laws. It did, however, move in a Keplerian path about an invisible point which was in turn traveling in normal fashion about the other sun.

There was nothing intrinsically surprising about this discovery; the implication was plain. One of the two stars—it was not possible to tell which, since measures had been made *assuming* the brighter to be stationary —was actually accompanied by another, invisible object; the invisible point which obeys the normal planetary and stellar laws was the center of gravity of the star-unknown object system. Such cases are by no means unusual.

To learn which of the two suns is actually attended by this dark body, we would have to have more observations of the system, made in relation to one or more stars not actually part thereof. Some stars exist near enough to the line of sight for such observations to be made, but if they have been reduced and published the fact has not come to my attention. I chose to assume that the object actually circles the brighter star. That may cost me a point in the game when the facts come out, but I won't be too disheartened if it does.

There was still the question of just what this object was. In other such cases where an invisible object betrayed its presence by gravity or eclipse, as in the system of Algol, we had little difficulty in showing that the companion was a star of some more or less normal type—in the case of Algol, for example, the "dark" body causing the principal eclipse is a sun larger and brighter than our own; we can tell its size, mass, luminosity, and temperature with very considerable precision and reliability.

In the case of the 61 Cygni system, the normal methods were put to work; and they came up immediately with a disconcerting fact. The period and size of the orbit, coupled with the fairly well-known mass of the visible stars, indicated that the dark body has a mass only about sixteen thousandths that of the sun—many times smaller than any star previously known. It was still about sixteen times the mass of Jupiter, largest planet we knew. Which was it—star or planet? Before deciding on the classification of an object plainly very close to the borderline, we must obviously decide just where the borderline lies.

For general purposes, our old grade-school distinction will serve; a star shines by its own light, while a planet is not hot enough for that and can be seen only by reflected light from some other source. If we restrict the word "light" to mean radiation we can see, there should be little argument, at least about definitions. (If anyone brings up nontypical stars of the VV_2 Cephei or Epsilon$_2$ Aurigae class I shall be annoyed.) The trouble still remaining is that we may have some trouble deciding whether this Cygnus object shines by intrinsic or reflected light, when we can't see it shine at all. Some educated guessing seems in order.

There is an empirical relation between the mass of a star, at least a main-sequence star, and its actual brightness. Whether we would be justified in extending this relation to cover an object like 61 Cygni C—that is, third brightest body in the 61 Cygni system—is more than doubtful, but may be at least suggestive. If we do, we find that its magnitude as a star should be about twenty or a little brighter. That is within the range of modern equipment, *provided* that the object is not too close to the glare of another, brighter star and *provided* it is sought photographically with a long enough exposure. Unfortunately, 61 C will never be more than about one and a half seconds of arc away from its primary, and an exposure sufficient to reveal the twentieth magnitude would burn the image of 61 A and B over considerably more than one and a half seconds' worth of photographic plate. A rotating sector or similar device to cut down selectively on the light of the brighter star might do the trick, but a job of extraordinary delicacy would be demanded. If anyone has attempted such a task, I have not seen his published results.

If we assume the thing to be a planet, we find that a disk of the same reflecting power as Jupiter and three times his diameter would have an apparent magnitude of twenty-five or twenty-six in 61 C's location; there would be no point looking for it with present equipment. It seems, then, that there is no way to be sure whether it is a star or a planet; and I can call it whichever I like without too much fear of losing points in the game.

I am supposing it to be a planet, not only for story convenience but because I seriously doubt that an object so small could maintain at its center the temperatures and pressures necessary for sustained nuclear reactions; and without such reactions no object could maintain a significant radiation rate for more than a few million years. Even as a planet, though, our object has characteristics which will call for thought on any author's part.

Although sixteen times as massive as Jupiter, it is *not* sixteen times as bulky. We know enough about the structure of matter now to be sure that Jupiter has about the largest volume of any possible "cold" body. When mass increases beyond this point, the central pressure becomes great enough to force some of the core matter into the extremely dense state which we first knew in white dwarf stars, where the outer electronic shells of the atoms can no longer hold up and the nuclei crowd together far more closely than is possible under ordinary—to us, that is—conditions. From the Jupiter point on up, as mass increases the radius of a body decreases—and mean density rises enormously. Without this effect—that is, if it maintained Jupiter's density with its own mass—61C would have a diameter of about two hundred fifteen thousand miles. Its surface gravity would be about seven times that of the Earth. However, the actual state of affairs seems to involve a diameter about equal to that of Uranus or Neptune, and a surface gravity over three hundred times what we're used to.

Any science fiction author can get around that, of course. Simply invent a gravity screen. No one will mind little details like violation of the law of conservation of energy, or the difference of potential across the screen which will prevent the exchange of anything more concrete than visual signals; no one at all. No one but *Astounding* readers, that is; and there is my own conscience, too. I might use gravity screens if a good story demanded them and I could see no legitimate way out; but in the present case there is a perfectly sound and correct means of reducing the effective gravity, at least for a part of a planet's surface. As Einstein says, gravitational effects cannot be distinguished from inertial ones. The so-called centrifugal force is an inertial effect, and for a rotating planet happens to be directed outward—in effect —in the equatorial plane. I can, therefore, set my planet spinning rapidly enough to make the characters feel as light as I please, at least at the equator.

If that is done, of course, my nice new world will flatten in a way that would put Saturn to shame; and there will undoubtedly be at least one astronomer reading the story who will give me the raised eyebrow if I have it squashed too little or too much. Surely there is some relation between mass, and rate of spin, and polar flattening—

I was hung up on that problem for quite a while. Since I had other things to do, I didn't really concentrate on it; but whenever a friend whose math had not collapsed with the years crossed my path, I put it up to him. My own calculus dissolved in a cloud of rust long, long ago. I finally found the answer —or *an* answer—in my old freshman astronomy text, which is still in my possession. I was forcibly reminded that I must also take into account the internal distribution of the planet's mass; that is, whether it was of homogeneous density or, say, almost all packed into a central core. I chose the latter alternative, in view of the enormous density almost certainly possessed by the core of this world and the fact that the outer layers where the pressure is less are presumably of normal matter.

I decided to leave an effective gravity of three times our own at the equator, which fixed one value in the formula. I had the fairly well known value for the mass, and a rough estimate of the volume. That was enough. A little slide rule work gave me a set of characteristics which will furnish story material for years to come. I probably won't use it again myself—though that's no promise—and I hereby give official permission to anyone who so desires to lay scenes there. I ask only that he maintain reasonable scientific standards, and that's certainly an elastic requirement in the field of science fiction.

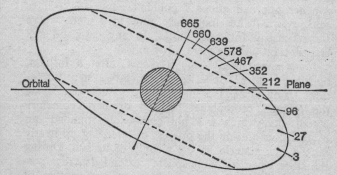

Cross section of Mesklin. Shaded portion represents Earth on same scale. Dotted lines are arctic and antarctic circles. Listed values of gravity (effective), represented by numbers at appropriate latitudes, are very approximate.

The world itself is rather surprising in several ways. Its equatorial diameter is forty-eight thousand miles. From pole to pole along the axis it measures nineteen thousand seven hundred and forty, carried to more significant figures than I have any right to. It rotates on its axis at a trifle better than twenty degrees a minute, making the day some seventeen and three quarter minutes long. At the equator I would weigh about four hundred eighty pounds, since I hand-picked the net gravity there; at the poles, I'd be carrying something like sixty tons. To be perfectly frank, I don't know the exact value of the polar gravity; the planet is so oblate that the usual rule for spheres, to the effect that one may consider all the mass concentrated at the center for purposes of computing surface gravity, would not even be a good approximation if this world were of uniform density. Having it so greatly concentrated helps a great deal, and I don't think the rough figure of a little under seven hundred Earth gravities that I used in the story is too far out; but anyone who objects is welcome if he can back it up. (Some formulae brought to my attention rather too late to be useful suggest that I'm too high by a factor of two; but whose formulae are the rougher approximations I couldn't guess—as I have said, my math has long since gone to a place where I can't use it for such things. In any case, I'd still stagger a bit under a mere thirty tons.)

I can even justify such a planet, after a fashion, by the current (?) theories of planetary system formation. Using these, I assume that the nucleus forming the original protoplanet had an orbit of cometary eccentricity, which was not completely rounded out by collisions during the process of sweeping up nearly all the raw material in the vicinity of its sun. During the stage when its "atmosphere" extended across perhaps several million miles of space, the capture of material from orbits which were in general more circular than its own would tend to give a spin to the forming world, since objects from outside its position at any instant would have a lower velocity than those from farther in. The rotation thus produced, and increased by conservation of angular momentum as the mass shrank, would be in the opposite direction to the world's orbital motion. That does not bother me, though; I didn't even mention it in the story, as nearly as I can now recall.

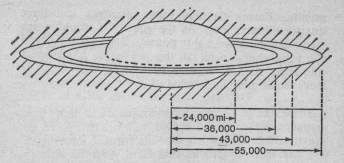

Scale drawing of Mesklin and ring system. Inner ring reaches to less than 1,000 miles of planet's surface; gaps are of corresponding width.

The rate of spin might be expected to increase to the point where matter was actually shed from the equator, so I gave the planet a set of rings and a couple of fairly massive moons. I checked the sizes of the rings against the satellite orbits, and found that the inner moon I had invented would produce two gaps in the ring similar to those in Saturn's decoration. The point never became important in the story, but it was valuable to me as atmosphere; I had to have the picture clearly in mind to make all possible events and conversations consistent. The inner moon was ninety thousand miles from the planet's center, giving it a period of two hours and a trifle under eight minutes. The quarter-period and third-period ring gaps come about twelve and nineteen thousand miles respectively from the world's surface. The half-period gap would fall about thirty-three thousand miles out, which is roughly where Roche's Limit would put the edge of the ring anyway. (I say roughly, because that limit depends on density distribution, too.)

On the whole, I have a rather weird-looking object. The model I have of it is six inches in diameter and not quite two and a half thick; if I added the ring, it would consist of a paper disk about fourteen inches in diameter cut to fit rather closely around the plastic wood spheroid. (The model was made to furnish something to draw a map on; I like to be consistent. The map was drawn at random before the story was written; then I bound myself to stick to the geographic limitations it showed.) I was tempted, after looking at it for a while, to call the story "Pancake in the Sky," but Isaac Asimov threatened violence. Anyway, it looks rather more like a fried egg.

There are a lot of characteristics other than size, though, which must be settled before a story can be written. Since I want a native life form, I must figure out just what conditions that form must be able to stand. Some of these conditions, like the temperature and gravity, are forced on me; others, perhaps, I can juggle to suit myself. Let's see.

Temperature depends, almost entirely, on how much heat a planet receives and retains from its sun. 61 Cygni is a binary system, but the two stars are so far apart that I needn't consider the other one as an influence on this planet's temperature; and the one which it actually circles is quite easy to allow for. Several years ago I computed, partly for fun and partly for cases like this, a table containing some interesting information for all the stars within five parsecs for which I could secure data. The information consists of items such as the distance at which an Earth-type planet would have to revolve from the star in question to have the present temperatures of Earth, Venus, and Mars, and how long it would take a planet to circle the sun in question in each such orbit. For 61 Cygni A, the three distances are about twenty-eight, thirty-nine, and sixty-nine million miles, respectively. As we have seen, 61C's orbit is reasonably well known; and it is well outside any of those three distances. At its closest—and assuming that the primary star is 61A—it gets almost near enough to be warmed to about fifty below zero, Centigrade. At the other end of its rather eccentric orbit Earth at least would cool to about minus one hundred eighty, and it's rather unlikely that this world we are discussing gets too much more out of the incoming radiation. That is a rather wide temperature fluctuation.

The eccentricity of the orbit is slightly helpful,

though. As Kepler's laws demand, the world spends relatively little time close to its sun; about four fifths of its year it is outside the minus one hundred fifty degree isotherm, and it is close enough to be heated above minus one hundred for only about one hundred thirty days of its eighteen-hundred-day year—Earth days, of course. Its year uses up around one hundred forty-five thousand of its own days, the way we've set it spinning. For practical purposes, then, the temperature will be around minus one hundred seventy Centigrade most of the time. We'll dispose of the rest of the year a little later.

Presumably any life form at all analogous to our own will have to consist largely of some substance which will remain liquid in its home planet's temperature range. In all probability, the substance in question would be common enough on the planet to form its major liquid phase. If that is granted, what substance will meet our requirements?

Isaac Asimov and I spent a pleasant evening trying to find something that would qualify. We wanted it not only liquid within our temperature limits, but a good solvent and reasonably capable of causing ionic dissociation of polar molecules dissolved in it. Water, of course, was out; on this world it is strictly a mineral. Ammonia is almost as bad, melting only on the very hottest days. We played with ammonia's analogues from further along the periodic table—phosphine, arsine, and stibine—with carbon disulfide and phosgene, with carbon suboxide and hydrogen fluoride, with saturated and unsaturated hydrocarbons both straight and with varying degrees of chlorine and fluorine substitution, and even with a silicone or two. A few of these met the requirements as to melting and boiling points; some may even have caused dissociation of their solutes, though we had no data on that point for most. However, we finally fell back on a very simple compound.

It boils, unfortunately, at an inconveniently low temperature, even though we assume a most unlikely atmospheric pressure. It cannot be expected to be fruitful in ions, though as a hydrocarbon it will probably dissolve a good many organic substances. It has one great advantage, though, from my viewpoint; it would almost certainly be present on the planet in vast quantities. The substance is methane—CH_4.

Like Jupiter, this world must have started formation with practically the "cosmic" composition, involving from our viewpoint a vast excess of hydrogen. The oxygen present would have combined with it to form water; the nitrogen, to form ammonia; the carbon to form methane and perhaps higher hydrocarbons. There would be enough hydrogen for all, and plenty to spare —light as it is, even hydrogen would have a hard time escaping from a body having five thousand times the mass of Earth once it had cooled below red heat—at first, that is. Later, when the rotational velocity increased almost to the point of real instability, it would be a different story; but we'll consider that in a moment. However, we have what seems to be a good reason to expect oceans of methane on this world; and with such oceans, it would be reasonable to expect the appearance and evolution of life forms using that liquid in their tissues.

But just a moment. I admitted a little while ago that methane boils at a rather lower temperature than I wanted for this story. Is it *too* low? Can I raise it sufficiently by increasing the atmospheric pressure, perhaps? Let's see. The handbook lists methane's critical temperature as about minus eighty-two degrees Centigrade. Above that temperature it will always be a gas, regardless of pressure; and to bring its boiling point up nearly to that value, a pressure about forty-six times that of our own atmosphere at sea level will be needed. Well, we have a big planet, which should have held on to a lot of its original gases; it ought to have a pressure of hundreds or even thousands of atmospheres—whoops! we forgot something.

At the equator, *effective* gravity—gravity minus centrifugal effect—is three times Earth normal. That, plus our specification of temperature and composition of the atmosphere, lets us compute the rate at which atmospheric density will decrease with altitude. It turns out that with nearly pure hydrogen, three g's, and a temperature of minus one hundred fifty for convenience, there is still a significant amount of atmosphere at six hundred miles altitude if we start at forty-odd bars for surface pressure—*and at six hundred miles above the equator of this planet, the centrifugal force due to its rotation balances the gravity!* If there had ever been a significant amount of atmosphere at that height, it would long since have been slung away into space; evidently we cannot possibly have a surface pressure anywhere near forty-six atmospheres. Some rough slide-rule work suggests eight atmospheres as an upper limit—I used summer temperatures rather than the annual mean.

At that pressure methane boils at about minus one hundred forty-three degrees, and for some three hundred Earth days, or one sixth of each year, the planet will be in a position where its sun could reasonably be expected to boil its oceans. What to do?

Well, Earth's mean temperature is above the melting point of water, but considerable areas of our planet are permanently frozen. There is no reason why I can't use the same effects for 61C; it is an observed fact that the axis of rotation of a planet can be oriented so that the equatorial and orbital planes do not coincide. I chose for story purposes to incline them at an angle of twenty-eight degrees, in such a direction that the northern hemisphere's midsummer occurs when the world is closest to its sun. This means that a large part of the northern hemisphere will receive no sunlight for fully three quarters of the year, and should in consequence develop a very respectable cap of frozen methane at the expense of the oceans in the other hemisphere. As the world approaches its sun the livable southern hemisphere is protected by the bulk of the planet from its deadly heat output; the star's energy is expended in boiling off the north polar "ice" cap. Tremendous storms rage across the equator carrying air and methane vapor at a temperature little if any above the boiling point of the latter; and while the southern regions will warm up during their winter, they should not become unendurable for creatures with liquid methane in their tissues.

Precession should be quite rapid, of course, because of the tremendous equatorial bulge, which will give the sun's gravity a respectable grip even though most of the world's mass is near its center. I have not attempted to compute the precessional period, but if anyone likes to assume that a switch in habitable hemispheres occurring every few thousand years has kept the natives from building a high civilization I won't argue. Of course, I will also refrain from disagreement with anyone who wants to credit the periodic climate change with responsibility for the development of intelligence on the planet, as our own ice ages have sometimes been given credit for the present mental stature of the human race. Take your pick. For story purposes, I'm satisfied with the fact that either possibility can be defended.

The conditions of the planet, basically, are pretty well defined. There is still a lot of detail work. I must design a life form able to stand those conditions—more accurately, to regard them as ideal—which is not too difficult since I don't have to describe the life processes in rigorous detail. Anyone who wants me to will have to wait until someone can do the same with our own life form. Vegetation using solar energy to build up higher, unsaturated hydrocarbons and animal life getting its energy by reducing those compounds back to the saturated form with atmospheric hydrogen seemed logical enough to me. In the story, I hinted indirectly at the existence of enzymes aiding the reduction, by mentioning that plant tissues would burn in the hydrogen atmosphere if a scrap or two of meat were tossed onto the fuel.

The rest of the detail work consists of all my remaining moves in the game—finding things that are taken for granted on our own world and would not be true on this one. Such things as the impossibility of throwing, jumping, or flying, at least in the higher latitudes; the tremendously rapid decrease of air density with height in the same regions, producing a mirage effect that makes the horizon seem *above* an observer all around; the terrific Coriolis force that splits any developing storm into a series of relatively tiny cells—

and would make artillery an interesting science if we could have any artillery; the fact that methane vapor is denser than hydrogen, removing a prime Terrestrial cause of thunderstorm and hurricane formation; the rate of pressure increase below the ocean surface, and what that does to the art of navigation; the fact that icebergs won't float, so that much of the ocean bottoms may be covered with frozen methane; the natural preference of methane for dissolving organic materials such as fats rather than mineral salts, and what that will do to ocean composition—maybe icebergs *would* float after all. You get the idea.

The trouble was, I couldn't possibly think of all these things in advance; time and again a section of the story had to be rewritten because I suddenly realized things couldn't happen that way. I must have missed details, of course; that's where your chance to win the game comes in. I *had* an advantage; the months during which, in my spare hours, my imagination roamed over Mesklin's vast areas in search of inconsistencies. Now the advantage is yours; I can make no more moves in the game, and you have all the time you want to look for the things I've said which reveal slips on the part of my imagination.

Well, good luck—and a good time, whether you beat me or not.

About the Author

Hal Clement (Harry Clement Stubbs) was born in Massachusetts in 1922. He has been a science lover from early childhood, at least partly as a result of a 1930 *Buck Rogers* panel in which villains were "headed for Mars, forty-seven million miles away." His father, an accountant, couldn't answer the resulting questions, and led little Hal to the local library. The result was irreversible brain influence.

He majored in astronomy at Harvard, and has since acquired master's degrees in education and in chemistry. He earns his basic living as a teacher of chemistry and astronomy at Milton Academy, in Massachusetts, and regards science-fiction writing and painting as hobbies. His first two stories, "Proof" and "Impediment," were sold when he was a junior in college; their impression on Harvard's $400 per year tuition secured family tolerance for that crazy Buck Rogers stuff.

He has since produced half a dozen novels, of which the best known are *Needle* and *Mission of Gravity*. His reputation among science-fiction enthusiasts is that of a "hard" writer—one who tries to stick faithfully to the physical sciences as they are currently understood. Like Arthur C. Clarke and the late Willy Ley, Clement would never dream of having a spaceship fall into the sun merely because its engines broke down. He can do his own orbit computing, and does.

He leads a double life, appearing frequently at science-fiction conventions as Hal Clement and spending the rest of his time in Milton as the rather square science teacher with a wife of twenty-five years and three grown children, Harry Stubbs. He does occasional merit badge counseling for the Boy Scouts, has served on his town's finance committee, and is an eleven-gallon Red Cross blood donor.